Unhinged CRAVINGS

Unhinged CRAVINGS

WICKED CRAVINGS
BOOK FOUR

JL JACKOLA

Paperback ISBN 978-1-960784-60-5
Electronic ISBN 978-1-960784-61-2

Distributed by Tivshe Publishing
Printed in the United States of America

Cover design by Tivshe Publishing

Visit www.jljackola.com

Also by J. L. Jackola

UNBOUND PROPHECY SERIES

Ascension

Descent

Surfacing

Submerged

Riven

Adrift

UNBOUND PROPHECY NOVELS

Unbound Kingdom (the trilogy omnibus)

Orlaina (an Unbound Prophecy prequel)

UNBOUND KINGDOM TRILOGY

Severed Kingdom

Cursed Kingdom

Prophesied Kingdom

Wicked Hues Series

The Forgotten Hues of Skye

The Coveted Hues of Skye

The Shattered Shades of Crimson

The Impossible Shades of Crimson

The Endless Shadows of Pete

Welcome back to the world of wicked cravings where morally gray is the norm and cravings are hard to resist.

Unhinged Cravings is a mafia romance with darker aspects than the first three books, so be prepared to expect:

- Explicit sexual content
- Language
- Threats of s. a. and unwelcome touching (not by the mmc)
- Trafficking (not by the mmc)
- Past trauma and physical abuse (again, not by the mmc)
- Panic attacks and mental health representation
- Violence and death

For those who crave the complicated bad boy.

Chapter One

EMERSON

Waves crashed against the shore, leaving trails of froth as they receded. The sun left a soft warmth on my skin that opposed the violent splashes of crimson that corrupted my vision. On the other side of the country, my brother was celebrating. The thought of my brother having any amount of pleasure in his life scratched at my insides like spikes dragging down sheet metal. A wedding. As if he deserved a moment of happiness. He'd been so quick to ruin mine twenty-five years ago that his actions had made us the enemies we were today. I had turned my back on him, building my empire in Seagate, far from his territory and from him.

"Our men are in place, boss."

I didn't bother to look back at Pack, my second, feeling his tension and knowing his eyes were scanning the deck out of habit. Even with men on the ground making rounds and another guarding me at the end of the deck, he was on high alert. We all were. I scraped my hands through my hair. Years of war brewing between Greyson and me had led to this moment. But it wasn't one I had anticipated, no matter that he likely thought it was. Things were out of my control, and this was my last attempt to rein them in before I lost everything. That left my future hinging on what took place in the next twenty-four hours.

"Good. The plane is scheduled to depart at five a.m. Make sure the two at the hangar take out the guards tonight and don't move from their posts. I want no fuckups."

"Got it. The other three will take surveillance until Tides arrives. Only then will they move to ambush. There will be no mistakes. We've gone over the plan and accounted for any unexpected turns."

My hand swiping down my face, I said, "Once I make this call, he'll have his security on high alert. Our men need to strike quick and lethal. My brother is the best on the east coast for a reason. They are not to underestimate him. It's imperative they leave him alive and conscious. I want him to know what I'm taking from him. If they fuck that part up, I'll kill every one of them."

"They know the importance of the mission. We all do."

I gave him a nod, my worries still not completely quieted. There were too many factors, and two of the men I'd sent were still green. That's why they were the decoys, taking the place of the guards they would kill and going in first. My seasoned men would do the real work. I should have sent Pack, but with so much at stake here at home, he'd stayed to ensure my protection.

"Let me know the minute you hear anything."

Staring back out at the ocean, I pulled my phone from my pocket. As much as I needed to make this call, it would alter what scraps of necessary politeness existed between my brother and me and obliterate it completely. Unless my plan worked. This plan was one that would force him to do the one thing I'd avoided for twenty-five years: talk. Sure, he knew how to contact me, but we had spoken only a handful of times in necessity, with nothing more than curt warnings. This time, I needed his full attention. I needed him here, on my turf, begging and desperate. The advantage had to be mine for this to work. And the only way to do that was to have leverage. Something he valued more than his pride—Riley Brinks.

Walking into the house, I placed my phone on the bar and poured myself a glass of scotch, contemplating the move I was about to make. This game was dangerous, and it was one that could backfire on me. There was a high probability he would kill me, but I flourished in risk. Death held no sway for my consideration. I faced it every day.

My teeth gnashed as I thought about Greyson. I knew him well enough to expect his next move. He wouldn't buckle to my threat, and he was too cocky to change his plans. Too proud to let me think I made him nervous. That would be his downfall and leave him only one option—to come crawling to me.

With a chug of my drink, I dropped the glass and picked the phone back up. Ready to make the call that would change everything, and content that I would have my brother's coveted prize and the advantage in my hands soon.

Chapter Two

GREYSON

Riley threw me a smile from across the room. The bustle of her dress had fallen again, and her friend Casey was huffing about it as she fixed it. Riley blew a strand of her ebony hair from her face as she laughed. She looked like a princess, my princess. The day had been perfect and seeing her walk toward me, the train of her dress following her as she held her brother's arm, had been the most memorable moment of my life followed by the one when she'd returned to me. It had only been a few months since that day, but each day that passed only brought me more happiness because they involved Riley. I'd brought her in on all the parts of my business, amazed at how she picked right up. I hadn't had a partner since the falling out with my brother, but Riley was my partner in every way.

"You keep my sister safe, Tides," Mason said, coming to stand next to me. He was the part of the deal I'd bristled at, but we were making it work. We had to because Riley was too important to us both for it not to.

"That's all I've done, Brinks."

I glanced at him, noticing how his eyes lingered on Casey.

Downing the rest of my drink, I said, "You getting any sleep tonight?"

He swiveled his alcohol before taking another drink. "Fuck off, Tides."

I shrugged, "Just saying, I know that look. Trust me, it's the same one I give your sister."

"Asshole," he mumbled as I walked away. Casey was Tyson's sister, and that seemed like a complication, but then again, so was loving your enemy's sister and that had worked out.

As I crossed the dance floor, my intention was to steal Riley away and tell them I didn't care about her bustle because I was just going to rip the damned dress from her anyway. We were leaving for our honeymoon in the morning, and I planned to make love to my new wife until Den came to take us to the airport.

My phone rang, and I considered ignoring it. This was my wedding day, after all. But habits are hard to break, and I answered, bringing it to my ear as I walked through our guests.

"Speak."

"I hear congratulations are in order, brother."

I froze, standing in the middle of the dance floor, my eyes scanning the room and catching Mason's. He was sharp, his expression becoming serious as he read my own. He made a beeline to me as I said, "Emerson."

"She's quite a beauty, Grey. Too bad my man had a taste of her before you sank your cock into her."

A growl rumbled through my chest, accompanied by the tightened grip on my phone.

"What do you want?"

"This is your warning. You may think your empire is safe, little brother, bringing Mason Brinks into your fold. It's not. I'll take what you covet, and you'll have no choice but to bow to me. Enjoy your honeymoon."

He was gone before I could respond. I dropped the phone

from my ear, looking over at Riley. He'd shattered the peace of the day, the contentment I'd held for that brief time ripped away by his words.

Riley met my eyes, hers creased with concern.

"Who was that?" Mason said, and I turned to him.

"My brother."

"Your brother? You have a brother?"

"Unfortunately, Emerson is my older brother."

"And why do you look like I need to worry about that?" Tension played in his features.

"Because he doesn't go by Emerson Tides. I'm the only one who still knows that name. To everyone else, he's Cade Slaughter."

He took a step back. "The leader of the Bad Omen?"

I flicked a strand of Riley's hair from my suit jacket. "Yes. The leader of the Bad Omen is my brother. A man who hates me with a passion. And the feeling's mutual."

He looked over at Riley, then back at me.

"I'll protect her, Mason. I promise you. No one will ever lay a hand on Riley again."

"What did he want?"

I watched Riley as she crossed the room, her green eyes deep with worry.

"To threaten me under the guise of congratulations. I need to change our plans. If he knows about the wedding, he'll know about the honeymoon." How he knew those things was something I would need to uncover. If there was a mole in my family, I would burn him out and send him back to my brother piece by piece.

"Take my plane. I can get you a room at the island where Tyson and Angie had their wedding."

My alcohol swished in my glass as I thought about that stark of a change. It would throw Emerson off, but it was far from what I had planned.

Riley was almost to us.

"Fuck," I muttered. I didn't like running and this looked like I was running. But pride was no longer my concern. Riley was, and I would do what was necessary to keep her safe. Even if it meant letting my brother think he had me on the run.

"Fine." I took a swig of the whiskey, letting it smooth its way down my throat. "We'll leave tonight instead of in the morning."

He took his phone out, saying, "I'll make it happen. Enjoy telling my sister you're changing plans on her. That should be fun."

Rolling my neck, I ignored the urge to punch him before he walked away. His plan made sense and as much as I hated to admit it, if my brother wanted to sabotage my honeymoon, changing the destination and the departure would throw him off. He wouldn't expect me to deviate because that's what he would do. He was the one who took chances, who rushed into things. I was the levelheaded one, patient and unyielding. Changing course like this was not something he would expect from me.

"Grey?" Riley said, coming over to me.

I gave her a smile, her presence calming me. "Everything's okay. Your brother has it handled. What do you think about going to the beach for our trip?"

Her forehead crinkled with confusion. "But you wanted to go to the mountains."

And I had. I'd booked the lodge, arranged for a chef to prepare our meals, booked the ski slopes, and a slew of other romantic things.

"We just got through winter. I don't know why I thought staying in the cold was a good idea. Besides," I said, pulling her to me, "this will give me a reason to see you in a bikini again." Although the restraint needed to keep from killing every man who looked at her would make the decision even more brutal.

Her head tilted, and she gave me a curious look before saying, "Okay, I don't care where we go, as long as I'm with you."

I motioned for Den, who made his way to me. "Change of plans. We're taking Brinks' plane and I'm taking my bride to the beach after we finish with this foolishness."

Riley pouted her lips at the comment, and I gave her a hard look before she said, "Is there something you're not telling me?"

"Yes, but I'll explain when we're on the way because I tell you everything, right?"

"Right," she said, giving me a kiss.

"Care for a dance, Mrs. Tides?" I asked, watching as the concern fell from her eyes, her smile beaming.

"Of course, Mr. Tides."

I walked her away, looking back at Mason, who nodded. I would never have believed it, but I trusted Mason. I'd let him handle whatever my brother had planned while I enjoyed my new wife. I'd deal with what remained of the mess when I returned.

Drawing Riley against me, I held her close as we danced, losing myself to her presence. This was our life, the life she'd chosen when she'd chosen me. It was one where danger hung in the air all around us, where threats lingered in the shadows, but it was one where I would protect her with my life because no one was getting near her again. Riley was mine. And if I had to kill my brother to keep her safe, I wouldn't hesitate to pull the trigger.

Chapter Three

AVA

Weddings had never been my thing, but Riley's wedding tempted me to change my mind. Sleek and sophisticated, it was everything I wasn't and everything Riley and her new husband were. Greyson Tides. Leave it to my new friend to land the most eligible bachelor in the city.

I straightened the gray scarf I wore around the waist of my black bridesmaid's dress. Of course it was a black and white wedding. As if putting me in all black didn't make me stand out even more than I already did. Riley had argued that black was my color until I'd argued back that this wasn't a rock band T-shirt or a pair of leggings.

There had been two bridesmaids, me and Angie—a tall, gorgeous strawberry blonde who looked stunning in her dress, with the gray sash emphasizing her tiny waist. I peeked over my glass of wine at her. Her husband, Tyson, had his enormous hand behind her back and was whispering something in her ear. That man frightened me. It was like every muscle under his suit looked like it was straining to break free.

The maid of honor, Casey, was in a matching dress, but she filled it out in curves that were closer to mine. Her cuteness juxtaposed Angie's model potential, which left me the odd woman out with my pink streaked hair, tattoos, and nose ring.

"You look like you want to crawl under the table with a bottle of tequila," my Uncle Den said, coming to stand beside me.

"If I have to wear this dress much longer, I will."

"It won't be much longer. They're leaving tonight instead of in the morning."

I turned my eyes to him. An equally massive presence to Tyson, I should have guessed my uncle did more than manage money for Greyson's firm. The truth had come out after Riley spilled the beans about Greyson's actual job. My uncle was a henchman. The right-hand man for the most notorious mob boss —if I had been aware of who any of them were—and today, his best man.

It had taken me time to recover, but when I pieced things together, it made more sense than it should have.

"Why?"

"A threat. They're taking Mason's plane instead. I'll be leaving with them, but I'll make sure someone escorts you home."

I rubbed away the nudging of fear for Riley, still adjusting to the deadly world that had unfolded around me when the truth came out.

"What about Greyson's plane?"

"Grounded for now. Mason's team will take it home in the morning."

Damn. Casey and I had decorated the plane as a surprise. Stocking it with Riley's favorite chocolates and a few extra bottles of champaigne.

Greyson gestured to Den from across the room. "Gotta go, kiddo." He gave me a peck on the cheek, then stalked across the dance floor.

Kiddo. He made me laugh because even though I was thirty, he still called me kiddo.

Riley threw me a quick wave before Greyson pulled her away.

If she had thought they'd have time to say goodbye to everyone, she was wrong.

I made my way to the bar and rested my elbow on it as I watched them rush out the back door. "You look entirely too depressed for this event," the bartender said, setting a wineglass in front of me. He was cute, with shaggy brown hair and big brown eyes. He held up two bottles of wine, and I pointed to the pinot grigio.

"I'm not a wedding person," I admitted, tugging at my hair that Riley had insisted needed to be styled so that pins were digging into my scalp. With her no longer present, I let it down.

The bartender, Billy, continued talking to me until I had downed two glasses, and the party was winding down.

"I'm done for the night," he said, hanging there for a minute.

I glanced over, seeing one of Greyson's men waiting for me. Gesturing to him with my head, I told Billy, "I have an escort."

"Hmm, a lot of that going on here tonight."

"Yeah, comes with the territory."

"Wanna ditch him?" he asked, his thick brow arching.

The wine had gotten to me, and he looked entirely too delicious not to play with. I chewed the side of my finger, thinking of my options. I knew it would be difficult to ditch the guard, but I thrived on taking risks and this was a challenge I wanted.

"Yes. Did you drive?"

"Yeah." He pulled his car keys out and held them up for me to see.

"Perfect. Meet me in the parking lot in ten minutes."

His mischievous grin had my thighs twitching before he left out the main door of the ballroom.

Tugging my scarf from my waist, I looped it around my neck, holding onto both ends as I walked up to my bodyguard.

"I need to use the girls' room and then I'll be ready to go."

He gave me a silent nod and followed me. That took plan A

out of the picture. But Riley had chosen an old estate for her wedding and the bathrooms had been added on the side of the estate lined with windows. And I'd noticed earlier that someone had cracked open the window in the women's room to let in the spring air.

After some finagling, I got the window open enough to crawl through and within minutes was racing across the parking lot to where Billy stood waiting. Was it dangerous to leave with a stranger? Sure, but I didn't let fear rule my life anymore, and Billy looked yummy. Plus, I knew of just the place for us to have some fun.

MAYBE THE WINE was in control because breaking into Greyson Tides' hangar had to have been the most idiotic thing I'd done. He'd likely kill me if my uncle didn't first. And since I knew who he was, killing me was a possibility.

Thanks to Casey, I knew where the hangar was, how to get in, and how to open the plane door. It seemed odd that the guards who had stood outside the hangar last time were nowhere to be seen. Maybe they'd all been at the wedding and were now where Riley and Greyson had gone.

"Shit, this is amazing," Billy said as he used his phone as a flashlight.

"Ignore the balloons," I said, pushing one aside. "This was a surprise for the happy couple."

"And we're going to enjoy it instead?" he asked, coming closer to me.

"Definitely." I pulled him by the tie and kissed him. I'd never had sex on a plane, but I fully intended to add that to my list of accomplishments.

My back pressed into the side of the seat, and he shoved his hands up my dress, yanking at my panties.

"We have all night," I said, bringing one of his hands up and putting it on my breast.

"So you want to blow me first or let me do you first?"

My insides knotted because both sounded good. He tugged the strap of my dress down and cupped my breast, pulling at my nipple ring and groaning. His phone fell, the light extinguished when it landed upside down.

"Damn, you're sexy."

"Wait until I'm riding you," I replied, eliciting another groan from him.

A movement in the shadows had me pausing, but he didn't notice, as he thrust his hand between my legs. It would have made me squirm with anticipation, but the shadow moved, and I pushed his mouth from mine.

"What's the matter, baby? You changing—"

A thud and he quieted, his body falling over just as I screamed. A hand wrapping over my mouth cut my scream short. Another hand picked my body up. Years of self-defense classes surfaced, and I broke free, but as I ran to the door, I hit a mountain of muscle.

"Bitch," the other man said, and his hand shot out and wrapped around my neck. I clawed at his fingers, kicking and flailing, but he was too big.

"Don't kill her. The boss wants her alive."

"Well, you were supposed to keep Tides conscious."

"Not so tough, is he? Maybe all those rumors about him are just lies."

Oh God, they thought I was Riley. I tried to tell them they had the wrong woman, but the chokehold he had on my neck made it impossible.

"Knock her out and let's go before someone finds us. I thought they weren't supposed to arrive until the morning."

"Looks like it's our luck they decided to consummate their marriage on the plane tonight instead."

They had to be idiots. I looked nothing like Riley, and Billy was far from Greyson Tides. Although it was so dark, I supposed it was easy to make the mistake. Something wet covered my mouth and nose, and I plunged into darkness.

Chapter Four

EMERSON

I paced my foyer as two of my men stood alert and ready. The call came in early that morning. They had captured Riley earlier than expected and were on their way back. Within minutes, the front door opened. Without turning, I waited for my men to bring her before me. She was struggling, a string of swears coming from her that would make the hardest of my men cringe. A black sack covered her head and draped down to her chest where the tip of a tattoo showed. With her hands bound in front of her, I could see another tattoo of a butterfly on the inside of her wrist. Bare arms led to the straps of her black dress and a gray scarf hung down the front.

I stepped closer, my brows scrunching as I tried to remember details of any visible tattoos on my brother's new wife and why she would wear a black dress that looked nothing like a wedding dress.

"Shut up and get on your knees," I told her, nodding to the two to force her down.

"If you think I'm sucking you off, asshole, you might want to rethink it. I bite."

Pack snickered, and I shot him a look.

"Force her down," I told them, walking closer to her.

She fought more, but didn't stand a chance against the brute force behind her. I heard the sharp hiss when her knees hit the tile floor. My men stepped back, and I yanked the hood from her. Rage blinded me and the hood crumpled in my hand.

"Who the fuck is this?" I snarled at my men.

"Tides' new wife."

She laughed. "I tried to tell them."

Grabbing her by the hair, I yanked her head back. "Keep your mouth shut or I'll kill you right now."

I pulled a chunk of her blonde hair up, including the pink strands, and looked back at my men. "Does this look like black hair? And why the fuck would a bride wear a black dress?"

"It was dark, boss. We thought she changed after the wedding."

I drew my gun and shot him straight through the eyes. Her scream accompanied the flop of his body. She tried to get up, and I clamped my hand down on her shoulder.

"Shit, boss. She was on the plane with Tides."

I turned the gun to her, pressing it against her forehead. "Who are you, and why were you with my brother?"

"It wasn't Greyson," she stuttered. "He and Riley took a different plane. This guy was the bartender and if these two imbeciles hadn't interrupted, I would have gotten laid."

I tried not to react because my urge to laugh was warring with my need for retribution. Walking around her, I approached my other man.

"I gave you one job. The most important job of your career. Bring me Riley Brinks. And what did you do?"

"Boss, the plane was dark."

"And that didn't give you pause? Make you curious as to why Greyson Tides would need his own plane dark?"

"We thought he was gonna fuck her."

My teeth ground loudly before I brought the gun up and shot

him. He stumbled back, clutching his chest, and I sent another bullet through his head.

His body fell in a lump right behind the woman, who was screaming again, holding her ears.

"Stop that incessant screaming before I drag your face through his brains."

She shut up just as I placed my gun to her temple. "You have three seconds to tell me who the fuck you are and why I should let you live."

"I'm Ava Shelton. Riley is my friend. I was her bridesmaid, and my uncle works for Greyson."

"Doing what?" I asked, her value rising with each admission.

"He's like a right-hand man. He was his best man at the wedding."

Gun lowering, I stooped in front of her. Big brown eyes, the color of golden caramel, looked back at me.

"You just bought yourself time."

A relieved breath fled from her lungs.

"Take her to the guest room," I told Pack, tucking my gun in my pants and rising. "She'll be staying with us for a while."

"What? You can't do that." She got to her feet, and I turned on her, grabbing her scarf and looping it around my hand so that it cut off her airway.

"I can do anything I want. You've got fire and I appreciate that, but I'm an inferno that will swallow your fire whole and decimate it."

The scarf unraveled but remained in my hand as I shoved her toward Pack. "Play by the rules, Ava Shelton, and you'll live until my brother comes to rescue you. Push me, and I'll send your body to him piece by piece. I'm sure your uncle would appreciate that."

I walked away shoving the scarf in my pocket, hearing her bitch but not caring to listen to what she was going on about. Rubbing my temples, I questioned if this was a good idea. She was bound to push my buttons and given the high stakes, my tension was so tight I would snap. I pulled my jacket off before pouring myself a glass of scotch.

Fuck ups. I had nothing but fuck ups on my team now. Unseasoned and making novice mistakes. Pinching the bridge of my nose, I cursed my situation. It had been my doing and now I was paying the price, my empire hanging in the balance.

Pack returned a few minutes later. "She's in the north wing. I've got two men outside her door."

"Good." I sat, planting my elbows on my desk.

"You think killing them was best, Cade?"

Eyes lifting slowly, I studied him. He was the only one I ever let question my methods. One of the few I still trusted.

"Yes."

"So what do we do now?"

"We wait for my brother to discover she's missing. I'm sure someone will go to the hangar since it seems they changed plans. Brinks and Raines maybe. They'll inform him and he'll call me. Then..." What then? Convince my brother to talk to me, to believe me. I sat back in my chair, staring out the window. Maybe he'd listen. "Talk to your contact in Bridgeville. See if they went to their destination or if they changed the itinerary altogether. My brother doesn't make swift changes like that."

"You mean he didn't make changes, boss. He's married now, and that's enough for him to do things differently."

"Confirm that and let me know what you find out."

"And the woman?"

With a sigh, I took the scarf out of my pocket and let it drift through my fingers, saying, "Leave her where she is for now. She's our prisoner, but treat her like a guest. Make sure she has food and whatever she needs."

"What if Tides doesn't respond?"

I looked back up at him. "Then I kill her."

Chapter Five

GREYSON

The plane touched down, and I brushed Riley's hair from her face. She was curled over me, her legs on my lap, her head on my chest. It didn't look close to comfortable, but I hadn't wanted to move her.

"Time to wake up," I told her as she blinked her eyes at me. They sparkled in the light streaming in from the windows.

"Are we here?" she asked with a yawn.

"Yes, now give me my phone." I held my hand out. She'd taken it from me and turned it off, breaking my rule that calls come first. But she'd straddled me and weakened my defenses as she'd unhooked my pants. When her hands had guided me into her, the phone was the last thing on my mind.

Thinking of it caused a reaction she noticed, and she gave me a knowing smile.

"Give me the phone, baby girl, or I'll edge you on the rest of the day until you're begging to come."

Her eyes narrowed and those lush pink lips pouted just enough for me to reach down and grab one between my teeth. Dragging them across it, I said, "Now, Riley," as my hand slipped between her legs.

"You're cruel," she said.

"I know I am."

My fingers slid further, and she huffed, grabbing the phone from her side and slapping it into my other hand.

"Boss, it's all clear."

I gave Den a nod and drew my hand from between her legs. "I'll finish that when we get to the room."

"You'd better." She continued talking, but the influx of messages and missed calls held my attention.

"Grey?" she asked as my worry grew.

Mason's urgent texts had me dialing him immediately.

"Bout time," he grumbled when he answered.

"What's wrong?"

"We've got trouble. There was a break in at your hangar. We found the bartender from the wedding bound and gagged, a nasty bruise on his temple. He snuck in with Ava." My eyes flew to Den as Mason continued, "They took her."

"Who?" I growled, digging my hands into the leather.

"The Omens. They thought she was Riley."

The leather ripped and Den came over to me. He knew me well enough to measure the changes in my moods, and this one was dangerous.

"Why do you say that?" I said, trying to keep my voice steady.

"Because they knocked the guy out and waited for him to come to. When he did, they told him if he wanted to see his wife again, the Omens were waiting to talk."

I scraped my hand over my face, glancing at Riley, thankful it wasn't her but worried for Ava.

"What the fuck does that mean, Tides?"

"It means my brother needs something." It was the only reason he would have left a message like that. Emerson was vicious. If he'd wanted to kidnap Riley, he would have just taken her and not left a message. Would have enjoyed watching me squirm as I tried to find out who had her. "Have them fuel the plane up," I told Den. "We're going home."

Riley let out a complaint until I silenced it with a finger. "How long can you and Raines stay?" I hated having to involve them, but my instinct told me if Emerson was desperate enough to attempt kidnapping Riley again and leave the man his men thought was me alive, then this was big.

"We can stay a few more days."

"Good." I disconnected, my mind piecing things together. A botched kidnapping was not like my brother. The Omens were strict, calculating, and cold. When they struck, they struck hard, annihilating families and hitting them where they were most vulnerable. But this had been sloppy. As had the instances involving Mason's girl and Tyson's wife. Sloppy was not something my brother did.

"What's wrong, boss?" Den asked, and my gut twisted at what I was about to tell him. Riley shifted next to me. I was about to destroy Den with the news of Ava's kidnapping and obliterate Riley's happy ending to a wedding that had been fraught with wrong turns. First, moving it forward and not giving her the Christmas wedding she'd wanted, then further moves when Tyson was shot, leaving the party early without goodbyes, and now this. It made me want to turn the clock back and start over, to undo the mistakes, but as I'd learned with past mistakes, there was no going back. No matter how much regret they caused.

Nausea sat in my stomach, threatening to spill. There were so many things I needed to process about the last few hours. How had I gone from hands groping my body to blood splatters and dead men? I sat on the side of the enormous fourposter bed, thinking this room was too extravagant to be a prison. The furniture was a dark mahogany and included a large dresser and two nightstands. The cool mint color gave a strange calm to the overwhelming sense of doom that sat in my chest. Even the matching bedding gave a false sense of tranquility.

I didn't know who these guys were, other than their leader was Greyson Tides' brother and he seemed unhinged. The brain matter in my hair made that apparent. Thinking about it had my skin crawling, and I made my way to the bathroom. I desperately needed a shower and maybe it shouldn't have been my priority given I was a prisoner in a madman's house with two dead men not far from my room, but the idea of chunks of brain in my hair and on my back made it my priority. Plus, I did my best thinking in the shower.

Looking around the bathroom, I spotted all the necessities: soap, shampoo, towels, a toothbrush and toothpaste, a comb. He had expected to kidnap Riley. I picked up a bar of floral soap, my nose crinkling at the potent smell. Had this all been for her? It seemed strange to give her or me amenities and such a fancy prison.

The walk-in shower was large enough to fit three people, the shower head like something I imagined they had in five-star hotels. Stripping, I grabbed a less smelly bar of soap from the counter and some shampoo and conditioner with a vanilla scent. The water was luxurious when I stepped under it, and I let it calm the nerves in my muscles. Only with my hair and body completely drenched did I let reality enter my mind. Doing so threatened to undo everything I was—steadfast, smart, quirky, bold. I took risks, looked fear in the eyes and laughed, went to haunted Halloween rides just to laugh at the actor chasing me down with a rubber hatchet. I walked home from work at night armed with years of self-defense training and a can of pepper spray, head held high and shoulders back.

Nothing had scared me in years. Until today. I hadn't let it show, too proud to let that man see me tremble, but I had been terrified. He shot those two men within seconds and with no remorse. What would he do to me?

I washed my face, forcing myself not to think about it. My uncle would find me. Riley would insist on it and Greyson would do it for my uncle and for her. But what would happen to me until then? This man was a mafia boss. I knew little about the business except what Riley and Uncle Den had told me, but I knew enough from observing Greyson to know this guy was the boss. From the way he carried himself, to the rolled sleeves of his white button down and his tattooed arms. And he was Greyson's brother. One who had some kind of grudge against Riley's new husband. Enough to kidnap his wife...or attempt to.

The water warmed my face as I tried to think of a way out. I could try to fight my way out, but they had guns, and I didn't know the first thing about shooting a gun. They had taken my phone and locked me in this room. Turning the water off, I dried myself with the softest towel I'd ever felt. I peeked at the tag, wondering how many paychecks something like this would cost me. Bartending didn't pay enough. I knew that for sure. Once I wrapped it around me, I headed into the room, finding clothes in the drawers. Once again, it astonished me that there were so many things here, as if he had planned this out and wanted Riley to be as comfortable as possible.

I dug around, looking for something to fit me. These clothes had likely been bought with Riley in mind. She was tall and thin. While I was only about two inches shorter than her, I had significantly more curves. She also dressed differently from me, and they had shopped with that in mind. No T-shirts, no ripped jeans, no tank tops.

I picked out a pair of jeans and looked at the tag. There were four pairs, and these were close enough to my size. Rummaging through the shirts, I found a gray V-neck T-shirt that would suffice. The top drawer of the dresser held a variety of underwear and bras. There was something icky about that, but I brushed it off and found a pair of undies that barely fit. They were clearly for someone with less ass and ended up looking like a thong on me. The bras were all too small, fit for Riley and not my C cups. It wouldn't be the first time I went braless, but usually I did so with purpose. There was no chance of hooking up with a hot guy here and thus no purpose in flaunting my breasts.

The room had one window, and I studied it, wondering why this hadn't been my first thought instead of showering. But I never thought the way others did or followed the norm. I tried to open the window, pushing at it, but someone had painted it shut and there was no movement. I contemplated breaking the glass, but I was certain guards stood outside my door and would hear it. No matter how I continued to pry at the window, it didn't budge more than a miniscule amount. When my hands grew tired, I cased the rest of the room, then crawled into the bed. The stress of the night caught up with me and my eyes closed within no time.

THE SOUND of the door opening drew me from sleep. I blinked at the bright sunlight that flooded the room.

"Boss wants you to join him for breakfast."

I rubbed my eyes, then looked at the man. His suit stretched under his bulging muscles, large veins protruded on his neck, giving it a square look. He had light brown hair with some strands that shone blonde, and his skin was tan. The sun hit his green eyes, making them almost gemlike. He would have been attractive but for the intense grimace.

"Tell him I'm not joining him." I flopped my head back down and turned over.

"He's not gonna like that answer and you won't like his response."

"I'm sure I won't, but seeing as I'm his prisoner, I don't want to eat with him."

An unexpected chuckle had me glancing back at him.

"Can't wait to see his reaction when I tell him that."

He left, and I heard the door lock behind him. I used the bathroom, then snuggled back into the bed and pulled the blanket up. The sound of the door slamming open interrupted my attempt to go back to sleep. Heavy footsteps followed, and I opened my eyes. My captor lurched over me, his jaw so tense I wondered if it would dislocate.

"Did you not understand my reply?" I said, closing my eyes again. A thought crossed my mind that maybe I shouldn't antagonize a man who could kill me with his bare hands.

"Did you not understand that my request did not give you an option for a reply?"

I peeked an eye open. "That completely defies the definition of the word request."

His teeth made a grinding noise before he ripped the blanket off me and picked me up. I was over his shoulder, my head hanging upside down, questioning what had just happened before I could think.

"Put me down," I said, kicking my legs. He held them tighter. "You've got to be kidding me."

"I don't joke," he grumbled.

"Maybe that's your problem." I dug my elbow into his back and rested my chin on my hand, watching the hall go by and the smirk on the guard's face. I stuck my tongue out at him, which only made the smirk grow.

"I didn't know I had a problem."

I snorted. "I don't even know you and I can already name five."

We passed through a wide, open living room with floor to ceiling windows that looked out at the ocean. I couldn't stop my inhale nor my stunned, "Where are we?"

"Seagate," he replied, not stopping.

Seagate. My elbow slipped, and my chin crashed into his back. Oh God. If we were in Seagate... I swallowed down the terror that I had just been smart mouthing a man deadlier than Greyson Tides. My uncle had explained the territories to me over dinner with Riley and Greyson. I'd had an abbreviated version of it but the one thing they stressed was the reason they were bringing me into the know and placing a guard with me twenty-four seven. I was Riley's friend, and that made me a target. No one had known Den was my uncle. He rarely visited, only called and ensured I had everything I needed. But Riley and I spent time together, and that made me a target.

With my introduction to the territories came the reason extra security was necessary, the reason Riley had run back to Treemont months before and why they had moved the wedding up. The Bad

Omen. A family worse than any other. One who infiltrated other families and took them down until they owned the entire province of Seagate. And their leader was a man who showed no mercy. Drugs, human trafficking, extortion, the list went on. I knew Greyson and my uncle weren't clean, that Riley's brother wasn't clean. I understood enough to know criminal activities funded their lives, but somehow this man's rap sheet made their doings look like charity work. It was the human trafficking that struck me the hardest and from Greyson's clenched hands that night, it was one of his deal breakers. Riley had explained to me that he and her brother had a no harm to women or children policy. A line they would never cross.

The man now carrying me through his mansion had no such line.

He dropped me into a chair, and I scrambled to get away. Catching me, he slammed me back into it.

"As mouthy as you were earlier, I expected you to give me your list of my problems," he said, walking to the other side of the table.

I went to rise, and he threw me a look that scalded me with the command to stay seated. The terror I had tried to hide the night before was now twofold, and I kept my hands in my lap to hide their shake.

"Awfully quiet now, Ava." My name fell from his mouth with a seduction that slinked under my skin.

Taking a moment to look at him, I found barely any similarities to Greyson. They had the same striking blue eyes, but this man had ebony hair with thick waves, and his features were different, sharper in the jawline with a squarer chin. His body was larger, with muscles that didn't like the fit of his shirt. I couldn't help but admit that I liked it because it left nothing to the imagination. This man was like a walking god.

One who kills people and kidnaps and sells innocent women, I reminded myself, pushing away the nervous thought that he could do the same to me.

"You're the head of the Bad Omen." My voice came out as a squeak, but at least it worked.

He picked up a knife and buttered a piece of wheat toast.

"Just figured that out?"

"What's your name?" This time my voice was steadier.

He sat back and took a bite of his toast. The thought that I'd never seen a man take a sexier bite of bread flitted through my mind and I frowned, wishing we were back in the dark foyer where I couldn't see how good looking he was.

Killer, Ava.

A terse, simple answer. "Cade."

"Cade Tides?" I tipped my head, trying to understand why that didn't sound right.

His laugh was a deep baritone. "I don't use that surname, and Cade is my middle name. My parents liked posh things and my name was one of them."

"And what was that?"

"Emerson." As quick as he said it, his expression turned like he hadn't expected to be so honest.

"Emerson Tides? Now that has a ring to it." I picked my fork up and took a bite of the scrambled eggs on my plate, trying not to roll my eyes back in my head and moan. They were so much better than the ones I made.

"Don't call me that or I'll cut your tongue out."

I chomped down and bit my lip so hard it drew blood. His brow arched when I jerked back at the flare of pain.

"Would you really?" I asked, dabbing my mouth with a napkin and hiding the blood. "Aren't I too valuable for you to kill?"

Please say yes. Please say yes.

He took another bite of his toast, and I watched the movement of his jaw muscles, followed by the flick of his tongue over his lips. My thighs should not have clenched, but they did.

The crust dropped on his plate, the motion slow compared to how fast he rose and had his hand wrapped around my neck. Thumb pressing on my airway, he brought his face close to mine.

"Don't ever think you're too valuable to kill. No one holds that worth to me."

His irises were so shaded they almost looked navy, something that shouldn't have been passing through my mind when he literally held my life in his hand. They searched my eyes, looking for fear, but I doubted he'd find it because, as much as he terrified me, he intrigued me. And as scary as having his hand around my neck was, facing fear had always turned me on. It was the reason I had snuck into the hangar that night with Billy. There was only one fear I had yet to conquer, and this man wasn't it.

I chased the high of danger. And Emerson Tides was the ultimate danger.

My lips parted at the irrational thoughts and his eyes dropped to them before they flicked back up. He shoved me away and straightened, tugging at his sleeves as he avoided looking at me.

"Next time I request your presence at a meal, consider it a command."

"I'm not really into commands," I said absently, rubbing my neck and hating how the impression of his touch lingered.

His silence had me lifting my sight to him. Shit, had I just said that out loud? This man was a killer, and I was saying flirty things to him. A call with my therapist was necessary at this point. I cringed, realizing the routine of my life was now in flux and my weekly session would not happen.

"I don't give a shit what you're into. When I tell you to do something, you will. I have no qualms about sending you back to my brother in a body bag as a wedding gift."

He stormed away, leaving me with the towering guard.

"Is he always so chatty?" I asked, taking another bite of eggs and trying not to think of all the ways my life was going to shit because I foolishly wanted to have sex with a guy on a plane. There was my job and then school. I was so close to finishing and missing time would jeopardize my degree. It had taken me years to decide to go to graduate school and now I stood to lose all that I'd worked for. Not to mention therapy and my meds. I'd already missed one dose.

My hand shook at the thought as the guard replied, "You caught him on a good day."

"So this is him in a good mood?" I said, feigning calm.

"You don't want to see him in a bad mood."

After he'd shot those two men the night before, I was certain I didn't want to witness his bad side. Bad side in bed? That might be worth it.

Shut up, Ava. I was going to strangle myself if I didn't stop fixating on how gorgeous my captor was.

"So, when I'm done eating, what then?"

"Then it's back to your room."

Twisting my mouth, I mumbled, "My prison."

He didn't respond and with a sigh, I continued to eat my breakfast, avoiding the empty space across from me.

Chapter Seven

The waves crashed on the shore below as I stood on the deck. Ava was under my skin in a way I didn't like. I didn't know why I had wanted her to eat with me, but curiosity drove me to it. Her refusal had fired me up, but I hadn't expected my reaction when she had peered up at me with those big chestnut eyes, pink strands of hair falling over her cheeks with the blonde ones. A pink gem sparkled in the side of her nose that I hadn't noticed the prior night. She was adorable, and I hated the thought.

But every time she opened her mouth, it was like a wildcat lived inside the cute exterior. The things she said with no hesitation and no fear. Everyone feared me, but if she did, she didn't let it show. Wildcat, that was the perfect name for her.

I rubbed my cheek and took my phone out, hitting the number I had hesitated to call. This plan had gone terribly wrong and now I had to pray my brother cared enough to come after Ava. If not, I would have to kill her and start over.

I'd ignored my brother's calls, enjoying the power in making him wait, knowing it would drive him mad. But it was time to make my next move.

Greyson picked up on the first ring.

"Emerson." The prick always used that name, never the one I had gone by since the day I'd walked out of his life. The day he'd stolen my girl from me and laughed when I'd walked in on them. Grabbing her head and fucking her mouth harder, like he was showing me his prize. It had been over two decades and I'd realized with time that she was just another fling, another woman in my bed, but the betrayal had left my pride wounded. I had loved her, and he had wanted to prove some stupid point, that she would turn on me in a heartbeat. Which she did with his coercion.

"Greyson," I returned, my voice flat.

"You have something of mine, and I want it back."

"Does your new wife know this one is yours, too? Does she share you with her?" The idea had my blood heating, a reaction I didn't understand.

"Fuck off. I'm not sleeping with her, asshole."

A bit of tension fled, and I pinched the bridge of my nose to bring it back. I didn't give a shit who Ava was sleeping with. She'd already admitted she'd been on the plane to screw the guy she was with. Why did I care if my brother was sleeping with her?

"Then she's of no value to you?"

"You know she is, or you wouldn't have taken her."

I wouldn't have taken her if my shithead men hadn't fucked up my orders.

"What do you want, Emerson?"

Rolling my neck, I said, "You."

The silence on the other end lingered. "What the hell does that mean?"

"It means I want you in Seagate so we can work out an agreement."

"An agreement on what? You stole my wife's friend—"

"And your henchman's niece."

He grumbled before he said, "There is no agreement here.

Either fly her home alive and unharmed or I will bring my full force down on you."

Which was exactly what I didn't want. I was weak, my empire vulnerable, something he didn't know because all indications pointed to me stirring trouble in his province and in Armina.

"A simple negotiation, Greyson."

"Don't pull that shit on me. I tried to negotiate years ago, but you were too stubborn to listen."

"You mean when Tina's mouth was around your cock?"

"Fuck you. That was twenty-five years ago. You should have let it go, but instead you decided that some bitch who spread her legs for everyone we knew, including me, was worth turning your back on family."

"Family doesn't fuck his brother's girl."

A heavy sigh followed by, "There's no talking to you, Emerson. You're blinded just like you've always been. And it's too late now. Your hands are too dirty, your deeds too warped for me to ever consider reconciling with you."

My hand clenched the deck rail, splinters piercing my skin.

"Send Ava back and stay in your province. Otherwise, I'm coming to get you. I have a score to settle with you for what your man did to my wife. Oh, and I'm sure Brinks will be more than happy to come along with Raines."

"You would bring those children to fight your war, Grey? Is that how weak you've become?" My rage was blinding me, my words not thought through, but they were out before I could stop them.

"Send her back—"

"The only way I'm sending her back is in pieces. You have two weeks to make your decision. In that time, I'll keep her alive and unharmed and you will keep your men and Brinks out of my territory. Two weeks and when I call again, you'd better have the right answer or she's dead."

I disconnected and slammed the phone against the rail. Two

weeks? There was no explanation as to why I had given him that deadline. It was too long. Enough time for him to bring an army to my door or enough time for me to fall for the pesky woman who was currently my hostage.

THE SCOTCH SOOTHED MY MOOD, and I took another gulp, resting my head back in my chair. Waves crashed against the surf, the moon streaming between clouds to cast long shadows over the sand. This was my favorite place to come when I needed to think. My deck perched high over the cliff with nothing to block the view. Woods surrounded the eastern side of the house, a long stretch of manicured grass on the front and western side. But the backside was all shoreline.

A scream broke the silence, high pitched and desperate. It clawed into my chest and severed my ability to breathe. My glass crashed onto the wooden deck as I ran into the house, following the trail of screams. Over and over, they pierced my ears, rising the closer I came to Ava's room.

The door was open, and I drew my gun, finding Pack staring at the bed. Ava was thrashing, the covers tangled around her body, her hands scratching at the air like they were digging for something.

"I found her like this. She's having some kind of nightmare," he said, frowning.

"Well, wake her up."

Another scream, this one so guttural it ripped through me. I moved toward the bed, but Pack stopped me.

"It's not good to wake somebody from a nightmare."

Jerking my arm away, I looked back at her.

"Go, I've got this." I tucked my gun in my pants as more

screams poured from her. They were getting more desperate, her voice cracking from the strain on her throat.

Pack left, and I heard him pushing my other men from the room before the door closed. If I couldn't wake her, I didn't know what to do. She looked so fragile, so wounded, her face contorted with terror and pain. I had killed, taken body parts, bloodied faces, tortured enough to recognize it. Most times, it fed me, but not this time. I wanted to wipe it from her.

On instinct, I crawled into the other side of the bed and wrapped my arm around her, drawing her flailing body into mine. This was not something I did, comforting a hostage, comforting anyone. I didn't make connections or hold women for any more than necessary. I was cold and brutal, taking what I wanted and reciprocating pleasure only when I was in the mood, but something about holding Ava seemed natural.

A broken whimper caused a twinge in my chest. I brushed her hair from her face and murmured, "Shhh. You're safe." A complete lie, but one that came out with surety.

She continued to thrash for a few more minutes until her body calmed and she fell further against me. I pulled her closer, spooning her and hating how nice it felt. The floral scent of her shampoo greeted me, and I buried my face in her hair, breathing it in. Another whimper, quiet and sad, came from her and no matter how I wanted to remove myself from her bed and the situation, I didn't want her to suffer anymore.

Suffer? When had I gone soft and worried that a prisoner was suffering? Anger surfaced, a need for self-preservation taking over until her hand covered mine and pulled it toward her face. Positioned between her breasts, I couldn't help but notice the weight of them, the softness and how unbound they were. Shit, she still wasn't wearing a bra. I'd realized it when she was at breakfast, her nipples pressing against the fabric of her gray T-shirt with the outline of her nipple rings prominent. Her brazen attitude had threatened to make me hard, but that sight had done the job. She was everything I'd never considered in a woman but was now craving.

The thought had my pants growing uncomfortably tight, and I tried pulling my hand away, only to have her stop it. She was not letting me go. I was certain she had no idea who was holding her, or she would have been slathering me in snarky comments and kicking me out—like she held the power in any of this.

Giving up my fight to leave, I scooted up so my body completely eclipsed her frame and rested my head on the pillow. Sleep never came easily to me. My mind was overactive, my worries incessant. But something about holding Ava silenced the voices and let sleep in. Something I didn't realize until a smart-assed voice broke my peace with, "Is this how you get your thrills? Sneaking into women's beds and feeling them up, Emerson?"

She really needed to stop using my real name. Only my brother did that, and it pissed me off more every time he did. But I let it go, finding something cute about the way she said it. Cute?

I blinked my eyes open, suddenly aware that I was palming her breast and not disliking the fact that her nipple was completely taut below it.

"I don't have to sneak into women's beds," I groused, removing my hand even though I'd really wanted to tug on that nipple ring and hear what sounds it evoked.

"No? You just force them into yours?"

"Fuck you," I grumbled, rolling onto my back and trying to get my bearings.

She turned toward me, something I hadn't expected, and I squinted at her. She looked even more adorable when she woke up. Her hair was tussled, her eyes a lush chestnut, a fresh flush on her cheeks. I wiped my hand over my face, questioning how I'd lost my mind in the last twenty-four hours.

"Why are you in my bed, Emerson?"

This woman had no fear other than what she experienced in her dreams. She was bold and sassy. Fearless or pretending to be.

What had happened to her to cause a nightmare that vivid and terrifying? An instinct to kill whoever had left that damage surged, and I shoved it away.

"It's Cade, and it's my bed, not yours."

Her brow quirked, and I noticed a divot where a piercing should have been. Was there anywhere on her body that wasn't pierced? The possible answer to that question had me throbbing. Ava Shelton was a woman unlike any who ran in my circles, and the urge to flip her over and discover every tattoo and piercing fought for dominance.

"It's my bed while you have me imprisoned and I like Emerson. You don't look like a Cade." She smirked and tiptoed her hand up my chest before I grabbed it and pushed it away. "Now tell me why you're in my bed."

"Only if you tell me why you think it's smart to flirt with your captor." Because that's what I was. A man who would kill her if my brother didn't come through. A tug of doubt had me suddenly questioning my plans.

"I'm not flirting," she said, laughing. "This is how I always am. In your face and loud. If you don't like it, then send me home."

"Good try, but I'm not sending you anywhere." And why had I not gotten out of the bed? Damn it, this was bad. I sat up and ran my hand through my hair, sensing her eyes on me. "I'm in your bed because you were having nightmares."

A startled intake of air had me looking over at her. She scrambled from the bed and, for the first time since she'd come into my life with her attitude and brash remarks, she looked scared. Hand rubbing her neck, she said, "I did?" Her voice was meek, and I tipped my head at the difference.

"Yes, a violent one."

"Shit. You need to send me home. Please." Her eyes pleaded with me, but I ignored the plea, rising from the bed and smoothing out my pants.

"No." Gathering my senses and remembering who I was and why she was here, I turned my back on her and walked toward the door.

"Please, Emerson."

That plea seared me, and I squeezed the door handle. "No."

I opened the door, but her words stopped me. "Did you hold me all night to soothe my nightmares?"

Teeth gritting, I glanced back at her. I couldn't afford to get attached to her. No matter that after this brief time, I could already sense it happening. "I only did it to stop the incessant screaming. The screaming stays in the basement. If you keep it up, I'll lock you down there where I keep my enemies until they can't endure my torture and die."

I ripped the door open and stomped out of the room, waves of crimson blinding me. This was who I was, the cruel bastard who everyone feared. Not some nice guy who held terrified women through the night to chase away their nightmares. Not some weak man who fell for women in a day or cared if his hostage was comfortable.

Heading to my room, I convinced myself that this had been a moment of weakness. That I would avoid her for the next two weeks. But by the time I had pounded my aggression out in my gym, she was back on my mind where she stayed until I knew there was no avoiding her.

Chapter Eight

GREYSON

Gentle fingers smoothed the tension from my shoulders before Riley's head rested on my back.

"They're waiting for you," she said, her hands wrapping around my waist.

I took them in mine and brought them to my lips. Never had I held something so precious as Riley now was to me. Thinking she may have been the one in my brother's hands and that this wasn't the first time she'd almost ended up there made my stomach knot.

Green eyes, dark with worry, looked back at me when I glanced over my shoulder at her. Turning, I pulled her closer.

"What did he say?" she asked.

I had stepped away to take the call with Emerson, leaving her in the main room with the others. The ass had ignored every call and text, making me wait until he was ready to talk. It was a move I would have made. I was the calm one, he was the impulsive one.

"Nothing good." I gave her a quick kiss, wishing I had the time to savor it and more of her. But with her brother and Tyson waiting, not to mention Den, who was the most unnerved I'd ever seen him, now wasn't the time to indulge. "Come on."

I led her out to the living room. Den's pacing was wearing a path in the floor near the windows. Mason was on the couch, a drink in one hand, his other around his girl, and Raines was in the chair with his wife sprawled on his lap. Apparently, we all came as a package deal now. It wasn't the life to bring a woman into, but I didn't have a choice with Riley, and I'd found she took after her brother in ways that still surprised me. Calculating and smart, she saw things I missed, looking at situations with a critical eye that surpassed even mine. Casey had taken down a pack of Bad Omen to save Mason. And Angie...well, as obstinate as she seemed, I had a suspicion Raines didn't have any choice but to include her.

"I have two weeks," I said, walking into the center of the room.

Mason leaned forward, swirling his drink in his hands. "Two weeks to what?"

Rubbing my temple, I said, "To decide. Me or Ava."

Tyson pushed Angie to the side. "What the hell does that mean?"

"It means I hand myself over to my brother or he kills her. He'll call me for an answer and if I give him the wrong one, she's dead."

"Fuck," Den muttered, his pacing stopping.

"Why two weeks?" Angie said, staring at her nails. "Even I can make a decision in less time than that. Do I want a French manicure or just tips? The pink shoes or the black ones?"

The muscles in my jaw tightened. "Why are you even here?"

"Because she's a bitch and won't satisfy me if I leave her out," Tyson said, biting her ear and eliciting a giggle from her.

My head had ached before, but now it was becoming a migraine. "This is not shoe shopping. This is life or death. Not a fucking manicure."

"But she has a point," Riley said, "as much as I hate saying that." Angie threw her a look that Riley returned without flinching. "Two weeks is a long time in our world." Our world. I loved her more every day.

"I'm inclined to agree." Mason took another swig of his drink. "These are the Omens we're talking about. They don't give time-lines. They act swiftly and with intent. Something's off."

"Something's been off," Casey added. "Everything about this has been off since they kidnapped me and Angie."

I scratched my jaw, thinking about all the careless mistakes and miscalculations. "No, since Clint Randall," I mused. Riley shivered, and I brought my hand around her waist, pulling her over to me. There were still nights she woke up from nightmares I couldn't free her from. All I could do was hold her close and soothe her until she fell back to sleep. Not even I had the power to take her memories away. "He went rogue. Or at least I thought he had. He botched everything he did. He had every opportunity to kill you, Brinks. Why not just do it when he was in your inner circle?" I patted Riley's ass, which garnered me a grimace from Mason, then walked over to my bar. Pouring myself a glass of scotch, I continued, "He failed at killing Riley the first time." She cringed, and I gave her an apologetic look. "And the second time, he screwed up again. I thought he was going rogue on the family, but what if he wasn't? What if he was just sloppy?"

"How so?" Raines asked.

"He took the time to call me. My brother would never give up the pleasure of telling me he had Riley and allow one of his men to make the call. It was a novice move."

"Or a move that came from someone without the constraints of the Bad Omen." Angie said. "A rogue man like you said."

"No." Mason's brows knitted, his hand tight on his glass as he thought it through. "A rogue would have kept his mouth shut and taken her somewhere. Raped and killed her or kept her hostage until he was done with her."

Riley rubbed her arms. "Can we stop talking about me like I'm not here?"

"Shit, sorry, Ri." Mason looked genuinely apologetic.

"I know," Casey said, hopping from her seat and taking Riley's hand. "You have wedding gifts to unwrap. Angie, I know how much you love comparing yourself to others, so why don't you join us and see if Riley got better gifts than you?"

Tyson snorted, and I heard an *oomph* that told me she had likely elbowed him. But my eyes were on Riley.

"We were going to open them together," she said, conflict in her features.

"Go. Presents aren't really my thing. I only like giving them."

She gave me a small smile as Casey dragged her away, Angie chattering behind them about how she'd wanted some ice cream machine.

"I had to get her that damned machine and I've seen her use it once," Tyson complained, rolling his neck as he stood and stretched. "So you two think what? That there's something off with the Omen?"

"Casey suggested that a while ago, remember, Ty?"

I raised a brow, taking a swig of my drink. "She was the one who noticed?"

"Fuck off, Tides."

Smirking, I ignored him and said, "My brother hasn't had more than a two second conversation with me in years. Now he wants to talk, and that has my alarms up. There's something off."

"What did he do to you?" Raines asked.

I stared down at my drink. "It's what I did to him. A young, foolish move I thought would prove a point."

They waited for more, and my expression soured. "Let's just say I knew his girl liked to sleep around and I proved the point."

"You fucked your brother's girl?" Tyson said with a chuckle.

"She gave me a blow job and I kicked her out once I made my point." Even saying the words sounded crass now. I was no longer that man, hadn't been in a very long time. Enough time to regret my actions, but not enough to mend the destruction they had caused.

"I hope you didn't say that to my sister," Mason said, almost growling.

I sat in the other seat. "Your sister knows everything. We have no secrets. Not anymore." But it had taken almost losing her to confess it all to her.

"So, what do you think is off?" Tyson asked, setting his glass down and steering the conversation back.

"I don't know, but two weeks is a long time for Emerson. That tells me he wants me to think about his proposition and maybe more." I took another drink. "Maybe it's time to piece together whatever it is we're not seeing."

"And if we don't?" Mason asked. This was my fight, but Riley's connection to Ava made it theirs, too. That didn't mean they were running the show, and that Mason had deferred the next move to me, told me he understood the hierarchy. Ava was my man's niece and although I hadn't been in her life before, Den was the closest I had to a best friend. That made this my battle to direct and to win.

"Then we bring our force to Seagate and take my brother down."

Chapter Nine

AVA

ringing my hands, I paced the room and avoided looking at the bed. Emerson had held me through my nightmares. The most feared mob boss in all the provinces. A man who probably killed puppies and most definitely killed people with the same hands that had been wrapped around me when I woke. I rubbed the space between my eyes, trying to convince myself that I'd disliked waking up to that. To hate how safe and warm I'd been. How hard and large he'd been.

"Stop it, Ava," I muttered, making another trail across the room. "He's a killer who abuses women."

But he had done nothing to me to substantiate that claim. Hadn't laid a finger on me except...well, except his hand around my neck and the gun to my head.

Exactly, my know-it-all side huffed.

He had held me all night, though. And I couldn't get that thought from my head unless I considered the reason for his actions. My nightmares. I needed my meds and soon or every night would be the same. I stopped my pacing, tilting my head as I considered how I didn't dislike the idea of waking that way again.

Smacking myself on the forehead, I grumbled at my bad decision making and went back to pacing. The door opened, and I jumped, grabbing my chest.

"Do you people ever knock?" I asked my guard whose name was Breaker. I'd made the mistake of asking about the name, only to regret it when he told me he enjoyed the sound of bones breaking.

"No."

Putting my hands on my hips, I asked, "What if I was changing?"

"Then I'd get a show and see what those tits look like without the shirt in the way," he responded with a shrug.

Gaping at him, I crossed my arms to cover my chest. Maybe I should have tried squeezing into one of the smaller bras. Spilling over the edge might have been a better choice.

"You're gross," I groused.

"Never said I wasn't. The boss wants to see you."

"Great." I rolled my eyes, trying to ignore the excited butterflies in my stomach. Butterflies? Since when did I get those, and why would they swarm over the man who had kidnapped me? Ugh, I hated my confusing body sometimes.

My guard grabbed my elbow and pulled me down the hall and through the large living room, out onto the patio.

"You don't need to pull her arm out of socket, Breaker."

If those butterflies had annoyed me earlier, they had me eager to reach into my gut and pulverize them now. Emerson looked too hot for someone I should hate. He wore a black button-down shirt with the top buttons open to show his tan chest and tattoos. His sleeves rolled partway up his forearms, exposed more tattoos and muscles that had me salivating. The shirt rested against even more muscle, and I didn't even want to gaze down at his pants, especially after last night.

I caught my uncouth gaping in the reflection of his sunglasses and quickly closed my mouth. With a firm yank of my arm that sent me stumbling slightly, I gave Breaker a nasty look.

"That's cute, Ava," Emerson said as Breaker laughed and walked away. "I think you frightened him with all that angst."

He didn't have to remove the glasses for me to sense his eyes graze over my body. It was like hands sliding down my skin and I moved my arm awkwardly to cover my breasts, knowing my nipples had beckoned to the call of that heated gaze.

"You wanted to see me?" I asked, staying in place.

Removing the sunglasses didn't help my cause. His eyes were bright blue in the morning sun. I could have stood there all day drinking them in.

"Come sit down. We need to talk."

Shit, no, we didn't. "I'm good," I said—a complete lie— pivoting to walk away.

"Ava." That was not the voice of the man who had comforted me. That was the voice of a lethal killer. The one I kept warning myself was behind the tempting exterior. "Sit."

My muscles tensed, and I debated my choices. I didn't like being told what to do, but one glance at him let me know I didn't have a choice in the matter.

"I told you I don't like commands," I complained, taking a seat and thumping into it. "You want to talk, then talk."

He slid a plate over to me and a glass of orange juice. Scrambled eggs and toast with jam.

"Do you eat anything but toast and eggs?" I asked, not moving.

"Only when I want to cook something else."

My jaw dropped again, and I snapped it closed. "You cook?"

He gave me a smirk that had my insides melting. "Why? Am I not supposed to know how to cook?"

I gave up on my pouting when my stomach growled. Lifting the fork, I replied, "It's just not something I would expect someone like you to do."

Did Greyson cook? Or Riley's brother? That Tyson guy looked entirely too large and terrifying to stand behind a stove.

"Someone like me?"

I raised my eyes, seeing the curiosity in his. Swallowing, I said, "A mob boss." I figured it was the less messy answer.

"Hmm. I didn't realize there were limitations on our abilities." He took a sip of his coffee and waited for my response while he placed the mug back on the table.

The coffee smelled delicious. Not thinking, I reached over and took the mug, bringing it to my lips as his brow rose.

"Mmm," I moaned before realizing the sound had slipped from me.

One awkward moment and one flash of desire mixed with tightened jaw muscles later, he said, "If you wanted coffee, I could have gotten you a cup."

My hands still wrapped around the mug, I lowered it, saying, "This will do, but tomorrow I'll take my own...unless you want to share."

He snatched the mug from my hands and mumbled, "I don't share."

"Is that why you hate your brother?" I asked.

That jaw clenched even more and the words, "Something like that," came out muffled by it.

I'd hit a nerve and considering who I sat across from, I wanted that nerve soothed quickly. Rising, I walked to the edge of the deck and looked over the railing. "It's beautiful," I said, staring down at the private beach. Enclosed by rocky cliff sides, the shore fed into crashing waves that danced as they turned to a frothy surf.

"It is," he said, too quietly for a man of his force.

I peered back at him, and he dropped his eyes to his coffee cup before holding it out to me. "Here."

"No, it's fine. I shouldn't have—"

"Take the fucking coffee."

My hands went to my hips, and I scowled at him. "Don't be so fucking rude."

It might not have been the best response since I was standing across from my ruthless kidnapper on the edge of a deck that was too many stories up to count.

But he chuckled and held it out further. "Take the coffee, Ava."

Thrown off, I let my hands fall. It was almost like he was two different people. Walking over, I took it from him, my fingers touching his briefly, but long enough to set those butterflies into another frenzy.

"You've got a mouth on you," he said, resting back in his chair as I took my seat again.

"I do. It gets me in trouble sometimes."

"I bet. You're like a damned wildcat."

"Untamed and unhinged," I said, grinning over the rim of the cup.

"Something like that." He shook his head, and I looked back out at the view.

"I've never been to the ocean," I admitted.

"Never?"

I turned back to him, seeing the curiosity there. "Never. I didn't grow up near the ocean and it didn't seem worth the two-hour drive to get to the shore when I moved to Bridgeville." I lowered the mug. "Why do you live here?"

He sat up and rested his elbows on the table, clasping his hands in front of him. "It makes for a distraction from life, I suppose. There isn't much beauty in my life, so this suffices."

I picked at the handle. "No beautiful women in your bed every night." Unsure where that question had come from, I focused my sight on the mug handle and avoided his eyes.

He snorted. "Not every night."

My eyes flew up as something in my chest became uncomfortable. "But some nights," I said, hating how I had wanted him to say something different.

The corner of his mouth lifted. "When I'm in the mood. I

suppose it's different when you have a boyfriend you can sneak onto airplanes and fuck."

The way he said fuck left my core heated. That he was fishing for my status as much as I had been for his had me confused. "He wasn't my boyfriend."

He waited for more, his stare penetrating.

Grinning, I said, "He was the bartender from the wedding. I don't do boyfriends; they get too clingy."

"So, you don't do commands, and you don't do boyfriends. There are so many things to unpack there, wildcat."

My heart beat out of rhythm, halting my breath momentarily. This was bad and wrong, and I was enjoying it too much. I suspected he was enjoying it just as much.

"I doubt that," I said, finding my voice.

Dropping his arms and leaning further in, he said, "What were you dreaming about last night?"

The sudden change of topic had me flustered. "I...nothing," I stuttered, lowering my eyes again.

"Ava." That commanding tone had returned.

Pushing my chair back, I rose. "Nothing. It was just a nightmare."

"That wasn't just a nightmare," he countered, rising as well.

I walked away, hearing his steps behind me. Prisoner. That's what I was, no matter how comfortable our talk had been, or how gorgeous he was. But I didn't know how long I would be here and if the nightmares were returning, they would get worse.

Halting my steps, I turned back, finding his solid chest right in front of me. I looked up at him, only then noticing how he towered over me.

"I need my meds," I said, hating that I had to ask. Straightening my spine, which only gained me a half an inch, I added, "Or else they'll continue."

"The nightmares?" His brows creased and concern lined his blue eyes.

"Yes. The medicine I take helps keep them away. I need to take it three times a day, and I've missed two doses already."

Pulling his phone out, he said, "Do you know the dosages and the name of the medication?"

"Yes."

"Good. What other meds do you need?"

I couldn't help but stare at him. "You're going to get my medicine for me?"

"Just tell me what you need." He hit a number and brought his phone to his ear. A man's voice answered after one ring. "Reach out to your supplier. I need..." He looked at me.

I gave him the name and dosages, then listened as he repeated them.

"And?"

The specifics on the one I took for panic attacks and my anxiety were next. I didn't know if I would need the one, but given my situation, it was a likely chance.

"That's all?" he asked, as if he expected more. I'd thought I had given him plenty.

I nodded, yet he waited.

"What?" I asked, putting my hands out.

"No birth control?"

I slammed my mouth shut too hard and the shock of my teeth clanking made me cringe. "I don't need it. Unless you're planning to do something..." I backed up, remembering who he was and that reputation that had bothered the other bosses. Swallowing too loudly, I took another step back, seeing the understanding in his eyes.

I needed to get out of there. This game of flirting was nothing more than a way to ease me in before he sold me off to someone or passed me around to his men. Fear hammered me, and I spun on my heels and ran.

"Damn it. That's all," I heard him tell whoever was on the phone as I passed through the deck doors.

His hand was on my arm, stopping my movement and spinning me around before I got further.

"Ava, stop."

A stern warning, but one I didn't want to heed because the thought of being traded and used terrified me like nothing had before.

I tried pulling away, but his other hand took my free arm, and he tugged me toward him.

"Let me go, Emerson. Please. You can't do that to me. I'll fight you and whoever buys me. I will not stop fighting until I'm—"

"Stop." He glanced up at Breaker, who had been blocking my way out of the main room to the door that stood not far from him, then dragged me back out to the deck.

Dragged was the best term because I dug my heels into the floor and clawed at his hands. Shoving me toward the table, he looked down at his hands, grumbling, "Fucking calm down. Goddamn you're a wildcat." He sucked his bloody knuckle, his eyes dark as they stared me down.

My chest was heaving from my struggle, but with his focus on his knuckle, I made a break for it. His arm came out and slammed into my stomach. My back hit his chest hard enough to knock the air from my lungs when he flipped me around. A firm hold kept me from wiggling.

"Settle down, wildcat." This time, his voice was low and gravely, a sound that caused an annoyingly warm sensation between my legs.

"Why should I? You must think I'm a fool. Well, I'm not, Emerson Tides. I'm smart and on to you."

He chuckled, an unexpected reaction and one that only further infuriated me.

"You think that's funny?"

"I think it's funny how you have the nerve to call me by a name only my shithead brother calls me. And that you think you've got me figured out."

My body was enjoying his arms around it entirely too much, and I relaxed further into him. His voice against my ear informed me of where my body's allegiance fell when he said, "I find it humorous that you can look so adorable and sweet, yet there's a fucking wildcat with wicked words and sharp claws underneath."

The heave of my chest was entirely too noticeable. "So I'm adorable?" Oh no, there I went again, flirting with a man I was just running from. This man was eviscerating my common sense.

He removed his hand and flicked the messy knob of hair on the left side of my head. I had ripped strips of fabric from a shirt in my room and used them to tie my hair up in two knots.

"With pink streaks and these things? Not sure there's another word that accurately describes you."

Huffing, I said, "I'd take beautiful or gorgeous. Adorable makes me sound like I'm a kid." I glanced over my shoulder at him, my forehead scraping against his stubble. "Oh no, don't tell me you're into kids."

The yank to my knot caused an uncensored yelp.

"No, I'm not into kids. What the fuck is wrong with you?"

"Just checking if I needed to add something even more disgusting to your rap sheet."

A noise similar enough to a growl came from him, eliciting a fuzzy sensation in my stomach. Wiggling from his hold, I turned to find his features stiff. His eyes flicked to my chest, and there was a slight tick to his jaw.

"You know, if they bother you so much, you could get me some clothes that fit. I'm sure you've noticed, I don't have Riley's figure and these," I cupped my breasts, "do not fit her B cups."

He shook his head, the corner of his mouth tugging toward a smile. "I'll have Jill get you clothes."

"Jill? Is that one of those sometimes sleep overs?"

Wiping his hand over his face, he muttered, "You're a handful. No, she's my housekeeper, and she picked up the clothes you now have on."

"Housekeeper with benefits?" *Shit, Ava, what are you doing?* I was frightened of this man ten minutes ago and here I was back to the fishing again.

Another head shake. "Never let her hear you say that." He pinched the bridge of his nose. "I have a meeting to attend." He motioned for Breaker. "Finish eating, then Breaker will take you back to your room."

"Still a hostage, huh?" I said, walking over to my food and considering how cold it likely now was. Instead, I grabbed the coffee, not caring if it was cold. I turned and looked at him as I took a sip, but what I saw in those blue orbs wasn't playfulness or even anger. It looked more like regret before he blinked it away.

"That's what you are, Ava." He pulled the cuffs of his shirt down, a move I found intriguingly sexy, my eyes trailing the movement of his hands. "You need to remember that."

Breaker stepped out onto the patio, and Emerson turned away from me. As he neared the threshold, I said, "I suppose you'll need to remind yourself of that as well, Cade." His steps faltered at the use of his alias, but he didn't respond.

I dropped into my seat with a sigh, picking at the cold food and missing his company.

L ight flickered above us, the snapping within the fading bulb in tempo with my rising heart rate.

"What do you mean, my men already picked up the shipment?" My fists opened and closed as I tried to contain the ire that was currently shading my vision with bright streaks of red.

"Yesterday," Ronnie said, tugging at his neckline and gulping. "Said they were your guys, and that you sent them early."

"My guys?" I snarled. "And just how did you know they were my guys?"

"Their tattoos. They all had it, showed me as proof."

I held back the roar that threatened to escape. Letting him or my men see me out of control would only worsen the situation.

Adjusting my collar, I stepped toward Ronnie, a supplier I had worked with for years. Who I had never had issues with...until now. The nervous tugging at his shirt continued, his eyes darting to my hands, then back up. My six three frame dwarfed him but to his credit, he didn't move. If he had, he would have been dead already.

Placing my hand around the back of his neck, I said in my calmest voice, "When have I ever sent someone in my place to inspect a shipment?" Putting pressure on his jugular, I squeezed. "When has that ever fucking happened, Ronnie?"

"N...n...never Cade."

Releasing him, I patted his chest. "You gave my merchandise to someone else." I had my gun pressed to his temple within seconds. "And you're going to replace it, or I will take my time putting bullets into every part of your body, including that small dick of yours. Enough bullets to make you suffer, but not enough to make you die quickly. Then I'll take a seat and watch as my men remove every finger, every toe, every tooth." I knocked the butt of my gun on his forehead. "How many hours of torture do you think you can stand, Ronnie? Because I just lost a few hundred grand and I need you to know the pain of that loss as if it were your own."

His face had gone stark white, his eyes now so large they looked like saucers. Tucking my gun away, I gave him a light smack on his face.

"Get me my product, Ronnie. You have two days, or I'll return with a bottle of scotch and prepare to be entertained by your screams."

As I exited the warehouse, Pack stepped in stride with me. My other men were far enough ahead and behind me for him to talk.

"You think it was them, boss?"

"I know it was."

The thorn in my ass and the reason I was now forced to grovel to my younger brother. My punch on the roof of the car left an indent.

Pack opened the car door for me, saying, "Get in, boss. It's not safe out here."

I glanced at him, seeing his eyes flicking around. He was on alert for good reason. This was war and I was the target. My empire was the target.

"Let's see if they've gotten to my other suppliers," I said, getting in. It was bound to be a long day. Four more stops and my mood had already soured. I needed a drink and a little of Ava's smart mouth. That mouth was enough to make me want to strangle her, yet every time she opened it, she enthralled me more. I rubbed my eyes. Everything about her enthralled me, which was a dangerous thing. Maybe I should have just killed her.

"You good, boss?" Pack looked at me through the rearview mirror.

"Yeah, just trying to clear my mind."

He returned to driving, but I could tell he wanted to question me, knowing me enough to spot my weakness for the spirited minx locked in my home. But we weren't alone, and he knew better than to say anything.

Staring out the window at the passing streets, I thought about how good it had been to hold her. I hadn't had a woman in my bed in too long and those had been one-night stands, nothing more than a night of release. Attachment wasn't for me. My life was too dangerous and busy for a woman, but something about Ava had me craving more. Not just a fling or a heated fuck. More. And I had never wanted more.

Shit, the woman had been in my life for two days and I couldn't get her off my mind. I didn't want to think about what would happen after two weeks with her. Resting my head back, I tried not to think about it. She was my hostage. Nothing more. Collateral damage if my brother didn't agree to my meeting. A bargaining chip if he did.

I needed to avoid her, to stop insisting she eat with me, to leave her locked in her room. Disassociate myself from her. But as the day went by, the meetings better than my first but still tiring, my mind was back on her.

Toweling my hair dry after a much-needed shower, I picked up my phone, seeing Tuck's number. He was my go-to for medication when our supplies ran low. Pack was the closest we had to a doctor, with enough experience now to extract bullets and stitch my men up. Tuck was who I went to for the supplies he needed to keep our makeshift operating room stocked.

"Tuck," I answered, throwing my towel into the bathroom.

"I can get the meds, but it will take a few days. My contact is out of the province, but assures me he'll have it in three days."

Damn. "Three days? That's too long."

"The first drug is the problem. It's difficult to get. What do you need it for, anyway? It's some heart medication."

I rubbed my neck. "No, that doesn't make sense. It's for nightmares."

"Huh, that's not what my contact said. Who's having nightmares?"

"Nobody. Just get it for me."

Disconnecting, I did a search for the medication, finding the same answer Tuck had given me until I added nightmares to my search. The result was not what I had expected. I brought the phone closer, questioning what I'd found. Not only did the drug help with heart issues, psychiatrists used it when working with PTSD patients who suffered from night terrors.

I read the article several times. PTSD? What had Ava gone through to give her that? And those nightmares I had assumed were because I had shot two men next to her and put a gun to her head, had nothing to do with me. Something had happened in her past that still haunted her in her nightmares.

Throwing my phone on the bed, I grabbed a T-shirt and pulled it over my head while I walked from my room. Breaker was off duty, but Vin stood guard in front of Ava's room. He gave me a nod, and I opened Ava's door.

"You people need to learn to knock," she complained behind a book I assumed she must have convinced one of the guys to get her. "Seriously, I could be naked in—" She halted her words, her eyes peering over the edge of the book.

I noted the sweep of her eyes over my body and couldn't stop my smirk. This was the first time she had seen me out of my regular attire of dress shirts and slacks.

"You dress down nicely, Emerson."

So, she was back to my name. Hearing her call me by my alias had been akin to a dagger piercing my skin, and I'd hated the sensation.

I had intended to come in and demand she tell me why she needed to take a medicine prescribed to patients with PTSD, but as she lowered the book, the words escaped me. She had freed her hair and blonde and pink curls hung loosely around her neck now. I had called her adorable, and she was right to question the term because she really was beautiful. With doe eyes that hid the viper below, a splash of freckles dusting her nose, and a mouth that screamed to be kissed.

"I can't get the medicine for a few more days," I stated, ignoring her comment and pushing away the thoughts of kissing that mouth.

Her expression fell so fast, I hated that I had wiped away her playful smile. "Oh." A simple reply that told me enough.

"Do you have a heart condition, Ava?" I asked. My normal method of demanding answers had escaped me. The idea of making her tell me something that would bring that haunted look she'd had in her sleep back again killed me.

"No," she replied with a laugh. "Unless I developed one with as many times as people have barged into my room unannounced."

"My room," I said, closing the door behind me and walking further into the room.

Her brow lifted. "Until you let me go, it's mine. Now, if you have nothing better to say, then I have a hot date with this boring mystery." She lifted the book back up.

"Then why are you taking a drug for patients with heart problems?"

"I have my reasons, as does my doctor."

"And those reasons are?"

"None of your business." Her face stayed behind the book. "All you need to know is that they help my nightmares."

But it was the reason for those nightmares I wanted to discover. My hands clenched thinking about what the causes might have been and an urgent desire to slice open the person behind them mounted in my body.

With no reason to explain the rash command that followed, I said, "You're sleeping with me until I can get them." The moment the words were out, I wanted to take them back. It was like my filter had broken and the faucet of shit I would never have said or done continued to run free.

This time, she lowered the book.

"Excuse me."

"Get up. You're sleeping in my room with me until you're back on your medicine."

"There's really no reason for that." Her cheeks held a pink tint to them.

"There are many reasons for it, including the fact that I don't want to lie awake all night hearing you scream from the other side of the house. Nor do I want you scratching yourself up like you were doing last night." Her eyes flicked to her arms where the faint sign of scratches still showed before she tucked them under the covers. "If I'm stuck holding you all night to keep your mouth shut and your body still, I'll do it in my bed where I'm more comfortable."

Excuses. That's what they were. Excuses to cover some unfounded worry I couldn't silence and a need to hold her again. I was half tempted to ask if she was a witch, thinking she must have put a spell on me to make me this soft.

Her lips curved, a mischievous gleam entering her eyes. "Is that what you tell yourself to rationalize an excuse to feel me up again?"

My jaw ticked, the tendons in my neck tightening. Whether in irritation at her assumption or that she saw right through my excuses, I couldn't pinpoint. "If you'd prefer to sleep in the basement where I torture my enemies, suit yourself. It's soundproofed down there and no one will hear your screams."

She scrambled out of bed, the devious look faltering.

Eyes tracking the curvy bare legs that led to panties that were tight and lacy, my breath faltered. "Why aren't you wearing the pajamas I provided?" My words came out in a broken rasp.

She tugged at her shirt, succeeding in only covering a fraction of her hips. Not enough to cover the trail of ivy tattooed on her right one. She was sexy. Beautiful, adorable, and sexy. My pants tented uncomfortably and there was no way to hide my reaction.

"Because they're sized for Riley, who does not have thighs, boobs, or an ass like mine. Not to mention she's like a giraffe compared to me." Riley was the kind of woman I had gravitated to in the past, but after seeing what those curves looked like on Ava, I was quickly developing a new taste. With a waist that made a delectable arc I could almost imagine my hands enveloping, she was endowed in every rounded part of her body.

"Jill will be here tomorrow to get you new clothes," I said, averting my eyes before I lost control and pinned her to the wall. The urge to have her body under mine was almost primal. Tugging my T-shirt over my head, I threw it at her. "Put this on."

She fumbled, dropping it as her lips parted and her eyes traced my chest before landing on that damned hard-on that wouldn't go away. They flicked down to the shirt quickly, and I watched her lean over to get it, trying not to strain my neck to see what her ass looked like in that position.

"Fuck," I muttered, swiping my hand over my face. "Cover up. I don't want the men seeing you like that." It was the truth. I was already feeling out of control and a feral need to kill anyone who saw her body was roaring through me.

She rolled her eyes. "Turn around."

Brow furrowing, I asked, "Why? You going to try stabbing me in the back?"

"If I thought I could, I already would have," she snapped.

"I'd like to see you try." I turned around and crossed my arms. "Why am I turning around?"

"Because I don't want you seeing my tits when I take my shirt off and put this one on."

I peeked back. "Why don't you—"

"Turn!" Her arm folded over her breasts before I could see them, the fabric of my shirt blocking them but leaving the rounded edge of cleavage in sight.

If I hadn't been hard before, I definitely was now. Shit, what was this woman doing to me? What was I doing to myself? I should have moved her into the basement. Or left her in this room, instructing my men to make sure they kept her fed and alive. Avoided her. That's what I should have done, but I didn't think there was any way I could avoid Ava. It was too late; she was in my thoughts too much and a craving had developed. Unhinged and out of control, but it was there and difficult to ignore.

"You don't give the commands," I told her, continuing to stare her down.

"Please turn, Emerson. I don't want to sleep with layers of shirts on. It's hard enough having one on."

Fuck. Fuck. Fuck. Don't ask her, I warned myself, but my mouth didn't listen.

"You sleep naked?" It sounded like I had just hit puberty.

"No, but topless." She held my gaze a bit too long. Like a challenge. Heat seethed in me at the look in those brown eyes.

Silence. Long, heavy silence. With unspoken words and that damned challenge. Almost like she was daring me to grab her and take her against the wall like my body was craving. I broke the connection, turning and cursing myself for being so weak. Ava was my prisoner. That was it.

"Damn. If you thought I was adorable before, any hope of

looking like a mature adult has gone out the window with this look," Ava mumbled.

She stormed past me, book in hand, shaking her head and continuing to mumble. Hand going to her wrist, I turned her around. Something I shouldn't have done because seeing her in my shirt was a mistake. Giving it to her had been a mistake. No, coming to her room had been the fatal error. Everything else was just residual idiocy.

Although she was tall, my shirt fell to her knees, the size and the length too much for her frame. It hung over her breasts, the material gathering so that I could see her nipples protruding along with the outline of the nipple rings I wanted desperately to reach out and tug. My thumb rubbed her wrist in the same path I desired to smooth over her nipple.

"What?" she said, swallowing a bit too loudly. My eyes rose from where they'd been devouring her body, and there was a twitch in my jaw that matched the one in my pants. "Nothing." I released her, and reached behind her to open the door, my body moving closer to hers with the action.

Her eyes searched mine. What she was looking for, I wasn't sure. But I hoped she didn't see the battle that was waging inside of me. Warring to keep seeing her as my hostage instead of someone I wanted in my bed. Which was exactly where I had commanded her to go.

"Walk," I said, scraping my hand through my hair.

"I don't know where I'm going."

Huffing, I pushed her aside, expecting her to follow me.

"Rude," she muttered, and I shot a look back at her over my shoulder.

"If you want to keep your tongue, I recommend keeping your mouth shut." *Unless it's around my dick.* Fuck, I needed to stop. It had to be the situation with the merchandise and everything else that had kept me on edge the last few months. That's why I was so off kilter and why my mind couldn't focus.

She stayed silent as I led her through the main room and to the other side of the house.

"What's down there?" she asked when we approached the stairs that led from the living area to my room. The hallway continued well past the stairs.

"The garage and the entrance to the basement." I gestured for her to go ahead of me. Not because I was worried she would bolt for the garage, but for a better view of her legs. Perverse reasoning, I knew, but it was too tempting not to. "Don't get any ideas, either," I told her as her eyes lingered on the hallway. "I have men posted outside it."

"Doesn't mean I couldn't steal a car and run them over with it." Her eyes sparkled with amusement when they returned to mine.

My lips thinned. "Try it and I'll show you why people fear me."

She didn't flinch. Instead, she took a step closer to me and stood on her tiptoes. Her head tilted, revealing the soft arc of her neck, before she brought her fingers to my chin.

"I don't fear you, Emerson."

Bold, brash, and beautiful. I was screwed. I'd known this woman for two days and she was already breaking down my barriers.

I grabbed her wrist and closed the remaining distance between us, then forced her to step back until the wall stopped her. Her lips parted, and I fought the need to kiss her, even though it was raging through me. Letting her think I was, I moved my face closer, hearing the hitch of her breath and noting her pulse race in the wrist I had pinned against the wall. Sliding my cheek along hers, the scent of her skin tantalizing me, I brought my mouth to her ear and snarled, "You should fear me, Ava. Because whatever it is you think I am, I'm not."

"Then tell me who you are," she breathed, her chest heaving against mine.

I was too close, and the temptation was too high to just ravage her here in the hallway. To take her like I wanted and touch every inch of her, kiss every bit of ink, play with every piercing. Just the thought had me so hard I was aching.

Dragging my cheek back left my lips so close to meeting hers that it took every ounce of strength I had not to move them the few centimeters needed to devour her mouth. My other hand was above her and I dug my fingers into the wall to keep from dropping it into her hair.

Pulling away but still maintaining my stance of power over her, I said, "A dangerous man with hands that are stained with the blood he's spilled. Don't think because I've been kind to you I'm anything but a killer, Ava."

The blink of her eyes was her only reaction.

"Now get your ass up those stairs before I change my mind."

"You still don't frighten me."

My hand fell, my fingers digging into her soft hair. With a handful in my grasp, I pulled, forcing her head back further and enjoying her sexy exhale entirely too much.

"I should." Tired of restraining my urges, I released her wrist and scooped her up, throwing her over my shoulder.

Her shriek was rewarding, and I chuckled as I walked past the stairs and further down the hall.

"Wait. Where are you going?" Worry edged her voice, feeding the ruthless part of me.

"You chose not to go up the stairs, so I changed my mind."

Tension left her body rigid. "But you can't do that."

I opened the door to the basement, saying, "I can do anything I want. I'm your captor, Ava. Your jailer. Not some bartender at a wedding." My mood turned further at the thought and the next one. "Did you even think about what he could have done to you? Running off with some strange guy you just met?"

She let out a laugh. "And I'm flirting with the man who held a gun to my head two days ago and killed the men who took me. I don't live my life like some sheltered schoolgirl. I like danger."

Releasing my hold on her, I placed her back on her feet and studied her. The moment of fear was gone and the confident pain in my ass was back. The fear had reminded me she was here for one purpose. But this side of her was one I wanted to play with, to explore.

"Are you going to take me into your dungeon and lock me away?" There it was. A flitting of fear behind the façade of confidence.

Taking her elbow, I dragged her behind me down the first few stairs. The change in her was instant. She scratched and pulled to get free.

"Please, Emerson," she begged, a sound I normally enjoyed from my victims but detested hearing from her.

Pausing my steps, I peered back at her. Terror lined every part of her features and a sudden need to erase it from her stalked through me.

"Please. I'll stop flirting. I'll stop talking back. Whatever it is you dislike, I'll stop. Just don't lock me down here."

What had happened in three small steps to turn my wildcat into a broken, pleading woman? My wildcat? That was new.

I turned and took a step up. Darkness from the basement spilled around me, but the light from behind her splayed out to give her an angelic look. Light to my darkness. The contrast was stark. What was I thinking, letting myself get close to this woman who was so different from me? So full of life.

Terror still darkened her eyes, and I wanted to take it from her, to replace it with the vibrance they usually held.

"Don't do any of those things," I said.

"Okay, I'll stop. I promise."

I halted her words with a finger to her mouth.

"No, don't stop any of it. There's nothing I dislike."

Taking her arm, I noticed how badly it was shaking. Her

entire body was trembling at the thought of being locked down there. I brought her hand up, watching it quake.

"See," I said. "You were wrong. I do frighten you." Normally, that would have excited me, but not this time. Not with her.

"You don't," she said, her voice meek.

"Keep telling yourself that." I turned her around. "Go, you're not spending the night down here."

She was up the stairs before I could contemplate the brief urge to smack her ass. Wiping my hand over my eyes, I again questioned how comfortable I was with this woman. As if I had known her my entire life and not just two days.

"Are you always this slow? How do you manage to kill anyone when you move like an old man?" The fear was gone, replaced by her usual sass.

I stalked out of the basement and slammed the door behind me. "Did you just call me old?"

Hands on her hips, she said, "Well, you are in your forties, right?"

"And how old are you that you think that's old?" She was younger than me, but it wasn't until she answered that I realized just how much younger.

"I'm thirty." She crossed her arms and waited for my response.

Fifteen years younger. Not as much of a difference as my brother and his new wife, but it was still big enough.

"Don't make me throw you over my shoulder again," I grumbled.

"I'd like to see you try." There was that challenge in her eyes again.

I shook my head and walked to her, throwing her over my shoulder before she could even complain.

"There's that wildcat," I said, smoothing my hand up her calf before I could stop myself. "Flirty and bold."

"Well, you did say I shouldn't stop."

"That I did."

On the last step into my room, I lowered Ava to the floor. She teetered for a moment and grabbed my arm to steady herself. I stood there frozen, looking down into her piercing eyes and drowning in them. The air in my lungs seemed non-existent, my pulse so slow I should have been comatose. I might have been for all I knew because, in that moment, nothing seemed to exist but the spirited woman in front of me.

"I dropped my book," she said, finally breaking the intensity of the moment.

Frowning, I glanced behind me, not seeing it.

"Can't you go without it? Where did you get a book, anyway?"

"I may have convinced Breaker to get me one." She must have noticed my muscles go rigid. "Don't say anything to him. I think I annoyed him so much he figured shutting me up was worth your wrath."

Nothing was worth my wrath and my teeth were grinding. Prisoners didn't need books. But Ava did. If I didn't know how Ava was, I would have considered making Breaker pay for heeding her request.

"I'll get it in the morning."

Those arms crossed again with a roll of her eyes to emphasize her annoyance with my answer.

"Are you serious? It's after midnight. Why are you even still awake?"

Her eyes crinkled with amusement. "I bartend at night. This is early for me."

"Bartender?" That was an unexpected piece of information.

Shrugging, she explained, "It pays well and leaves me time during the day for class and studying."

My head tipped to the side as I contemplated her words. "You're a student?" Another unexpected admission.

She scratched her nose, her stance relaxing. "Grad school. I took a few years off to play, then took my uncle's offer to get my master's. He offered to pay for school and my apartment if I moved to Bridgeville and closer to him."

So he could keep her safe. And it was likely my brother who had footed the bill for school. The thought conflicted with my hatred for him.

"Of course, now that you've derailed my life, I'll have to plead forgiveness and hope they don't throw me out." The attitude was thick.

"My brother owns that city. They'll look the other way, trust me."

I didn't give her time to answer. The book was on the floor in the hall, near where she'd started fighting our descent into the basement. I paused, looking at the basement door. She didn't fear me, but she feared what was down there. Or maybe the basement itself. Granted, it was nightmarish, and the ghosts of my past deeds haunted it.

By the time I returned to my room, I found Ava standing in front of the floor to ceiling windows that lined the one side of the room. I threw the book on the bed and moved next to her.

"It's so beautiful here," she said with a slight melancholy. "Open and endless."

I looked out at the view. The waves pounded the shore below. The tide was high and so they battered against the rocky alcove. A half-moon spread its golden light into a long stream over the ocean, highlighting the peaks and frothy curves.

"A silent predator," I said. "Beautiful from the outside, but potentially deadly. Its rip currents could drag you under, its waves could break your bones and flood your lungs, and its creatures could devour you."

I sensed her gaze fall to me, but continued to look ahead. "Like you?" she asked so quietly, I almost didn't hear her.

Snorting, I replied, "I'm far from beautiful and far more deadly."

"I'm not convinced."

This time I did turn to her, but she was gone, strolling across the bedroom and jumping into my bed. She crossed her legs and looked at me, a devious smile on her face. My mind screamed that this had been a mistake. That I needed to pick her back up and take her to her room. I could tolerate the sounds of horror that came from her room, ignore the need to rush in and calm her. But I couldn't do it. I wanted her there, in my bed and in my shirt. Wanted that smile and the wildcat that lived behind it.

"That's my side of the bed," I grumbled.

"No, it's mine. I always sleep on this side. You slept on that side last night and you were fine."

And just like that, my aggravation returned. "Get on the other side of the bed," I said, stomping over to her.

"No." She crawled further into the bed, a move that left my balls throbbing because it was so sexy. Sliding under the sheets, she picked her book up and ignored me.

"You're not sleeping on my side of the bed, Ava."

"I am, and nothing you do can make me change sides."

I clawed my fingers through my hair. She was so frustrating, yet I adored and hated it at the same time.

"What is so important about that side?" I asked, feeling the muscles in my jaw sharpen.

"Why is it so important to you?"

"Because I put my gun and my phone on the nightstand."

The book lowered and her eyes shifted over to the other side of the bed where a second nightstand stood. Damn it.

"And your reasoning?" I asked, skulking to the other side and knowing she was winning this argument as much as I despised admitting it.

"I don't like sleeping on the side near a door." Her voice was low, like she didn't want to admit the truth.

I looked over at the door. She wanted to be as far from the door as she could while she slept. My fist clenched as I pieced together a reason for that reaction. What had happened to her to cause that fear? I couldn't help but think it had to do with her nightmares.

Pulling my gun from the back of my pants, I stared at it for a moment, realizing she could have grabbed it while I'd carried her. Could have shot me and run. A stupid, dangerous mistake, but then I seemed to make plenty of mistakes when it came to her.

I placed it on the nightstand along with my phone and got into bed, staying on top of the sheets.

She picked her book back up and returned to reading, and I couldn't help but consider how comfortable this seemed. We could have been a married couple turning in for the night. But we weren't. We were hostage and captor. A captor who was quickly falling for the hostage he should have avoided from the moment he saw her.

Chapter Eleven

AVA

Someone moved the book from my hand. I vaguely registered it along with the whispered, "Goodnight, wildcat," once he repositioned my body so my head was on the pillow. My eyes were too heavy to open, sleep having cast its spell on me, but I knew it was Emerson. A man who continued to pique my curiosity, although I thought it might be more than that now. No matter that two days seemed like too short a time to find the cold, cruel mafia boss everyone feared endearing.

The thought drifted away as I fell further into sleep's grasp. My dreams were gentle, flickers of blue eyes the color of a clear summer's day, baritone words that settled too comfortably in my drifting mind, a smirk that left my knees weak. But the calm slowly shifted, and a sense of dread crawled up my spine. Darkness crept in even as I backed away from it. I swiveled to run, but a brick wall faced me. Familiar and constricting. Red bricks the color of dried blood with scrapes across them, the markings of days that passed.

Turning back, the darkness eclipsed me, and I gasped for breath, terror striking like a venomous snake and forcing the scream from my locked lungs. I ran through the blackness, up the stairs. One, two, three...ten and a door. Locked and restricting. I pounded at it, screaming as the dark compressed its heaviness into my skin like an oily substance. Something skittered below the stairs. Pings and creaks my rational mind told me were nothing, but in the pitch, there was only my overactive imagination to create the monsters lurking below. I screamed and scratched, clawing at the door. My nails tore, my skin ripped, and my tears fell.

Something wrapped around my waist, and I bellowed out a cry as that terror hit like the wall tumbling onto me. The stairs collapsed, yet still the surrounding sensation continued.

Safety, my mind whispered, and I relaxed into that pressure.

Streams of light broke through the darkness, my fall cushioned by a gentle tide that swept me to shore. The sun shone down on me, and I blinked my eyes at it. The sensation, that presence that told me I was safe, that nothing would hurt me, continued and I let my tension go, noticing it slide from me, taken away with the tide. I relaxed further into the hold, letting it encompass me and knowing I never wanted to lose it.

The sense that something was missing woke me. I blinked my eyes, adjusting to the sunlight flooding through my window. The window in my prison, not in Emerson's room. Sitting up, I rubbed my eyes and looked around the room. He had moved me at some point, but I remembered his touch in my nightmare this time. The secure hold he kept on me as I'd fought my way from my memories had been solid enough for me to recognize. I rubbed my hand over my waist, missing his touch. The T-shirt he'd given me was still covering me and I brought it to my nose, smelling his scent that still lingered on it before I dropped it quickly.

I didn't want to recognize the feeling that fluttered in my lower belly, but it was difficult to ignore. This was something out of those dark romances Riley and I read. And I was the crazy female lead, falling head over heels for the corrupt mafia man within days of being kidnapped by him. This was madness.

Wasn't there some syndrome associated with victims and their kidnappers? Maybe that was what this was.

I fell back onto the bed, trying not to think of Emerson Tides and the undeniable effect he was having on me. He wanted to be hard and cold, but he wasn't that way with me. There were too many sweet moments, things he did and said that led me to believe this man wasn't as bad as everyone made him out to be. Or maybe he was different with me. I couldn't stop the smile that tugged at the corner of my mouth.

The door opened, and I quickly pulled my sheets up, giving Breaker a nasty look.

"Boss said to bring you breakfast if you weren't awake by ten." He placed a tray on the bedside table.

"Ten? It's ten already?"

He nodded.

"Where is he?"

"Meetings. He and Pack left with a few of the guys early this morning." He walked away. "Eat. Jill will be by soon."

He closed the door, and the familiar click of the lock assured me that Emerson had imprisoned me again. I sat back up and folded my legs under me, looking over the tray Breaker had brought.

Eggs and toast. I couldn't stop my laugh or the excited squeak when I spotted the coffee that was still warm. I brought it to my mouth, savoring the taste. The eggs were warm as well and I thought maybe he had instructed Breaker to warm everything up for me. A sweet gesture to add to the others.

When I was chewing the last bite of eggs, the door opened again. A woman entered the room, her auburn hair streaked with gray and pulled up in a stylish ponytail. She wore a pair of tight jeans and a mauve blouse that buttoned down the front. Stylish and attractive. If Emerson hadn't laughed at my questions about their relationship, I would have considered the jealousy that pushed at me was more than her looks and dressing skills.

Her flats clicked on the wood floor as she walked to the foot of the bed and stood there, peering down at me.

"Hi," I said, not sure if I should talk or continue letting her study me like a science project.

"So you're the one who has Cade acting so out of character."

I bit into a piece of crust and tilted my head. "Out of character?" I hated how my heart fluttered in response.

"Not his usual grumpy, demanding asshole self."

My brow shot up, and I almost coughed out the crust. "Should you be calling your employer an asshole?"

"I've known Cade long enough to get away with it." She walked around the side of the bed as I tried to adjust to hearing Emerson called Cade. It just didn't sound right to me, but I knew he let me call him by his true name and it wasn't something he allowed anyone else to do. Another check on the sweet side of his list. "Get up and let me see what I'm working with."

And she called Emerson demanding.

"If I'd known he wasn't kidnapping the tall, skinny one, I wouldn't have spent all that money. Now I'll have to donate all of it."

"Tall, skinny one?" I asked, her comment irritating me. Sure, I was rounder in places than Riley and a few inches shorter, but I liked my body and my curves, and I wasn't about to let her put them down. Besides, at five eight I didn't consider myself short.

"Yes. You have more body to work with. Curves are more difficult to shop for."

"Oh." There went the steam from my argument. I threw the sheets back and stood. Jill towered over me. She had to be almost six feet tall.

Her eyes flitted to Emerson's T-shirt, her lips twitching like she wanted to smile but it would be painful for her to do so. "That explains it," she murmured.

"I'm not sleeping with him," I snapped, not liking the condescending look she gave me.

"No? Why not?"

My mouth hung open before I could stop it. "He kidnapped me for one." A lame argument now that I recognized his smell and looked forward to seeing him. Not to mention, technically, I was sleeping with him until my meds arrived.

"Shame. You seem like the type of woman he needs."

I crossed my arms. "As opposed to what?" I asked, not really sure where this conversation was going or why we were having it.

She pushed me aside and began making the bed. "The women he normally sleeps with. Snobby, spineless, often brainless...at least the ones he bothered bringing into the house." Fluffing the pillow with a fervor fit for a boxer, she continued, "Most don't make it that far and haven't for a long time."

I wasn't certain that was something Emerson would want her to share. And I didn't like the sting of envy it caused. Like I was any better. I had my fair share of one-night stands, taking what I wanted and ghosting them if they got clingy. Commitment wasn't my thing, and I was beginning to think it wasn't Emerson's either.

She turned to me when she had mauled the pillow sufficiently. "You, on the other hand..." Her hand came out to tug one of my dyed locks. I had switched back to pink after playing with purple, thinking the pink flattered me more and was softer for Riley's wedding. "...have spirit."

"And you know that from the five minutes you've been in this room?" I said, hearing the sarcasm that emphasized the words.

"That and the grumbling he did when he called me. It takes a lot to get under Cade's skin, but you succeeded."

I scratched my head as she made a point of surveying me like an inspector. "He complained about me?" The thought soured my mood further. "He kidnaps me and has the nerve to complain about me?" The words I planned to volley at him when I saw him next would not be kind ones.

"See, that's what I'm talking about." She turned me around, lifting my shirt.

"Hey!" Glancing back at her, I pulled at it, but her hold was firm.

"I need to see what I'm working with here." Her eyes landed on the tattoo on my hip. "Yes, you're definitely something new for him."

This time, I yanked the shirt away and faced her. "I'm nothing more than a hostage he's using to bait Greyson Tides."

A sleek arch of her brow had me doubting my words. "We'll see." Twisting on her heel, she strolled back to the door. "I'm off to shop. I'm assuming T-shirts, ripped jeans, and flannel are your style?"

An indignant huff came from me as I gaped at her back.

"I'll try to improve on the quality of your wardrobe, but I'm sure whatever I get, you'll make it your own." An insult mixed with a compliment. Who was this woman?

"Why do you care?" I asked as she opened the door.

She peered back at me. "About your style?"

"No," I said, rolling my eyes. "If I'm something different for Cade?" It was so hard to say that name that didn't roll off my tongue as delicately as Emerson did.

She faced me, the morning sun from the window reflecting in her eyes. "I've known Cade since he moved to this province." That didn't make me feel better, and I imagined a torrid affair between the two in their youth. The idea had envy clamping down on my insides. "He takes, and he uses. He doesn't keep. But you, he's keeping."

"I'm just a pawn to get what he needs."

Eyes flicking to the tray from breakfast, she said, "You've been here for three days, Miss Shelton. How many times have you seen Cade?"

"I... A few," I admitted.

Her mouth lifted into a smile that held no judgement, only kindness. "Cade doesn't care if his enemies are fed or cared for."

"He expected Riley and had clothes and this room for her, not me."

"I'm not privy to what his intentions are or why he does things, but my guess is she held value. A trade is only worth it if the goods aren't damaged. Whatever he wanted by taking her necessitated keeping her cared for. But I can guarantee she wouldn't have left this room to eat breakfast with him, nor to share his bed."

"I'm not sleeping with him."

"I know, but Cade doesn't care if his hostages have nightmares, Miss Shelton. In fact, he prefers they do."

I stood staring at the door long after she left, not sure what to make of her or her words. It seemed strange that she would tell me those things and talk as openly as she did. She didn't know me, other than what Emerson must have told her. And he trusted her enough to tell her about my nightmares, unless she had found out another way.

I trudged to the bathroom, rubbing my temples to halt the headache all this thinking was causing. Emerson was a mystery to me, and his relationship with this woman—a beautiful, elegant woman who knew a lot more than an average employee should— had me confused and irritable. Not that I should have been irritable about any of this. I was a hostage, not a guest. Reminding myself of that didn't help.

Resting my hands on the bathroom counter, I looked at my reflection. The messy curls, the crust in the corner of my eyes that I wiped away quickly, and Emerson's oversized T-shirt. Definitely different from the women I imagined he had slept with. That slither of envy pierced me again, and I grimaced. Why did I care who the mafia boss who kidnapped me slept with? This was temporary and once Greyson and my uncle saved me, I would never see him again. It was as simple as that.

But if it was that simple, why did my chest hurt at the thought?

Jᴉʟʟ ʀᴇᴛᴜʀɴᴇᴅ a few hours later with bags of clothes, which she dumped on the bed. Breaker brought in a new tray of food, then hurried from the room. I dragged in a breath, savoring the smell of the soup that sat next to a turkey sandwich on wheat. My mouth salivated just at the thought of digging into it.

Jill was going through the bags, pulling clothes out in a flurry. I picked up a T-shirt that said princess on it and quirked my brow. "And this seemed like my style?" I asked, missing my clothes even more.

"They don't have many options at the gallery that scream punk goth girl."

I gave her a wounded look. "I beg your pardon, but I am not goth. I like to think of myself as cute and quirky."

She let out a sound like a snort before throwing a pair of jeans and a shirt at me. This one, at least, was a half-shirt. "Try those on. And..." She sorted through another bag before pulling out a few bras. "...these."

"Oh, thank God," I said, grabbing one from her. "These girls were getting sore hanging free for so many days."

"I wouldn't know," she grumbled, tossing a handful of panties into a pile. "I'll get these washed up. The rest you can deal with as they are. Go on, get dressed."

I walked into the bathroom and did as instructed, not bothering to argue. The bra fit perfectly, as did everything else. "How did you know my size?" I asked, zipping the jeans up as I emerged.

She crossed her arms and looked me over. Again, I felt like I was some experiment she was evaluating. "I have a knack for clothes. I went to school for fashion before I came to work for Cade."

"Why did you change direction?" I asked, taking the designer rip in the jeans that probably cost more than my entire wardrobe and widening it until my knee was hanging out.

"You did not just rip those," she scolded.

"I did," I replied, going through the pile of clothes. There were cute shorts, more shirts, and a few tight ones in colors I loved. I may have looked hardcore to some, and I got that sometimes at work with my tattoos and piercings, but black wasn't my only favorite color. I loved pinks and purples and—I dropped the clothes and yanked the dress buried at the bottom, pulling it out and staring at it—dresses. I adored dresses, but never got to wear them. Riley's bridesmaid's dress was the first dress I'd worn since I was a child.

I held the dress up, knowing my eyes were large as I considered just how Jill had known I would love it. Black silk edged with pink. It was the type of dress that hugged curves but, in a flattering, delicate way. Falling to my ankles with a slit that ran up to the mid-thigh, I could just imagine it with a pair of strappy pink heels. Just like the ones Jill pulled from another bag.

"Just in case," she said, taking the dress from me and hanging it in the walk-in closet I had paid little attention to. There was nothing in it. Jill had bought no dresses for Riley's stay. Only for mine.

"In case of what?"

She shrugged. "You never know." The smug look on her face told me she had already planned out when I might need it. Again, I wondered if Emerson knew how devious his housekeeper and personal shopper was. "Why don't you work on putting those away?" She pointed to the bed. "Just leave the things you don't want and the ones I bought for the other woman in the chair, and I'll get them later."

Steady steps to the door had me acting irrationally. When had I acted rationally since I'd been here, though? "Can you stay longer?" I asked, suddenly desperate for company.

She looked back at me, her eyes scrunched.

"It gets lonely in here and Em...I mean, Cade doesn't let me out unless he's here." She gave me an amused grin when I started to say Emerson's real name. "All I have is the book Breaker gave me."

"Breaker gave you a book? I highly doubt that." A few strides and she was picking up the book he had given me the day before. "Hmm." It was all she said before she turned to me. "Share your sandwich with me and I'll stay. But don't tell Cade I wasn't cleaning or I'll take all these clothes back and make you wear the clothes that were already here."

"It's not a pretty sight," I said, cringing.

"Must be something," she commented, grabbing the sandwich and holding half out to me.

We sat on the bed and talked, and for a few minutes I felt normal again, like I wasn't locked in the estate of a brutal mafia boss. A man I couldn't talk about without an annoying heat entering my cheeks. It turned out Jill differed greatly from what I had first judged her to be. She'd married one of Emerson's men right out of college, which led to her emersion into this life. That was all she told me before she questioned me about my life. I kept my secrets to myself, talking about school and Riley, my uncle and the years I'd spent trying to find myself. But nothing before then. And nothing about my nightmares.

Those were my secrets to keep. Ones I wouldn't give up, no matter how comfortable this façade of normalcy was. And that was all it was. A moment to forget I was a prisoner with no way to escape. It was easy to forget and every time I was with Emerson, that reality slipped away, just as easily as it did with Jill. But when she left, and I was alone in my luxurious cell, surrounded by mounds of expensive clothes, that reality returned, along with the heavy reminders that this wasn't right. That I needed to stop forgetting I was nothing more than a pawn to Emerson. A means to an end, no matter how it seemed I was becoming more than that.

Chapter Twelve

EMERSON

Another day of inspecting my warehouses and checking in with my suppliers meant another day away from Ava. As annoying as it was, I missed her company. Irritating was more like it. A woman I barely knew, who had been in my life for forty-eight hours and I couldn't get her off my mind. It was completely irrational. Madness. If I had known her for months, I might have been tempted to say the attraction made sense, that I liked this woman too immensely to ignore. Enough to have her in my bed, to want to hold her each night, to see her curled up in my sheets, have her smile light the crevices of my rotted heart. But I hadn't known her for months, so saying those things only made me sound like a feeble-minded teenager who was smitten with the new girl in his class.

"Boss?" Pack jerked me from my thoughts, and I found him waiting for me to get out of the car.

Clearing my head, I exited, snapping the lapels of my jacket and adjusting my cuffs. Pack flanked my right side while Vin flanked my left with two more of my men following behind. The wharf was busy, but this end belonged strictly to me and my business endeavors. Jimmy nervously paced in front of the warehouse door and my hackles rose. Jimmy wasn't a nervous man. He was smooth and calm, a viper slithering silently in the long grass, which was exactly why I had hired him.

"If I didn't know better, I'd say you have bad news for me, Jimmy. You know how I dislike bad news."

He stopped, his fingers fidgeting with his collar.

"The shipment didn't make it, boss."

Rage raked at me for release, but I kept it in check. "And why is that?" I asked, stepping into his space and snagging his shirt in my fists. "Because I expected to have that warehouse filled with cartons of artillery."

"I know, Cade." He swallowed, his pupils wide with fear. Jimmy feared little, but he knew to fear me. Had seen what I did to people who disappointed me.

With a violent shove, I pushed him through the door and looked around at the empty building. Another empty fucking building. "Where are my goods, Jimmy?"

Jimmy had his own team of men, all loyal and on my payroll, as long as he delivered like he always had. Two of them watched us, the tension clear in their stiff stances.

"Rhodes, tell him what you told me," Jimmy called to one of them.

The grinding of my teeth caused the man to flinch as he came over to us.

"The truck was here. It rounded the corner but stopped." He swallowed loudly, the only sign of nerves the man showed. Too bad I was one word away from blowing a hole in his head. "Someone threw the driver out the door and the truck backed away. We ran for it, but it was too far down. By the time we got to the end of the buildings, it was gone." The skin on my knuckles strained at the pressure. "This was on the body of the driver."

He handed me a paper, and I snatched it from him, surprised my skin hadn't split.

One line, three simple words. *It's over, Cade.*

Rolling my neck, I shredded the note. "Next time, you shoot out the windows, the tires, everything your bullets can hit, and you don't tell me you failed." My gun was out before he could register my movement. "For you, there won't be a next time, but your boss won't fuck up again."

I shot him between the eyes, then took out the second man in the building before turning my gun on Jimmy. To his benefit, he held his head high, awaiting his sentence.

"Clean up this mess and find my fucking shipment, or it will be your blood spilling next time."

"Yes, Cade."

After tucking my gun into my pants, I punched him, hearing the break of cartilage and seeing the spray of blood.

"You ever fuck up this bad again, you will beg me to use my gun and end your miserable life."

I stormed away, trying to maintain my composure when all I wanted to do was roar in frustration. They were destroying me. Dismantling my empire stone by stone and I had found no way to stop them.

"What do you want to do, Cade?" Pack asked as we drove off.

I had called in all my favors, used every resource, but nothing I had done had flushed them out.

"Double down on security at all the sites." I thought of Ava. The last piece on my chessboard. The most valuable piece. "And on the house. Run through everything again, all communication, all the videos, the itineraries. If there's even a small letter out of place, a number smudged I need to know. I want these fuckers and when I get my hands on them, I will spend days savoring their deaths."

I avoided seeing Ava until it was late. My mood was too volatile and the last thing I needed was a reminder of another weakness. And Ava was a weakness. A vulnerability I couldn't fortify. Her meds were due the next day, and as much as I wanted the nightmares to stop, I disliked the idea of not having her next to me.

Rubbing my temple, I opened her door to find her staring out the window. She had a pair of low-cut jeans on and a shirt that left too much of her skin uncovered to avoid that uncomfortable swelling in my pants as my eyes skimmed over her curves. She turned, and I fixated on the soft skin and the belly button piercing. A pink rhinestone at the top, a teardrop pink stone dangling on the bottom. I wanted to flick my tongue against it, then strip her down and tongue all the others I suspected she had.

The tip of her vine tattoo showed where the pants sat low on her hips, and an overwhelming desire to wrap my hands around those hips threatened to leave me out of control.

"You left me in here all day," she said.

I forced my eyes from her body, skimming over her crossed arms and the way the pose drew her shirt up higher.

"I can leave you in here any time I want. In fact, I can lock that door and never let you out again."

She cocked her head, her eyes sparkling. "Would you do that?"

"Keep giving me that attitude and I just might."

She let out something between a sigh and a snort before skipping to the side table and picking up her book.

"Did you really just skip?" I asked, walking further into the room.

"Yup. You should do it sometimes. It's fun."

"I don't skip."

"We'll work on that," she said, giving me a confident smile. "I like to play hopscotch sometimes, too. There's a board I spray painted in the alley behind the bar. We go out and play when we're on break."

There were too many things in that statement for me to take in at once. The idea of her playing kids' games on her break and going into a back alley at night were two. But how she so confidently stated we would work on something together, like this wasn't some temporary situation, like there was a future that extended past this was one I fixated on. It left a strange sensation in my steel heart.

Rubbing my chest, I decided not to tackle any part of her admission. "I see Jill bought you some clothes."

Her smile grew, and it seemed to throw a light all the way into the depths of my rotted soul. "She's great." She pulled a drawer open and took out what looked distinctly like the T-shirt I had given her before bumping it closed with her hip. "Did you know she still designs clothes? She's going to bring me some pieces to see."

She had walked past me and stopped at the door, peeking back at me. I was still trying to determine why she was bringing my T-shirt with her and why she made it sound like she and my housekeeper were best friends.

"Do you do this a lot?" I asked.

"What?"

I scratched my head. "Make friends?"

Her head went back in a beautiful arc as she laughed. "Yes. Another thing you should try." She gestured to the door with her neck. "Are you coming, or are we sleeping here tonight?"

Gaping was not something I did, but damn if it wasn't becoming a habit with Ava. "You're assuming I'm here to take you to my room?"

She batted her lashes, her mouth curving into a devious grin that I wanted to devour. "Am I wrong, Emerson?"

"Go," I grumbled, hating how she worked me into a frenzy that I couldn't ignore.

She skipped out the door, and I shook my head. I heard Breaker snicker. "Take the rest of the night off," I told him before calling to Ava. "Is this skipping thing something normal for you?"

"Nah," she said, twisting around and walking backwards. "It's probably from being off my meds for so many days."

"Great," I said as I pondered which medicine it was. Catching up with her, I caught her elbow and dragged her toward the kitchen. "Come on. I could use a drink."

She tugged her arm from my hold and stopped me. Standing on her tiptoes, she pulled my head down and for a second my heart slammed against my chest, thinking she was going to kiss me. She sniffed and said, "Another drink?"

"It's been a long day," I snapped.

With a laugh, she replied, "At least you weren't locked in a room all day."

I took her by the shoulders and studied her. Large golden-brown eyes met mine as the air thinned between us. Her lips parted and that urge to kiss her returned. I swallowed back the temptation.

"What would you do if I let you out of your room more?"

A flash of excitement in the gold. "I would sit on the deck all day and watch the waves. Maybe lay out on the beach, make sand-castles, curl up on this big couch and read a book."

My adoration grew, and I suddenly wanted to be there with her, carrying her out into the waves, smoothing my hand over her stomach and feeling the heat of the sun on her skin, packing the sand to perfect the castle walls. All things I had never done. I hadn't been in the water since my younger days, work taking up any time I had to live my life like she lived hers—with wide eyes and excitement, with fervor.

"Come on," I said, gently taking her elbow. She shifted the book, and I took it from her along with the shirt, placing them on the couch. I went to take her elbow again but a step ahead of her, my hand slipped so that it caught her hand instead of her elbow. I froze, my sight going to our hands before it flickered to her face. She continued to stare at our hands, and I could see her wrestling with what it signified, the simple slip of limbs that meant so much more considering who we were to each other. Prisoner and captor. Innocent and killer. Sunshine and darkness. Opposites in every way, yet there was something there that I was having a difficult time denying and after years of burying myself in a dynasty that was crumbling and denying myself the pleasure of attachment, I didn't think I wanted to ignore this.

Her fingers intertwined with mine, a slight smile lifting the worry in her features before her eyes met mine.

"A drink?"

I nodded, unable to make my mouth function. When I'd transformed from lethal killer to a man who couldn't form words, I wasn't certain, but it wasn't a good sign.

"I suppose a glass of wine will do. Maybe a snack? That dinner Breaker gave me wasn't up to par with what I expect from this luxury hotel." And just like that, she was pulling me from my spot in the room out to the deck, sliding the doors open easily, as if she had lived here her entire life.

"Not up to par? It was pasta Bolognese from a restaurant in town."

"Eh, not as good as the eggs and toast." She sat with a flourish and tucked her legs under her.

"Noted. I'll remember not to bother spending money at an upscale restaurant on you when you're happy with scrambled eggs."

Her laugh bounced against my ears. I rested on the rail, looking at her. The moonlight spilled over my shoulder to highlight strands of white in her blonde hair, which she had clipped up with a dozen butterfly clips I had to assume Jill had bought her. A few loose curls drifted in the breeze. For a moment, my breath escaped, and I fought the reaction, knowing what it meant and hating it.

"Stay here," I said, walking away, my footfalls heavy. "Don't think about jumping or trying the stairs. You won't make it far."

"You never know," she teased.

I left her there, signaling to Vin to keep an eye on her, but I trusted her even though I had no reason to. She could be playing me, preying on my weakness, but that would mean she knew my weaknesses. Considering smart mouthed women who talked too much and colored their hair pink were not my typical weaknesses, that seemed unlikely.

The kitchen was dark, so I threw the lights on and opened a bottle of wine. After pouring her a glass, I rummaged through the refrigerator and found a block of cheese. It was a juggling act to carry the plate of sliced cheese with crackers, her wine, and a fresh glass of scotch for me, but I managed.

Ava remained in the same spot, hugging her knees to her chest and staring out at the ocean. I took the moment to consider what this was. What I was doing bringing wine to my hostage and intending to hold her through the night. I didn't bother acknowledging the myriad of other things I was tempted to do to her. This wasn't right. It wasn't me. My hold on the glasses tightened as I remembered who I was. Ruthless, cunning, vicious. Not this man. Soft and weak.

"Emerson?" She had turned to me, her eyes keenly seeing my struggle. Lips lifting into an understanding smile, she said, "I'm not sure what we're doing either."

How she saw right through me was unnerving.

Rubbing her arms, she placed her cheek on her knees. "I should hate you, but I don't. I should fear you, but you make me feel safe. Every rational thought I have disappears when we're in the same room together. I don't know what that means but..." She bit her bottom lip, a crinkle forming between her eyes. "...I'm not so sure we should ignore it."

She seemed so young, so vulnerable then, and I had to remind myself that she was young. Fifteen years my junior, no matter how mature she came across.

I forced my feet to move. "It's just wine and cheese," I said. "Don't make it more than that." Cold and blunt, more than I had intended.

"That's better," she said, snatching a piece of cheese when I put it on the table. Her eyes rolled back, her neck tilting with them. I couldn't peel my sight from how sexy she looked, nor could I stop myself from imagining if that look was anywhere close to what she looked like in the throes of an orgasm. I tore my eyes from her, sitting quickly and taking a drink.

"I love cheese," she moaned.

Another gulp of my scotch. Fingers clenched on the glass. I needed to walk away, to send her back to her room, to avoid her until this was over. But I'd told myself that countless times and ignored that voice each time.

"All right," she said. "Tell me how you met Jill. She didn't divulge much and I'm curious."

Chuckling, I shook my head at how easily she lifted the mood. Like a ray of sunshine breaking through an overcast day. Resting back in my chair, I decided to just let whatever this was happen. I couldn't fight it because I couldn't deny how Ava affected me. Bringing out a side of me I hadn't known since before I'd turned my back on my brother and started my new life.

"She likes to think she's mysterious," I said. "I met Jill right after she graduated college. It was a few years after I set up shop here."

"Did you sleep with her?"

My head jerked to hers, and I narrowed my eyes at her. "I thought I answered that. Why do you even care?"

Shrugging, she said, "She seems like your type."

"And how do you know what my type is?" I asked, lowering my glass to the table.

"Tall, thin, brunette. Model figure with great fashion sense."

Her mouth twitched like she was denying a grin that wanted to emerge. She was toying with me, testing me. "Isn't that what most mafia types like?"

She tossed the corner of cheese into her mouth and gave me a look that challenged me to say differently. I couldn't. She'd pegged me. At least what I'd always gone for—long legs, thick auburn hair, and tight designer dresses. I'd sworn off red-heads since the debacle with Greyson, but I barely went for blondes unless they were too sexy to ignore.

But now. I wasn't so sure I hadn't looked for anything else because those things had led to meaningless affairs, one-night stands, sex in the back rooms of my clubs. Never anything serious, never anything that would leave me hurt. Not since the day that had changed my life. I had hardened myself and never let a woman close enough to me to even consider falling for her.

The realization slammed into me like the waves pounding the surf. Because none of those things compared to Ava. There was a comfort with her I had missed. Like being home or the times with my brother before our rift. A familiarity, a sense of peace. Full when I'd been nothing but empty for so long.

"So you think I fucked Jill and she what? Just sticks around for the occasional shot at my bed when I'm looking for a piece of ass?"

Wine squirted from her mouth, and she caught it in her hand, her eyes wide with surprise and humor.

"That's an attractive look. Is that how you won the bartender over?" I teased as she sucked the wine from her palm and wiped her mouth with her shirt.

"No," she said, brushing her hands together to get the residue off. "I won him over with my cleavage and my adorable attitude."

I threw my head back and laughed, something I hadn't done in so long it felt good.

"So, do you really use Jill for booty calls?"

Brows raising, I said, "Booty calls? Does anyone say that anymore?"

"Do you?" She laced the question with something akin to a need for me to say no.

I rested my elbows on the table. "No. I do not. I have never slept with Jill and yes, you clearly know my type."

Her smile dropped before returning, this time not reaching her eyes.

"At least, that's what I thought my type was." I swirled the alcohol in my glass, watching as it rose to the edge to escape. "I think I was wrong all these years."

"Really?"

"Why do you pick up strangers and sleep with them, Ava?" I could turn the conversation just as quickly as she could.

An inhale, sharp and deep. "I told you. I don't want attachment. Men are too needy."

"Do you think you wanted nothing more because it scared you?"

"No," she snapped.

"What kind of men do you like, wildcat?" I raised my eyes to see her, my reward a gorgeous crimson that rose in her cheeks.

"The kind I don't have to take home," she murmured. "Who take what I give them and leave."

"Who won't hurt you?" I was digging now, looking for a reason behind her nightmares. If it was a man who had cursed her with them. Who had hurt her.

Her brow quirked. "Isn't that why you do the same thing, Emerson?" Fuck. I didn't know how she saw through me like that. My teeth chomped down, straining the muscles in my face. Ava inched closer to me. "Maybe we're just two people who never knew what we wanted and always avoided telling ourselves we needed something different. So we didn't look and took what we could from people who wouldn't fill that need because admitting it was missing in the first place would make us vulnerable. And fuck if either of us ever wanted to be that way again."

I reeled back before I could catch myself. She had summarized all I'd just come to see in a few sentences. And she had admitted something that still didn't tell me about the trauma in her past, but confirmed it was there.

If I believed in the sort of thing that happened in romance movies, the instant love, the moment where the world came into clarity and there stood the woman who had brought me that clarity, I would have pinned that as the moment I fell in love with Ava Shelton. But I didn't believe in those things.

Clearing my throat, I said, "Jill married one of my men, Bobbie, right after she graduated. I warned him not to, but he didn't listen. Most of my men know getting involved with a woman is dangerous. This isn't the life to bring a woman and children into." If the abrupt change of subject back to our original discussion bothered her, she didn't show any reaction. "I took her on as my housekeeper when she couldn't find work and eventually added more responsibilities. It kept her safe and Bobbie happy. Bobby was shot on a job. Took a bullet to the heart and died instantly." She winced, her hand shaking as she lowered her wine glass. "I kept Jill on, paid for her house, her car, all her bills. Paid the tuition for their son. I did what I could once I hunted down his killer and let him bleed for days until I couldn't stand his whining anymore and gutted him."

Her skin paled.

"I'm not the good guy, Ava. I take care of my people..." Even if some stabbed me in the back. My mood shifted further. "...but I'm still a killer and a criminal. Don't forget that just because I can have a civil conversation and a drink with you."

"Morally gray."

"What?"

A smile formed. "You're what they call morally gray in the books Riley and I read."

"And what books are those?"

A beautiful flick of her fingers sent a crumb cascading through the air. "Mafia romances, bully romances, the really dark stuff."

"Good God. She married my brother and reads mafia romance books?"

"I guess she knew what she liked. A morally gray man who would burn the world down for his woman."

"Is that what you want?" I asked, leaning closer to her.

"If you mean a man who will avenge anyone who hurts me, who holds me through my nightmares, who makes sure I have hot coffee when I wake up late? Then yes."

The inhale I took was like the drag of a knife through my chest. "I kill people for a living, Ava."

"You killed a man who killed Jill's husband. Then took care of her like he would have wanted. I don't see the bad in that."

Rubbing my temples, I shook my head again. "You are something, Ava Shelton."

"Why?" she asked with a crooked grin. "Don't your sexy model women think the same way?"

I tilted my head, unsure if she was trying to goad me into something or if she was teasing me. "First, there's barely any talking when I'm with them." An uncomfortable fidgeting of her legs told me she didn't like that answer. "Second, they're not my women because I don't have a woman. And third, what makes you think they're any sexier than you?"

Her mouth parted, her eyes flitting up to meet mine.

"Or that you couldn't be a model?"

She snorted this time. "That's funny." She picked at a rip in her jeans—the one big enough for me to see her knee and half her thigh. Hardly something I would have attributed Jill to buying, but they fit Ava's personality.

"It's not," I muttered before finishing my drink. "Besides, just because you thought you knew my type, doesn't mean everyone in my business has that same type." I'd thought I did, but how wrong I was.

"I guess you're right." She pulled her knees back up to her chin. "You're the third boss I've met in a matter of months. I didn't know this world really existed except in my books and on screen. And here I am, captured by one. Kidnapped after attending the wedding of one—whose wife looks like a model, might I add. A wedding where her brother, another boss, walked her down the aisle and his girlfriend was her maid of honor. Talk about adorable. Casey is the definition of it and yeah, she's curvy and cute. And don't even get me started on Angie. Holy cow, she looks like she stepped out of one of those fashion magazines."

She was rattling on about how beautiful these women were, and it bewildered me. As confident as she was, as sure of herself as she seemed, she didn't see she was just as alluring. I had seen pictures of Tyson's girl, Angela Donelli, but I didn't know who Casey was. My intel lately had been lacking with my focus on other things. I had everything on the boss in the province north of mine, Donelli, including his daughter Angie. Ava was right. Angie was hot, but Ava was no less.

Dropping my glass on the table, I stood and stepped over to her. She was still going on about Tyson's girl and how she had fit perfectly in her bridesmaid's dress while Ava and Casey had to get theirs adjusted. Boring talk I couldn't care less about. Her words halted when I leaned over her chair, my face close to hers.

"Stop."

She drew in a breath. Her eyes studied mine, the moonlight sparkling in them. I wanted to tell her she was the most alluring thing I'd seen, that no matter the women I'd had in the past, none compared to her because they didn't come close. That I suspected I was falling for her because she was exactly what I'd never known I needed. To tell her I would trade every one-night stand I had ever had, every night of pleasure, for one hour of time with her, for one smile, one laugh, one word from her. But I didn't. I hovered there, so close, yet a distance remained because it had to. She was my prisoner and whatever this was couldn't happen. "I never want to hear you compare yourself to another woman again or I'll lock you in that basement." A flash of fear had my eyes creasing. There was something about the basement that frightened her other than the purpose it served me. The reaction she'd had the night before was too extreme. Yet she kept her secrets, just as I kept mine.

I backed up and held my hand out to her. "Come on, it's getting late."

She looked at me for another moment before she placed her hand in mine. A slight gesture but one that spoke of the trust she had for me, trust she shouldn't have had and that I would likely break.

Grabbing her shirt and book from the main room, I led her to my room, hating how normal this appeared and how I was looking forward to holding her. The medication she needed would be here in the morning and then she would be back in her room at night. It should have been a reassuring thought, but it wasn't. Instead, it left a strange ache in my chest. One I avoided acknowledging for fear of having to admit what it meant.

Chapter Thirteen

AVA

Stretching my limbs in a long cat stretch, I glanced over at the empty side of the bed. The bed in my room, not Emerson's. He had moved me again. It was almost like he could justify having me in his bed for only so long. Like waking up next to me would cross some line. Rubbing my eyes, I sat up and yawned. Memories of my nightmares sat on the cusp of my awareness, but I shoved them away, thinking instead of how his hold on me had brought me out of the darkness again.

The covers disturbed a note at the end of the bed, and I crawled over to it.

Get dressed and meet me on the deck. Wear shorts.

Commanding and just like Emerson. I traced the neat letters that formed the words. Elegant and formal, not like my chicken scratch.

After a quick shower, I pulled out a pair of jean shorts with frayed edges and a blue tank top, followed by a tan flannel shirt. Rolling the sleeves up, I decided to forgo shoes. My hair was still wet, and I hadn't worn makeup for days. Why bother with shoes?

At the door, I lifted my hand to knock and let Breaker know I wanted to come out. It was ridiculous to pretend all this was normal when the door to my room locked me in. A reminder that even if my captor infatuated me, I was still his hostage. Confusing didn't even begin to describe the situation. I scratched my nose instead of knocking, thinking again of that syndrome I had read about where the captive falls for her captor. Was that all this was?

Nothing more than some psychological condition that was making Emerson attractive to me?

My laugh was audible. There was no making Emerson attractive. The man was hot. Even thinking about him had my legs clenching. And I wasn't delusional. I knew who he was and what he did. Shit, he'd killed two men the night he'd kidnapped me. I wasn't fooling myself into believing he was a good guy, although I had discovered there were pieces of him that were good.

With an exaggerated exhale, I knocked on the door, hearing Breaker's heavy steps followed by the clicking of the locks. He opened the door, his eyes scanning my body before he gave me a goofy smile.

"Damn, you're pale. Like some kind of vampire."

"Screw you," I said, shoving by him.

"Seriously, do you ever see the sun?"

"Don't make me hurt you," I threatened. His laugh continued down the hall.

"You couldn't hurt a fly, little girl. Tiny and pasty." He laughed even harder and by the time we'd reached the main room, I'd had enough.

I hadn't been able to fight my kidnappers, but I had gotten a few kicks in. And there had been no option but to comply with Emerson that night. Not with a gun pointed at my head. But I hadn't trained in self-defense or beaten my knuckles bloody against punching bags to have some goon think I was a defenseless little girl. It was time to show Emerson and his cronies I was compliant because I wanted to be, but I would fight back if pushed.

Pivoting quickly, I threw his step off. He glowered at me, his massive frame towering over me.

"I am not a little girl," I snarled.

He snickered, and I hit him with an uppercut causing him to stumble back. Pain flared in my hand.

"Fuck," he grumbled at the same time as I rubbed the ache from my knuckles.

He came at me and my instincts kicked in. I shifted, allowing him to grab me from behind before taking him out. Three quick moves and he was on his back.

"Impressive."

I glanced up to find Emerson resting on the doorframe. He looked even sexier today. His hair was damp, a shadow of growth was on his face, and he wore a loose button-down with short sleeves that showed his sculpted arms and tattoos.

My attention diverted, Breaker threw me to the floor, pinning me.

"Enough!" Emerson bellowed.

"Ouch." I rubbed my head. "That hurt asshole."

The menacing expression on Breaker's face cracked as he said, "Never let your eyes off the target, little girl."

"Call me a little girl again and I'll lay you out again."

"Get the fuck off her, Breaker." Emerson's voice held a possessive quality, and I peered over at him, seeing how dark his eyes had become, like a midnight sky.

"You've got some moves," Breaker said, standing and holding a hand out to me.

"Go," Emerson said, shooing him off before I could take his hand. "Take a break. Our guest is due a scolding for inciting violence against my men."

"Eh, boss, she was just playing."

"No, I wasn't." On the floor still, I felt extremely small with the two of them standing over me. I'd never felt small, but now I did. "There was no play in that whatsoever."

Breaker let out another laugh and walked away. "I'll admit you've got some moves kid, but that would only give you a second to run before your pissed off attacker would hunt you down."

There was no replying to him. He was too far by the time I thought of one. I looked back at Emerson, who had his arms crossed over his chest.

"So, you're going to scold me? Is that some kind of punishment?"

His brow raised before he stooped next to me. Piercing blue eyes, now the color of the sky, bore into me. "You'll know when I want to punish you, wildcat."

My stomach knotted, my mouth going dry. That nickname was like a tongue against my clit and the way he said it left me incoherent.

"Uh huh," I mumbled.

Hand extending out to me, he kept his intense gaze even after I was standing.

"Don't try that again."

The warning was clear, but as he turned to walk out to the deck, I couldn't stop myself from saying, "Why not?"

He halted his steps and threw a look over his shoulder. "Because next time he'll hurt you and I'll have to kill him."

No hesitation. No teasing tone. The words were serious, the darkness in those blue irises lethal.

He looked away and his steps became steady again. "Come get breakfast. I have plans for you."

My spine stung from the flip Breaker had given me and I was still a little dazed, but I didn't know if it was from being tossed or from Emerson's words.

"Just Breaker?" I dared.

He shook his head, mumbling, "Any man."

I sucked in a breath as he sat at the table and picked up his coffee cup while looking out at the ocean. The opportunity to run was there. No guard stood over me. Emerson's back was to me.

But I didn't because that draw to the man who had just told me he would kill any man who hurt me was too strong. Either that or I had hit my head too hard.

Standing, I stretched my back, knowing I'd have bruises. They would be worth the tradeoff of showing them I wasn't some weak woman. A strand of my hair stuck to my cheek, still damp from my shower, so I pushed it away as I walked.

"You don't have to prove yourself to my men, Ava." Emerson placed his mug on the table, his eyes still on the horizon.

"I always have to prove myself. I'm a woman. Men see me as helpless and fragile."

His chuckle skittered across my skin like the delicate rake of nails. "You're anything but fragile. Between that mouth of yours and those fists, you can hold your own. That left hook is something Breaker won't underestimate again. It takes a lot to make that man even flinch."

I looked down at my sore knuckles, rubbing them. "Yeah, well..." I didn't know what else to say.

His hand covered mine, and my eyes flew to him to see his focus on my fingers as he smoothed his thumb over them.

"The punching bag is different from hitting flesh and bone."

"I'm fine," I said, wanting to jerk my hand away but enjoying the warmth of his touch too much.

He released my hand, turning back to the view and avoiding my sight. I sat across from him, eating my eggs and thinking they were now my favorite food.

"Did your uncle teach you those moves?" he asked when the silence was almost unbearable.

"Some," I said, wiping my mouth. After chewing the rest of my mouthful, I explained, "I never wanted to be vulnerable again..." *No, too much, Ava.* He caught the choice of words, his head tilting toward me. "I mean, Den insisted I know how to protect myself. He taught me the basics, but he worked a lot and having his niece tag along wasn't safe, so he did what he could.

When I went to college, I took a self-defense class and loved it. I took as many as I could and started working out at the local gym." A sip of coffee didn't break the intensity of his gaze. "I lived in some shady places when I left college. Uncle Den hated it, but I was stubborn, wanted to see how tough I could be." Wanted to look death in the face again and laugh at it. Wanted to prove something that didn't need proving. "And even now I work at a bar and walk home alone at two in the morning." Shrugging, I added, "I need to know how to protect myself because no one else can."

His eyes narrowed, catching my last words. They weren't necessarily true. My uncle would kill for me. Now I had Greyson Tides because of Den and Riley, and there were men I worked with who continually asked to walk me home, who stayed after their shifts to make sure I was safe when I closed up. There were good men in the world and some of them were in my life, but the bad one had overshadowed them for too long.

"If your guys hadn't drugged me, I would have beaten the shit out of them." I was hoping to erase his serious expression, but it remained. Unable to take it anymore, I looked away. I didn't want to talk about my past, to tell him my secrets. They were my burden, not his.

"Since you trust me enough to sleep in the same bed with me, do you think you could let me out of my cell more often?" I asked, changing the subject.

"We'll see."

"Boss, your company is here." I turned to see another of Emerson's men at the door. This guy stood about three inches shorter than Emerson and reminded me of a weasel. The only thing tough about him was the snake tattooed on his cheek and the scar that ran through his left eyebrow.

"Good. Keep an eye on this one." He rose, cracking his knuckles as he walked up to the man. "You one of Pack's new hires?"

"Yeah, started a few days ago."

Emerson didn't respond but stood there, holding his stare, his muscles tense below his shirt. "Show me." I could see the tension in his back.

The guy pulled his shirt up, and I peeked my head around to see the variety of tattoos. Embedded in one was the Omens marking.

"Guess Pack thought you were good enough to skip my approval. Make one wrong move and he'll be cleaning pieces of your brain off my floor."

The image was one I didn't want to imagine, but it was there now. Emerson walked by him and, without a glance at me, he walked away, leaving the man to babysit me.

I slumped back in my chair and chomped on my toast. Every time it seemed like there might be something more to this, Emerson reminded me of my place in his world. Hostage. I didn't know why I was having so much trouble remembering it.

EMERSON WAS GONE for a while and, in that time, the guard stoically stood vigil. I tried making small talk, but he wasn't like Breaker or Emerson's other guy, Pack. This guy stared at me like I was his prey, his beady brown eyes never leaving me. It made my skin crawl like it should have crawled this entire time. I pulled my shirt closer to stave off the chill he was causing me. Panic crawled into my throat. It locked down my lungs and seized my muscles. The all too familiar tingling started, like a swarm of bees in my limbs.

By the time Emerson returned, I was ready to bolt and run back to my room. Emerson dismissed him, and the air seemed to lighten. My anxiety, however, didn't, and I continued to stare at the space in front of me, frozen and helpless to fight the panic that now held me hostage.

"Ava?" Emerson's concerned voice came through the haze, but it wasn't enough.

I gasped for breath, my head swimming as I clung to my shirt.

"Ava?" Hands took my face, forcing my eyes to his, but still I was lost to the rise of adrenaline and emotion that overtook all other senses and functions. I heaved in breaths, my heart racing. "Ava, what's wrong?"

All I could see was the man's face, his eyes burning a hole in me. This wasn't some holiday, some fun excursion. I was a prisoner, and that man wanted me dead. I was going to die. The thoughts pounded me, and my body went weak, my pulse slamming in an unsteady rhythm as I panted, the air never reaching my lungs.

The sensation of a forehead resting against mine added to the soothing strokes over my back.

"Shhh," I heard. "No one's going to hurt you."

The steady caresses melted the frozen locks on my limbs, waking them up and quieting my thoughts. My body inclined toward him, the sound of the waves, the seagulls, the breeze returning to my senses along with the smell of salt air and Emerson.

He brought his hands back to my cheeks, the move causing my eyes to meet his. Embarrassment rushed me like a bull charging its target. Here I'd boasted about never wanting to look weak and I'd done just that. If I'd been on my medications, I would have noticed the impending threat of an attack, but this had come on so suddenly I hadn't been able to stop it.

"I... I didn't—" He put a finger to my mouth, stopping my words. The moment lingered, an unspoken need, a flush of desire ricocheting through me that matched the flicker in his eyes.

"Are you all right?" he asked, dropping his finger and

removing his hand from my cheek. His features sharpened. "Did he do something to you?"

The embarrassment faded, anger replacing it. I worked hard to maintain an image of strength and confidence, and then things like this would remind me I wasn't infallible. That the demons of my past would never go away. I brushed my hair back, looking away.

"No, he didn't. I'm fine. I just...your guy gave me the creeps, that's all."

He took my chin in his fingers and turned my head. "He'll never watch you again."

I twisted from his hold, pushing away so I could stand. A move that forced him to his feet. His eyes creased and I could see him trying to figure me out.

"You don't always have to be strong, Ava."

My eyes leaped to his. He read my emotions like he had known me forever. I didn't know how to tell him I had to be strong or the past would devour me.

"I know," I whispered, rubbing my shoulder against my ear and feeling too seen, too open, too vulnerable. "Where did you go?"

"We should talk about what just happened," he pushed.

"Why do you care? It was just a panic attack, nothing more."

He hadn't been able to control how his body reeled back slightly. But he covered it, his eyes shifting into that emotionless look he'd had the night I met him.

"Your medicine came." His tone cut, reminding me of who he was and who I was to him. Only a commodity. A trade. A pawn in some war he had with his brother. My sight flicked to the bottles on the table. I hadn't even noticed him bring them.

I grabbed the bottles, looking at the generic labels printed on them. No name, no indication of who they were for or where they had come from. Only a simple medication name with the dose.

"Take what you need, and I'll have Breaker return you to your room."

The disappointment reflected in his tone had me clutching the bottle with my shaking hand and peeking back at him. His blue eyes were hard, but I could see the emotion below the exterior. How I could read his expressions so well after so few days, I couldn't explain, but I could see what he didn't want me to see.

I placed the bottle on the table, staring at the things that had been my island in a sea that thrashed against me viciously for years with the goal of drowning me. Emerson's steps resounded in the silence and tugged at something inside of me. A desperate need to have something else as my island. To admit that my smiles, my jokes, my confidence were all lies. Falsities to build some fantasy version of me no one could ever hurt again. The island had gotten smaller over the years; the tide eroding it until only my uncle, my therapist, and the drugs kept it intact. And I'd told myself that was all I needed, but after three nights in Emerson's arms, I wasn't so sure anymore.

I stared out at the ocean, watching the waves slam into the shore as his steps grew further away.

"He reminded me of my stepfather." My words were so soft I wasn't sure if he had heard me, but the footfalls ceased. I rubbed my arms, a chill scraping past the fabric of my shirt. "He always looked at me the same way. Like he would eat me alive if he could."

I swallowed, never having told anyone this, only Den and the psychiatrists. "You asked where the nightmares came from." All the weaknesses I had fought for years to hide resurfaced. "They come from him." My voice broke, and I hated it. I didn't even know if Emerson was still there, but saying the words and voicing my living hell seemed like the right thing. A time for my secrets to spill even though I couldn't give one rational reason why this was the man who needed to hear them.

"My father left my mother when I was a baby. It destroyed

her. We moved from town to town, and she spiraled more each time. First alcohol, then drugs. By the time I was six, I was taking care of myself. It's a wonder she made it that long." I had hated my mother for years, but over time, the hatred changed to pity. "She remarried when I was eight. He seemed nice at first, but that changed quickly." My eyes dropped to my hands, seeing the tremble in them. I crossed my arms, tucking my hands under them. "I can't remember a day when my mother wasn't high or drunk or without bruises after that. My bruises he kept to places no one would question."

I sucked in a shaky breath, knowing the worst was coming. The darkness sat at the fringe of my sight, and I fought it. "When I was twelve, he started to look at me different. Leering stares, touches that made my stomach turn. He would catch himself and the creepiness would turn to anger. That's when he started..." The crack of my voice was like glass cutting it. I hated going back to that time. It hurt even after all these years.

Emerson's hands slid over my arms like a support structure that fortified me in ways nothing ever had.

"The first time he locked me in the basement, he left me there for hours. He broke the bulb and threw me on the glass. Then he closed the door. I was terrified and bleeding, but no matter how I pounded on the door, no one let me out. It became his favorite punishment, and soon my mother started using it. Hours at a time in the pitch black. Things would scurry at the bottom of the steps. I know now they were likely mice or bugs, but back then I imagined hell existed at the bottom of those stairs and the demons were climbing to get me."

Tears fell, and I rested on his chest. He said nothing, just gave me the space to talk and the time to tell my story.

"When I was sixteen..." This time the sob climbed free, and he rested his head on mine, rubbing my arms. "I was sleeping, and the sound of my door creaking woke me up. I pretended to be asleep, scrunching my eyes and praying he would go away. But he didn't. He came in and climbed on top of me." Emerson's hold grew tighter, and I could sense his muscles become taut. "I fought him, scratching and hitting, as he told me I had to satisfy him because my mother had passed out." My stomach churned violently. "I kicked him in the balls and ran. But he caught me and beat me before he threw me into the basement, telling me I could come out when I was ready to fuck him." I let out a raw laugh, remembering how sick and twisted he had been. "He left me in there day after day. My mother never came for me. School never looked because we had moved so many times to avoid any suspicion that they hadn't bothered to enroll me in the new school. There were no neighbors, and I had no friends. By the fourth day, my knuckles were bloody from pounding on the door, most of my nails had ripped from scratching at the wood, I was hungry and thirsty. Delirious and almost catatonic. My uncle found me that night. I had been writing to him for years behind my mother's back after finding out she had a younger brother. I lied in every letter, telling him we were the perfect family, but when my stepfather beat my mother so badly that she'd been bed bound for days, I finally wrote him with the truth and he came for me."

Salty air invaded my lungs with the deep inhale I took. "He saved me. Took me to the hospital, then to Bridgeville. My mother had been dead for two days. She overdosed, but I sometimes wonder if she didn't take her own life. I'll never know."

"And your stepfather?" Emerson's voice was one I recognized from the first night I met him. The ruthless crime boss.

"Dead. I didn't know how until I found out what my uncle did for a living."

The tension lifted slightly from his muscles.

"Den took me in, hired tutors to help me finish high school. Got me in psychotherapy and paid for college. Although now that I know he works for your brother, I suspect Greyson may have had a hand in paying for those things."

"Sounds like the asshole did."

I peered back at him, meeting those gorgeous cerulean eyes tinged with emotion.

"So that's why you don't like my basement? I thought it was all the things I do to my enemies down there."

"Nope," I said, feeling somehow lighter than I ever had. "For some unexplainable reason, that doesn't bother me. It's the basement itself. I will never own a house with a basement." A shiver ran through me. "So now you know why I need the meds and why I still dream of being locked in that basement every night, no matter how many years have passed."

"I thought maybe it was me. You know, killer, crime boss, kidnapper?"

Staring at him, I broke into a grin, and my mood lifted completely. "Did you just make a joke, Mr. Tides?"

He grimaced. "Don't call me that. My brother is the formal one, not me." His bright orbs searched mine. "Thank you for telling me."

I twisted around in his arms, and he backed up a step like the unexpected closeness worried him. His hands fell away, and I instantly missed the protective warmth they had provided.

"Don't go telling anyone my secrets," I teased. "I might have to kill you."

A laugh and a lopsided grin that erased all the trauma I'd drudged up left my lower body with an annoying flock of butterflies hurling through it.

"You may know how to defend yourself, but I wouldn't go that far."

My hands went to my hips. "You doubt my abilities?"

"Not at all. I doubt you could kill someone." His grin faltered. "It takes a lot out of you, and I'd hate to see something like that taint you."

Not thinking, I reached up and traced my fingers over his jawline. "You're not as tainted as you think."

He seemed taken aback before he removed my hand and said, "Take your medication, Ava."

"Are you still sending me back to my room or are you going to tell me why you wanted me to wear shorts today? Was it just to see my pretty legs?"

"Both," he said.

"Both? But I said three things, so which two?" I was pushing him, but he didn't seem to mind and the further we were from my confession, the better.

He shook his head. "There was a reason I wanted you to wear shorts and yes, I wanted to see your pretty legs, even though that wasn't the reason."

"Aww, you think my legs are pretty. I think that's the nicest thing you've said to me since you called me wildcat."

Pinching the bridge of his nose, he muttered, "What the hell did I get myself into?"

I took two of my pills, chasing them with a shot of coffee.

"Only two?" he asked.

"Yup. Anxiety and nightmares. The other is for panic attacks, but since I already had one of the damned things, I don't need it now." Out of habit, I looked at my arm, but my watch wasn't there. "Can you set a timer for me, so I take my next one at two? I don't have my watch or my phone."

He pulled his phone out without hesitation. After setting the alarm, he motioned toward the stairs with his head. "Come on. I have something for you."

"More? It's hard to top medication, Emerson."

He threw a look over his shoulder, and I grinned.

"So it's the little things that make you happy?" he said as I followed him.

"Definitely." Growing up with nothing left me with an appreciation for the smaller joys in life. My uncle's life was extravagant compared to mine, and it had made me uncomfortable. That was the reason I'd gone to college out of the province and roamed aimlessly for so many years before deciding to move back to Bridgeville. "You know your bedroom is the size of my entire apartment, right?"

He pushed in a code at the end of the deck, where the stairs led down to the shore. I took note of the man making rounds at the cliff-side off the left of the deck and turned my head to the right to see another one in the distance. I'd been watching them out my window, memorizing the pattern of their passes like my uncle had taught me. An odd thing for him to teach me at the time, but now I understood he was taking precautions. I was a liability in his line of work unless I knew how to survive. And after what I had been through, he wanted me to have the skills to fight back harder if there was ever a next time. A lot of good it had done me in this situation, but as Emerson turned and gestured for me to go down the stairs, a mischievous gleam to his eyes, I thought maybe that had been a blessing.

Chapter Fourteen

EMERSON

Adrenaline still pumped through my veins even as Ava walked down the stairs ahead of me. There were times when my rage blinded me, but this time it scored me like a brand, shading my vision in splashes of crimson. I wanted to dig her stepfather up and bring him back to life so I could torture him again. I had suspected there was trauma behind her nightmares, but never had I considered it had been that. While I was thankful she had fought back and the man hadn't raped her, it did little to quell the ire in me for all the other things he had done. He and her mother. Neglect, abuse, torture.

I wiped my hand down my face, focusing on her instead. My eyes slid to the sway of her hips. Her shorts emphasized her round ass, and each swish eased the tension in my body.

The instinct to shield her from her memories as she'd spoken about them had been overwhelming. Before I could think, I had my hands around her, holding her like I did when she slept. Everything with Ava defied who I was. She brought out a side in me I thought no longer existed. A soft side that opposed the man I had built myself to be.

"Does this mean I have to climb all these steps to get back up?" she asked, her voice carried back to me on the breeze.

"Do you always state the obvious?"

"Do you always answer a question with a question?" she shot back.

Laughter bubbled up, free and light. That's what she did to me. She made me happy, and I hadn't been happy for years. She was like a ray of sunshine in my overcast world.

Ava jumped the last two steps, her feet sinking into the sand. She stared down at her toes as they wiggled. Her smile was brilliant, lighting her eyes to a golden hue. Face pointing to the sky, she closed them and breathed in. The sight mesmerized me. I could have stood there all day and watched her. She blinked a few times, then gave me a devious grin before she ran off toward the water.

Frozen in place, I soaked in the sight. The unhindered, carefree spirit she had. After all she'd gone through, she embraced life like I never had. With wide eyes and an open mind, savoring the small things I took for granted. I had lived here for fifteen years, yet never had the view been anything more than a backdrop. Now it was everything because Ava was there, chasing the waves as they hit the shore and laughing.

My chest tightened, an unfamiliar sensation seeping in, one I should have pushed away but couldn't bring myself to. She circled around, then splashed her hands into the water.

"Should I get you a swimsuit so you can go in?" I asked, trying not to picture her in a bikini that emphasized the flow of her curves.

"Oh, I don't know how to swim," she said, drying her hands on her shorts and walking from the water.

"How do you not know how to swim?"

She put her hands on her hips and tipped her head to the side. "Really? Let me see. Grew up in a province where beaches are a thing of myth. Sheltered and—"

"Okay, okay." I put my hands up in surrender as she sauntered closer to me. The sun lit the blonde in her hair, making the strands almost white. "I'll teach you." The words were out before I could stop myself.

Her mouth opened slightly, eyes scrunching. "I'm not sure we have time for that, Emerson." The words were like lead weights collapsing my shoulders. The truth that tied us. This was temporary and soon she would be gone. The idea caused that sensation in my chest to turn violent.

"True," I said, my vision slipping to the water.

"Why did you bring me down here?" she asked, bringing my attention back to her.

Why had I? An impulsive need, irrational and out of character. But then, those had been constant since the night I had met her.

"What is that?" Her sight slipped behind me to where I had tucked the things I'd asked Jill to buy for me on a whim yesterday.

"It's..." Shit. What was I doing? A desire for self-preservation surfaced, screaming for me to stop this. To force her back up the stairs and forget all of this. Forget that her smile sent warmth to barren crevices. That her spirit woke me, making me feel alive for the first time in over twenty years. That I wanted to make her happy, to hear her laugh, to see her grin and have her babble to me. Forget it all and return to who I had been before the night she crashed into my life.

She ran past me and over to the big tote of supplies for a day at the beach. A day I had planned for her and intended to spend with her. Canceling my meetings and setting aside my responsibilities and worries for just one day with her.

Dragging the bag to the middle of the beach, she spread the blanket out and dumped the contents onto it. Beach toys, sunscreen, a handful of books. I would never forget the excitement that lit her eyes when she lifted them to me.

"You planned a day at the beach with me?"

"I... You need some sun." That urge for self-preservation returned, and the answer came out more terse than intended.

"Mmm. So you're saying my skin is pasty? I'm not sure if that's a compliment or an insult, Mr. Tides."

I cringed, hating that formal name, but noticing that the inflection she put on it made it something more than just my father's name or my brother's.

"Not pasty, but definitely pale," I returned, heading back to the alcove where an umbrella and cooler sat. Jill had packed it when she had dropped the things off earlier in the morning. "I mean, you're not quite vampire material, but close."

She stuck her tongue out at me before picking a few beach toys out. Items in hand, she walked to a spot and sat in the sand. I set the umbrella up, trying not to dwell on how odd the action seemed to my everyday tasks. Picking up the sunscreen, I moved toward her.

"Put this on. I'm not pampering you if you get sunburned."

Squinting up at me, she frowned. "Are you pampering me now?"

I stooped, throwing the sunscreen into her lap. "This is me pampering, wildcat."

Her smile could have filled me more than the most expensive meal and left me sated for days. She obliged my request and put on the sunscreen before digging into the sand.

"So, Emerson Tides. How did you come up with Cade?" Her hands deftly shifted the sand into shapes.

Sitting across from her, I ignored the strange sensation of sitting on the sand in my slacks. Her eyes flitted to me, then back to the sand. "I needed an alias when I moved from Bridgeville. Cade was my middle name."

"Emerson Cade Tides?"

"Emerson Cadon Tides. Like I said, my parents liked names that sounded like we were wealthy."

"Were you?"

"Eh, middle class. We had enough to never go without. What about you?" I asked, wanting the attention off of me. "Ava Shelton. Any fancy middle names for you?"

Her hands stopped, and I worried I had brought her back to the nightmares, but she chuckled. "Avani Liliya."

"Avani? That's your first name?"

"It's on my birth certificate," she said with a shrug. "But I prefer Ava. No one but my stepfather called me Avani. If I could bring myself to change my name so I never have the reminder of him again, I would. But it's the only piece of the sober side of my mother I have."

I observed her. The strands of her hair had dried in the morning sun, and they slipped forward as she molded the shape of a dragon into the sand. Her brown eyes peeked up at me.

"Avani, huh?"

She gave me a nod.

"Maybe it's time you take your power back, wildcat."

Her inhale was beautiful, her eyes widening into chestnut orbs with hints of gold. She swallowed, and those irises held mine with an intensity that burned through me. "Maybe it's time we both do, *Emerson*."

The corner of my mouth twitched as I fought my smile and lost. "Maybe."

She went back to making her sand dragon, and I sat there, content to watch her work. Noting all the tiny mannerisms that made me adore her more—the way she bit her tongue between her teeth when she focused, the deft movements of her hands as they sculpted, how she itched her nose with the back of her wrist. All such miniscule things that I would never have bothered to care about, but with Ava, I wanted to store them all to memory.

For the first time in too many years, the stress of my present situation, the sins of my past, and the dangers of my future all faded into a silence Ava filled. She chatted about her classes, her intentions when she earned her master's, her love of all things art and the hours she used to spend in local museums that spurred her studies. And with every passing minute in her light, my darkness dissipated, leaving space for the emotions I'd been shielding in it to grow. At the thought, I should have walked away, left her there, left her to someone else to guard, and buried myself back in my work. But I couldn't do it.

AVA WAS CURLED up on the couch, exhausted from the day on the beach. We had stayed out the entire day, mostly sitting under the umbrella and talking as if we were on a first date and our roles no longer existed. I didn't know what to make of it, but if I didn't overthink it, I wanted more of it.

"Let her go where she wants in the house as long as she doesn't leave," I told Breaker.

His brow arched, and I knew what he was thinking. Like Pack, he'd been with me the longest. It was the reason I trusted him to guard her.

"Cut it out and go watch the front of the house. Get Vin on the deck so she doesn't go back out." I glanced at her one last time. "I'm going to shower."

I left them, heading to my room and trying to clear my head in the shower. What I was doing was dangerous and unlike me. I needed to focus. Ava was a commodity, nothing more. But no matter how I repeated the words, they didn't change the warmth that sat in my chest or the constant desire to touch her that hounded me like a craving I couldn't quell. It almost seemed like I was fraying at the seams.

Toweling my hair, I pulled on a pair of pants and took my phone out. After a few seconds of debate, I hit Greyson's number.

"I hope you're calling this late to tell me you're sending Ava home." He sounded gruff, as usual.

"Not gonna happen," I replied.

"Then what the hell are you calling for? Did you change your deadline? Because you're lucky I haven't brought my force down on your ass yet."

"You haven't because I'll kill her the second you do." This time, the words came out hollow. "You know what I want. You crawling up my front steps in less than two weeks."

There was a distinct growl on the other end of the phone, and I thought I heard a woman's voice. Riley. My new sister-in-law and the woman who should have been in Ava's place and all this confusion would never have entered my head.

"Touch a hair on her head and I'll keep you alive for years while I torture you."

"All talk, Grey. That's all you are. You don't stand a chance against me. Now shut the fuck up and tell me your guy really killed her stepfather."

I rubbed my hand over my face, hating the silence on the other end of the phone. Greyson and I had been playing enemies for decades, and this question made no sense to him. I shouldn't have asked it, but I needed to know. The thought of that man alive was eating at me and if he'd gotten away, I would hunt him down and drag him back so she could watch me rip him apart piece by piece.

A few more seconds of silence before he said, "What's going on, Mer?"

Even after over twenty years apart, he could still get into my head. Inseparable as kids, our parents had often joked about how we shared one mind. How the bond between us was so strong. Shit, it still was. Enemies or not, it remained, and I had spent years submerging it below my anger at him.

"Just answer the fucking question," I snapped, my grip on the phone so tight it cracked.

"His torso is in a lake, the rest of him we buried below a shopping mall in Creekwood."

"Did he suffer?"

More silence and I worried he would grow suspicious.

"Yes. Den locked him in the same basement he kept Ava in, then took a part of him for every day he kept her down there before the man bled to death. Weighed his torso down with bricks from the basement when he left it in the lake."

Relief surged through me. My brother and I were alike, so there should have been no question that if his man hadn't finished the job, Greyson would have done it for him. But I needed to hear it, to have confirmation that the man had suffered.

"Good. You have ten days before I want to see your pathetic ass in front of my gates or she's dead." I disconnected, hating how saying those two words cut me like a rusty blade. Throwing the phone on the bed, I raked my hands through my hair. Attachment was something I didn't do, especially with women. I took what I needed and walked away. Emotionless transactions, nothing more, and if they wanted more, they were greatly disappointed. But Ava had gotten past my barriers, chipping away at the locks within days until all my plans for her had morphed. I couldn't imagine killing her. I had a reputation as a heartless killer, one who shot and asked questions later. Yet I was hesitating, distraught over the idea that if my brother didn't bend, I would have to hurt her.

Like an injured dog backed into a corner, I resorted to punching back. Texting Breaker, I told him to make sure he fed her when she woke. I finished dressing and left through the garage, taking Pack and two others with me. Being away from her would help, and the club would give me a necessary distraction. At least I thought it would.

I owned several clubs through the province. Charter was the one I frequented. Upscale and catering to the more elite clientele, I preferred the atmosphere to the grittier options. The music blared, lights streamed, and women danced on the few poles strategically placed on the dance floor. Snapping my collar, I strolled through the club, making the rounds until I settled into a corner. Entertaining the brown nosing of the pathetic social climbers who wanted a piece of my attention and those who owed me money, I settled into my usual demeanor. Drink in hand, I caught the eye of a pretty brunette in a tight, sequined dress that clung to her body in all the right ways. She sauntered over and I nodded to Pack to let her by. Leaning over the table, her breasts deliciously displayed, she said something, but my mind fucked me over when it decided Ava's breasts were more tempting.

I blinked, taking another swig of my drink.

"What do you think?" she asked, clearly waiting for a response to some question she had asked.

Damn, she was sexy and from the look in her eyes, she was offering exactly what I needed, only she wasn't what I wanted. Against all rational thought, I swirled my alcohol in my glass and let my eyes rove over her body as she stood, thinking how she looked too thin and didn't have the hips I wanted to grip. I could have easily taken her into the lower part of the club and fucked away my cravings for the spirited blonde and pink haired woman in my house, but I knew it wouldn't help. That I'd be disappointed and somehow left feeling guilty because that amazing woman looked at me with eyes that trusted. Screwing some random woman in the dark corners of my club might damage that look, and the idea of that happening killed me.

Waving her away, I muttered, "Go find someone else to flaunt that sexy body to. I don't want it."

I gulped down the rest of my drink, averting my eyes from her gaping mouth. Rising, I adjusted my shirt cuffs and walked past her, hearing her complaints and ignoring them.

This was bad. Really bad. Pack said nothing as he drove me home and I stayed silent, my mind playing through why I had given up a night of sex with a gorgeous woman when any other night I would have used her until she left with wobbling legs and I was drained. That man seemed like someone else. A man searching for something and never finding it. Just like Ava had said. Searching for her all this time and now that I'd found her, no amount of temptation would compare.

It was late when I returned, and Ava no longer slept on the couch. I glanced down the hall where I knew she was likely reading and forced my feet to take me to my room. Standing under the shower and scrubbing off the smell of the club and perfume belonging to a woman I hadn't even touched, my mind drifted back to Ava. I wanted her desperately. To go to her room and ravage her, to have her come undone around me, to taste every inch of her and hear her scream in pleasure and not pain.

The thoughts flooded me, and I pictured her under me, skin to skin, mouth to mouth, our bodies moving as one. Stroking myself only worsened the need until a desperate hunger gripped me and my hand flew to the wall to stabilize myself. Every stroke I imagined was her pulsing around me, clenching in the throes of orgasm. My hand moved faster, my body rigid with the release that was so close it hounded me. Grinding my teeth, I silenced the roar that sought to flee as I came, splattering my desire for Ava on the shower floor, only for it to be swept away with the water.

Left only partially satisfied and irritated that I'd resorted to using my hand instead of taking the real thing from a woman who had been more than willing, I settled into bed. No amount of scrolling on my phone or answering emails helped to halt the sensation that something was missing. I looked over at the empty side of my bed, realizing only then that I had gotten into the side I never slept on, as if I had expected Ava to take my usual side. With a sigh, I looked at the time. One in the morning. Ava would still be reading. She was like me—a night owl. Her demons, like mine, made sleep a fleeting thing. I could count on one hand the number of nights I'd slept well, and they included the nights I'd held her through her nightmares.

With a sigh, I tossed my phone on my nightstand and threw the covers back. Pulling a pair of sweats on, I stalked from my room, annoyed at this newfound dependency for a woman who was only in my life by chance. An idiotic mistake. Or maybe a fortunate turn of fate. Whatever the reason, I knew two things: Ava would sleep in my arms tonight and I had completely lost my mind.

Chapter Fifteen

GREYSON

My phone shattered when it hit the floor, causing Riley to jump. I smoothed my hand over her leg, taking breaths to calm myself.

"Your brother?" she asked, her green eyes rimmed with concern.

She had come in mid-call, perching on my desk as she listened to my side of the conversation. Her soft skin calmed me, and I pushed my hand higher, the silky material of her nightgown scrunching with the movement.

"Unfortunately." Something was off. I sensed it in my bones, in that annoying connection I still had with Emerson, even after decades of our rift.

"Hey." Riley took my face in her hands and searched my eyes. She was too attuned to my moods. "Tell me what he said."

I brought my hand up and slid hers from my face, taking it in mine. A nagging thought kept returning to me and I let it churn in my head.

"Grey, is Ava all right?" Riley asked, too impatient to wait for my answer to her initial question.

Exhaling, I said, "I'm certain she is."

A frown marred her features. "Then why did he call?"

I sat back, taking her hand with me, the move forcing her into my lap where she curled up. My hand aimlessly caressed her leg as I spoke. "To ask me about her stepfather."

Her eyes crinkled as she tried to figure it out.

"You'll have to ask Ava when we have her back. It's her secret to tell, not mine." One she had clearly shared with my brother. But why?

"Then how would your brother know about him? I'm her friend and I don't," she said, voicing my thoughts.

My hand smoothed lazily over her leg, her soft skin soothing me. "I don't know. Den and I are the only ones who know." He had no choice but to tell me, getting my blessing to retrieve Ava when she was just a teen. She'd never known, but I funded everything, ensuring she had anything she needed after what the bastard had done to her. She assumed it was Den, although now that she knew me and knew Den worked for me, I was sure she had put the pieces together.

"Why would he need to know about her stepfather?"

"Good question. The man's been dead for fourteen years and before you ask, I can only tell you he deserved every bit of torture he received." Understanding lit her eyes, but as much as we shared everything, this was Ava's past, not mine. "It's out of character for Emerson to bother to ask something like that."

"Unless..." She chewed her lip, and I could see her thinking through it just like I was. It was a shame Mason hadn't brought her into the business earlier. She was smart, often seeing things from a perspective I didn't.

"Unless what?"

"Well, Ava is...well, Ava."

Even with the strain in my muscles, I couldn't help but chuckle. "And what does that mean?"

"It means she's fearless and captivating. Maybe he's falling in love with her just like I did."

This time, my laugh cascaded through the room. "Do I need to worry that you just confessed your love for Ava?"

She smacked my chest, and I pulled her in for a kiss. "A move like that has repercussions, baby girl."

Her blush was glorious.

"I think a few handprints on that delicate ass of yours are in order."

And it turned a violent crimson.

"Shush. I love her as a friend. You can't help but adore her and maybe he got into more than he expected by kidnapping her."

"He did because he thought it was you." The thought turned my mood, and my jaw ticked.

Riley rubbed her thumb over it.

"You forget who you're talking about, Riley. My brother doesn't have emotions. He's a heartless bastard who wants me for a stupid vendetta he has against me from when we were young."

Her sly grin had me scowling at her. "Sounds like someone else I know," she teased, her hand rubbing over my chest.

"I'm adding another smack to that punishment," I said, hating that she was doing what she did best and seeing things outside of my sphere of thinking. I was inclined to think she had been reading too many of the dark romance books I bought her. I'd had to convert my spare room into a library for her after she'd moved the collection I'd bought from her apartment and the one she had in Treemont. Not what I'd ever expected, but I would convert every room in my house if it meant I was on the receiving end of her reaction when I'd shown her the room as an engagement present. Priceless and embedded in my memory for life.

But that inclination to write off her thoughts warred with the two weeks my brother had given me and the feral tone in his voice when he'd asked about Ava's stepfather. That tone he usually directed at me the few times we'd spoken, but this time he hadn't. Throw in the fact that he insisted I wait two weeks before stepping foot in his territory and that he wanted to discuss an agreement with me, and I couldn't help but think something was off with my brother.

I picked Riley up and set her on her feet, rising to retrieve my phone from where it had hit the floor. The shattered screen was a reminder of my temper, but I could still dial Mason's number.

"Yeah," he answered, voices in the background.

"Are you with Raines?"

"Yeah. He and Angie are having a drink with us."

"Are you someplace we can talk business?"

"I can be. Want Tyson with me?"

"Yes." I thought about how keen Casey had been when we'd talked before. "And bring your girl."

"Then you're getting Tyson's, too. They come as a package deal now...much to my frustration."

"Just like you and Raines," I mumbled, responding to Riley's frown with a wink.

"Asshole," he grouched. I heard him yell to Raines, then the muffled sounds of them moving to another room.

Riley came over and looked up at me. "What's going on?"

"Just a hunch." I kissed her nose. "You're too observant to ignore."

"So you think he might be falling for her?"

Grimacing at the thought, I said, "Doubtful, but something's going on."

"We're all ears, Tides," Tyson said, on speakerphone.

"Give me the rundown again on your suspicions about the Omens."

"That was Casey," Mason said, giving credit to her as if it were a natural thing.

"Like I said, they're off," Casey's voice came through the phone.

"Hey Case!" Riley added over my shoulder.

A round of shouts of her name followed, and I rubbed my

head. "Can we focus? Tell me why again. Run the facts by me." I hadn't been involved in the Armina situations, so everything I knew came from Mason. Pacing, I listened to what she said, putting her on speaker when Riley threw her hands on her hips and gave me a look that told me I'd regret not including her. Since I had plans for her after this, I acquiesced to her demands.

Casey explained her thoughts on how sloppy the last attacks had been, confirming my thoughts on what had happened with Riley. Telling us that given everything she knew of the Bad Omen this didn't hold up to the reputation. There were too many mistakes, and they were too easy to defeat.

I scratched my head, her suspicions voicing my own.

"Rogue," I muttered, repeating what I'd said when Emerson had first taken Ava. It was a dangerous word in our world. "Clint Randall was the key. The place everything started. I know my brother. We've been enemies for longer than we were brothers, and he doesn't put up with sloppy men. Randall would have been dead after screwing it up the first time."

"So he went rogue," Mason said.

"Or maybe he didn't. If it's anything to know about Emerson...Cade, it's that he doesn't screw around and he doesn't make mistakes." Even when we worked together, he had been relentless.

"Then what's going on?" Mason said. "Both attempts in Armina failed and the reputation of the Omen is that they don't fail."

"Exactly." Riley let out a little whine when I released her, and I gave her a scolding look. "There's something off. The Omens don't give time, and my brother doesn't give a shit about anyone but himself."

"Yet he called you about Ava's stepfather," Riley mused aloud.

"What?" Raines was so loud, he sounded like he had grabbed the phone.

"Settle down Raines. Ava's stepfather was a bastard who my

man cut down when she was a teenager. But it's not something anyone knows. Not even Riley."

Silence on the other end lasted longer than I had expected, which told me they were all as confused as I was by the question.

"What did he want to know?" Angie asked.

"He wanted to make sure he was dead."

"How does that make any sense?" Raines asked, and I heard someone take a hard seat.

"So..." Casey started. "Either he's torturing her or falling for her."

Just like Riley had said. "What is it with you women that that's where your mind goes?"

"Let me guess, Ri said the same thing?"

"Yup," she answered Casey.

"Forced proximity, kidnapping. The perfect combination!" Casey's excitement was too much, and I had the urge to hang up on them.

"That's the most ridiculous thing I've ever heard," grumbled Mason.

"I'm inclined to agree, Brinks. But his tone wasn't menacing. If anything, it was protective." And he had to have known I would catch the difference. My head shot up, and I met Riley's eyes. "Maybe this is all connected. My brother wants to talk to me. That was his reason for the kidnapping. If someone's gone rogue..."

"Then he wants to ensure he takes them down without getting pinned for the sloppy mess they've made. The tarnished reputation they're making of the Omens," Mason finished.

"Exactly."

"And where does Ava fit into this?" asked Angie.

"I'm not sure, but if Casey and Riley are right, then this just got even more complicated and dangerous than it already was."

Riley's eyes grew large, as if she hadn't considered it.

"What do you suggest, Tides?"

"We stick to the plan. He gave us a deadline for a reason." A deadline that was difficult to honor. Keeping Den from barging into Seagate wasn't easy, but I knew my brother well enough to know he would be true to his word and kill her if we moved early. Although now I wasn't so certain he would. Regardless, I would honor the deadline because I suspected that reason had more to do with the woman he currently held hostage than anything else.

Complication was an understatement. If my brother was in trouble, if his empire was being sabotaged and Ava got caught in the middle of it, then I didn't want to think of the repercussions on all sides of the battlefield.

Chapter Sixteen

AVA

The words on the page continued to stare at me as my mind drifted again to Emerson. An entire day. He had spent the entire day with me. Not guarding me or torturing me, but playing in the sand and talking with me. I couldn't think of a day that had been any better except the day my uncle had rescued me. And when we'd tired of the beach, we'd spent the rest of the day watching terrible movies and munching on popcorn he made Pack get from the closest movie theater. I would have felt bad, but Pack joined us for one of the movies before my clearly irritating habit of guessing the plot twists annoyed him too much.

Falling asleep on the couch had not been my intention, but the hours on the beach had left me drowsy and before I knew it, I was alone on the couch and night had fallen. After Breaker led me back to my room, I opted for a long hot shower where the constant warmth in my belly at the thought of Emerson had me pretending my hands were his and hoping the shower muted my resulting moan. There was no other place to touch myself for fear of someone walking in on me.

And now, book in hand, my thoughts were still on him. The

shower time had not helped in any way. If anything, it had me craving the real thing even more. Groaning, I rested my head back and put the book over my eyes. This was horrible. I had orgasmed to the image of the man who had kidnapped me, and now I couldn't stop thinking about him. As if that was something new. An obsession had developed from the moment I laid eyes on him. The sound of the men dying behind me that first night returned, and I corrected that obsession to the next morning. No infatuation had developed on that first night. Only fear...that had dissipated the moment his blue eyes softened, and he spoke to me.

I returned to reading, forcing myself to focus and angry at myself for falling asleep earlier. When I was two chapters from finishing my book, there was a quick rap on my door, and Emerson's head peeked in.

"Knocking now? My status has improved if knocks have entered my world."

He gave me a smirk that erased any pleasure I'd had earlier and left me longing for more.

"Still awake, huh?" he asked, stepping in and looking around like he was in a room he'd never seen before.

"Yes," I said, hopping up from the bed. "And yes."

His brow raised when he noticed I was in his T-shirt again. I couldn't help it. The smell reminded me of him.

"What's the second yes for?" he asked as I handed him my book. His brow arched higher.

"Yes, I'd love to come keep you company because I can't sleep either."

I dug through the stash of books Jill had sent me, realizing too late that my ass was hanging out when I bent down. Swiveling, I caught the lick of his lips, the flare of desire in his eyes. This was so bad. I had just assumed he'd come to take me back to his room. And I wanted him to because I didn't like my empty bed now that he'd slept with me the last few nights. Ridiculous, I knew, but I had never been one to heed rational thoughts.

"Where did all those books come from?"

"Jill. Well, I guess you bought them for me, and she picked them up." I dropped the second book into his hand. "Thanks, I really love them. The boring mystery Pack brought me was dull without the smut."

"The smut?" he mouthed before he shook his head. "Why are you assuming I'm here to take you to my bed...to sleep..."

I reached up and closed his mouth, giving him a smile. "Because I just know."

"Well, what if I'm not?" It was cute seeing a deadly mafia boss struggle for words like a nervous teenage boy.

I crossed my arms, daring him to tell me I was wrong. "Am I wrong?"

He pinched the bridge of his nose. "Fuck, no you're not." His eyes dropped to the floor, and I could see the fight there. It was the same that I continued to have, the same that told me this wasn't right, but argued that it felt too right to ignore. "I can't sleep and just in case your medicine doesn't work, it makes sense to have you with me."

An excuse but one I latched onto because it gave me a reason to ignore the voice in the back of my mind screaming that this man had taken me from my home, my friends, my family.

"Oh, yeah. That's a good point," I said, lying because I knew I'd be fine tonight. He rubbed the back of his neck and again I couldn't equate this man to the ruthless killer I knew him to be. "Don't want to take a chance."

I walked to the door and opened it the rest of the way. "Should I lead?" I asked.

He snickered. "I thought you already were," he said, as if the timid man he'd been moments before was no more. "Why am I carrying two books?" he asked as he followed me out.

Another of my regular guards was on duty and his eyes darted between us until Emerson barked, "Patrol the north side with Johnson."

"Yes, boss."

I kept walking, knowing the route and surprised that he let me continue to lead. His steps were heavy behind me, his presence like a blanket on a chilly night. It slipped over me in an embrace I couldn't deny.

Running up the steps to his room, I continued my path to my side of the bed, noting how the other side was disturbed. The side he had told me was one he didn't prefer, but he'd taken it tonight. Perhaps out of habit or maybe some awareness that he would eventually collect me and I would fill that space.

I settled in and he stood over me, a perplexed slant to his eyebrows. "Don't get any ideas. This is to keep your mouth shut so you don't wake all of Seagate with your screams."

He handed me a book, but I shook my head and pointed to the other in his hand. His eyes drew in more.

"I have two chapters left in that one, so I need them both."

A roll of his eyes and the book was in my hands. He thumped to his side of the bed, leaving on his sweats and T-shirt.

"If you didn't want me here, why bring me?" I asked, flipping to my chapter.

"I didn't say that," he grumbled, picking up his phone.

My sight moved to him, but he avoided looking at me.

"So you did want me here? And it wasn't just because of my night terrors?"

"Read, Ava."

"Hmm."

He lowered his phone and finally looked at me. A wish, simple yet convoluted. To have him kiss me, to have his hands on my skin, his body against mine.

"Hmm, what?" he asked, disturbing my reckless thoughts.

"Nothing." I went back to my book, sinking some into the bed to get comfortable. I sensed his eyes on me, but I didn't turn back to him. The heaviness of that stare disappeared, and he returned to his phone.

We sat together, me reading while he worked or whatever he did on his phone. A comfortable silence sat between us, the sense that this was a natural thing for us. Two people who barely knew each other, whose circumstance was complicated and twisted, but who somehow needed each other even when they couldn't say it. Because I knew from the moods that crossed his navy irises and from my own slow descent into madness that we were heading to something neither of us could avoid.

I WOKE THE NEXT MORNING, my book laid open on the bedside table and the blankets pulled up over me. No memory of falling asleep, which told me I had drifted off while reading and Emerson had moved my book. The nightmares hadn't come, and I had slept peacefully. Too peacefully, only waking once when his arm slid around my waist.

Sitting up, I stretched and realized I wasn't in my room. He had left me in his, which seemed like madness considering I was his prisoner. Was this an opening to change things? I chewed my lip. No, because if it were, he would send me home. The air fled my lungs as an unexpected melancholy overcame me. As much as I wanted to be back home to my apartment, to Uncle Den and Riley, to work and school, it would mean not seeing Emerson. And that thought stung. I rubbed my chest, trying to fight off the sensation. It made no sense, but the ache was there, too prominent to ignore.

Shoving it away, I used the bathroom, thinking it looked too tidy. My bathroom at home was a mess of makeup and hair ties, lotions and body scrubs. Candles and bath bombs. Even the one I was using here was already a mess. This was like a blank slate—clear countertops, neatly hung towels. The only evidence it wasn't a showroom was the towel hung at the back of the walk-in shower. Normally, showers weren't that exciting to me, but this one was too fascinating not to look. It was massive, big enough for multiple people, and I stepped back out as the thought of him with another woman in it crossed my mind. The envy that leeched into my veins seemed inappropriate, but it was there, too irritating to ignore.

I considered taking my books back to my room but left them, like a mark that I had been there and might return. After peeking into his closet, which was nearly the size of my apartment, and running my hands absently over the plethora of suit jackets and pressed dress shirts, I denied my urge to sniff them for his scent. On my way out, something caught my eye, a bit of gray silk peeking from a drawer. Thinking it looked familiar, I opened the drawer. Amid the extensive collection of expensive watches and cufflinks was the scarf I'd worn the night he kidnapped me. I didn't know what to think of the warmth the sight caused in my chest or the fact that he'd kept a piece of me like a treasure.

Quickly closing the drawer, I gave in to the urge and brought one of his shirts to my nose, breathing in his scent before heading downstairs.

The creepy guard stood at the end of the hall, blocking the way to the garage, and I turned quickly from his heavy gaze. The joy that had been in my step turned to that nagging fear and I pulled at my shirt, suddenly self-conscious in just Emerson's T-shirt. Neither Pack nor Breaker were in the main room, nor were they in front of my room. As I showered and dressed, I contemplated what it meant. A show of trust? Or a test? But why would he test me unless the same convoluted emotions were swarming his mind like a hive of angry hornets like they were mine? I swore if my chest tightened at the sight of him one more time, I was going to impale it with something sharp.

My hair cutely tied in two knots, I padded from the room in my bare feet and ventured down the hall. I peered into the empty rooms that shared the hall with my room, surprised at how they were all furnished but seemed like they had never been used. The view from the room across from mine was as stunning as Emerson's view. It overlooked the ocean, unlike mine that looked out to the lawn with woods in the distance. Maybe he'd been worried I would jump to my death rather than stay in his grasp.

With a laugh at how ridiculous that sounded, I continued down the hall, walking into the front foyer for the first time since the night he'd taken me. No blood stained the marble floor, no evidence remained that two men had died there. In front of me, the front door stood unguarded. The crystal chandelier above me threw prisms over the wall from the morning sun as I stood there. A door with no guards, no one to stop me from running. I wasn't naïve. They were outside, patrolling or maybe waiting there. Waiting to see if I would risk it.

Risk. It was something I embraced, and days earlier would have taken. But now I hesitated. Emerson had left me alone, given me a taste of freedom, handed me his trust. If it was indeed a test, I didn't want to fail because I didn't want to disappoint him.

"What is the matter with you, Ava?" I muttered.

I twisted the fabric of my shirt. This was a chance to escape and yet I didn't want to because it would mean leaving the very man who had captured me. A man who was stirring emotions that shouldn't be waking. A man who had a side to him I didn't think anyone knew existed. And he had revealed that side to me, like it was the most natural thing. Because he and I were alike, living in solitary, keeping our secrets, living with our demons, and not letting others all the way in. We took what we needed to get us through and turned away from anything more than casual sex, anything that meant commitment and opening up. Searching without searching until we found each other.

The realization hit so hard that I had to sit. I drew my knees to my chest as my mind continued to contemplate that fact. Emerson and I had found each other, our paths colliding with one stupid mistake. If I believed in fate, thought it was more than something in the books I read, I would have called it that.

I didn't know how long I sat there, staring at the gateway to my freedom, sitting on the threshold between running and staying. Not accepting and accepting.

"What are you doing?" Jill's voice caused me to jump from the trance I'd been in. She sat next to me and inclined her head to the side while she looked at the door. "Is this some artsy thing?"

I snorted, glad to have a distraction. "Nah, just a good place to think." I tipped back on my elbows and stretched my legs out as I stared at the chandelier. "Why do rich people insist on hanging chandeliers in their houses?"

She laughed and reclined back with me. "No clue, but I'm glad I don't have to clean that thing."

We laid there on the floor of the foyer, staring at the chandelier and talking until a shadow passed over us.

"What the fuck are you two doing?"

Jill hopped up. "Sorry, Cade. I was keeping her company."

"Doing what? Staring at the ceiling? And her I expect to be sprawled out on a floor, but you?"

"Hey," I complained, not moving from my spot.

"Sometimes it's fun to just let go. You should try it sometime. Might do that grumpy demeanor some good," she told him.

"My grumpy demeanor is necessary." He turned his eyes to me before saying, "Pack is loose in the kitchen, Jill. You may want to stop him before he leaves a mess."

"Damn it," she mumbled. "I'll kill him if he so much as drops a crumb. I just cleaned in there."

She was off, running to the kitchen, leaving me alone with Emerson. His eyes flicked to the door, then back to me.

"I debated it." Guilt tainted the admission, and I wondered why I had guilt about escaping captivity.

"So you sat in front of the door?"

"Eh, I couldn't rationalize why I wouldn't just leave, so I sat down to contemplate my sanity until Jill came."

His cornfield blue eyes studied me. "And what conclusion did you come to?"

Grinning, I said, "That chandeliers are overrated."

His serious expression broke, and his laugh filled the space. I thought it might be the most perfect sound, and I didn't want him to stop laughing.

"Agreed, and I told the decorator that when I had the house built."

Frowning, I said, "And the decorator lived to walk away?"

He gave me a crooked smile. "I never said that. But the damn thing was up, and I wasn't about to waste money taking it down. I had fun shoving the leftover crystals into his eye sockets, though."

My stomach lurched and his smile grew.

"That's disgusting. Did you really do that?"

A shrug and a glint in his eyes told me I would get no confirmation. Shit, maybe I should have run. Morally gray was easier in books. This was real life, and this man just admitted that torturing someone was fun. That should have been a sign I was losing my mind. Maybe once my uncle and Greyson freed me, these confusing emotions would fade.

He stooped over me, his face coming into better view, and the thoughts quieted. My stomach settled, and my doubts stilled. No, I didn't think anything would fade once I was free. In fact, I suspected it would worsen.

"I'm not a nice guy, Ava. I'm the monster under your bed, the stalker in your closet, the beast in the woods."

Out of instinct, I reached my hands up and draped my fingers down his stubbled jaw. "No, you're not my monster. I've seen monsters and you're not one. Not to me, anyway."

It was difficult to read his eyes as emotion shifted through them, landing on something close to adoring surprise.

"Why didn't you run, Ava?"

The truth was too hard to admit. That I was falling for him against every screaming voice in my head. "I don't know what's happening here, Emerson, but it's too hard to run from. If that door had been wide open, I don't know if I would have run through it."

A crinkle formed between his eyes. "Why?"

"Because I think we've both been searching for too long."

His eyes flashed with understanding before they narrowed.

"Besides, this is like one of my books, and I'm curious to see what happens at the end."

Shaking his head, the perplexed shifts in his features relaxed.

"Did you eat lunch?"

Lunch? Shit, how long had I been lying there? "Nope, and I guess I skipped breakfast."

He rose and moved to stand above me, putting his hand out for me to take.

"If I'd known giving you the run of the house meant you would just stay in the foyer all day, I would have let you out of your room earlier," he teased as he pulled me to my feet.

I rubbed out my stiff back, thinking marble wasn't the most comfortable material.

"Well, you know me. Always surprising you."

"Yes, you are." We stood there, eyes locked for three breaths, before he said, "Let's get some food. I have to leave for another meeting soon and I don't want to find you laying in another part of the house with no food in your stomach."

My laugh was free and as I walked through the house with him, our banter falling just as freely, I knew I'd made the right choice.

Days and nights passed, a routine developed, and I spent my nights in Emerson's bed, my days with him when he was there. Like a couple, but one that didn't touch or kiss or say anything that would straddle the divide that kept those things at a distance —the true reason I was there and the train that was barreling toward us to shatter it all.

Emerson had gone to his office and told me to head to bed, but after finishing the last chapter in my book, I needed to grab another from my room. I should have just brought the stash to his room, but leaving them seemed like it left the line delineated, and it was blurring so much that I needed that delineation.

His T-shirt hung low enough that it covered my ass and part of my thighs, so I left my jeans behind and padded through the house. A light shone from the doorway of his office and, thinking he had finished his call, I walked toward it. He had told me no area of the house was off limits. I still couldn't leave, but I hadn't tried, and I didn't think I would.

As I drew closer, I heard voices. Halting my step, I started to turn away, thinking he was still on his call, but I froze as the conversation grew heated.

"And what are you going to do then?" It was Pack. His raised voice surprised me.

"I don't know," Emerson sneered, frustration emphasizing his words.

"This has to stop. She is a pawn. Your words, Cade. A pawn to get your brother here. She has no further use."

I swallowed back the hurt. They were words I'd told myself many times, but hearing them made them real.

"What happens if your brother doesn't comply? What then, Cade?"

Someone slammed their fist on the desk.

"Don't push me, Pack."

"Push you? That's what you need. You can't keep her if your

brother doesn't come for her. Will you do what's necessary now that you've been playing this fucked-up game with her?"

Another fist, but Pack continued, "Will you?"

"Yes," Emerson's growl slithered up my spine, causing the hairs on my neck to rise. "If he doesn't come for her, then I'll kill her."

The words ricocheted through my head, raising every alarm I'd been ignoring. I ran, heading straight to my room, where I slammed the door and rested my hands on my knees, trying to stop the panic attack that threatened to tear me apart. It had all been a game. Nothing had changed. I was still a means to an end for him. I lifted my head, trying to figure out a way to escape. I had to, or I'd be dead in days. Even if they came for me, he still might kill me. There was no guarantee. He'd told me he was a monster, and I had dismissed the warning.

I thought through my options. Men guarded the front door; I had no doubt of that. The garage entrance constantly had someone in front of it, and the deck led to the beach surrounded by rocky walls. My eyes landed on my window. I had spent the first day picking at the dried paint, but the window hadn't opened. Since then, I had marked the rounds of Emerson's men, knowing their schedule. The window was my only option.

I ran to my bathroom and grabbed the tweezers Jill had brought me. Stretching them until the metal spread, I took my new tool and dug at the window. Adrenaline pounded through my veins, and I prayed Emerson wouldn't come for me before I could escape. All the while, a pressure continued to build behind my eyes and my chest ached uncomfortably. His words had hurt as had Pack's and to know I'd given over to some delusion that this man cared for me... But he did. I'd heard it in his voice, the strain in his first answer to Pack. It wasn't enough to stop me from gouging at the dried paint like a frenzied animal. He would kill me.

Flakes covered my hands and the windowsill, and I put my

tool to the side. Pushing at the window, it gave some. I pushed and pushed, my muscles straining with the effort until, with a loud pop, it opened, sending me teetering forward until I caught my balance. The last patrol had walked by as I'd been picking at the paint, and I had ducked to avoid notice. I still had time to make a break for it before they returned. If I could make it to the woods, then I would have a chance.

The window was only a short drop to the ground, but my knees groaned at the impact, my feet reminding me I had idiotically forgotten they were bare. Too late now. I ran faster than I ever had, my sight on the woods as I wished the ache in my chest was only because my cardio routine had slipped recently.

Chapter Seventeen

EMERSON

"You're full of shit," Pack told me, crossing his arms and staring me down.

"And you're the only asshole I let talk to me like this. If you were anyone else, your tongue would be nothing more than a bloody stump."

He laughed. "I'm serious, Cade. Can you really do it after all the shit you've been doing with her? A day at the beach? Sleeping with her every night?"

"I'm not fucking her," I grumbled.

"Not yet, but that wouldn't be as bad as the real reason."

My eyes narrowed. "Watch yourself."

"No, this is too important. You have your hostage in your bed every night. You smile when you see her. Smile, Cade. I've known you for twenty years and I've never seen you smile like that."

I rubbed the back of my neck.

"Can you kill her? Because I don't think you can."

Neither did I. The thought gutted me. "No, I can't."

I fell into my chair, rubbing my temples.

"Then what are you going to do? She was your winning card, and now those threats are empty ones."

"Greyson will come. He won't leave her with me, neither will her uncle. I won't need to kill her because they'll get her."

"And can you let her go?" There was no judgement in his question, and I looked up at him.

"I don't know." He was the only one I trusted to hear that admission.

His phone rang, and he glanced at it before answering. The concern in his eyes changed the air in the room.

"We've got a problem, boss."

I stood quickly, tension high in every muscle.

"Ava escaped. She's running across the west yard."

All thoughts of our prior conversation vanished, and a myriad of emotions jutted at me. She'd run away. Left me as easily as if there was no connection there, as if she hadn't laid on the foyer floor and told me she'd stayed because there was no more searching. As easily as if her smiles had been false, her words hollow.

"Cade? What do you want them to do?" He still had the caller on the other end waiting for instruction.

The west lawn was off her bedroom, but I had left her in my room. She had waited for me to leave, then made her escape.

"Shit. Tell them to stand down. I'll get her."

I bolted from my office and ran through the house toward her room. Throwing the door open, I saw the open window.

"Damn it, Ava."

Her silhouette moved under the moonlight. She was too close to the woods. My initial hurt morphed to horror. We had traps throughout the woods. I couldn't have my men monitor every inch of them, so we'd laid traps in specific spots that my men knew to avoid but Ava didn't.

I jumped from the window and took off after her. She hadn't even changed and with her bare feet, her pace was slower than mine. The five miles I put in running almost every day made my strides longer and my pace faster than hers.

"Ava, stop!"

She glanced over her shoulder, terror in her eyes before she sped up. I pushed harder as she gained on the woods. Just as the woods swallowed her, I reached out and snagged her arm. She tumbled, and I went down with her, trying to pin her under me. Nails scratched, punches flew, and I remembered how she had disabled her stepfather. Pinning her flailing legs with mine, I tried to make sense of what she was screaming.

"You won't kill me, damn it. I'll fight you. I won't stop."

"Ava, I'm not going to kill you."

She fought harder, and I had to give her credit. She was strong, her hits calculated, and it took all my skill to block them until I captured her wrists and pinned them to her sides. Still, she struggled, her body bucking, her mouth continuing to spew swears and insistences that I was planning to kill her.

"Ava, stop fighting me. I won't hurt you."

"You're going to kill me," her voice broke, her fight simmering. She looked exhausted. Her skin was flushed and her eyes wild.

"I promise you, I have no intention of killing you."

Her chestnut eyes searched mine. "But you said...I heard you tell Pack."

"Were you listening to my conversation, wildcat?"

Sight flitting from mine, then back, she said, "You told him you would kill me."

I sighed. "It was a lie."

Her muscles went slack, and I rolled from her, resting my head on the ground. "Don't run," I told her. "If you go any further, you'll lose a foot, or worse. The woods have traps."

She made a strange squeak but didn't move.

I ran my hand through my hair. "I have a reputation to uphold, but it's crumbling." Admitting the truth was easier than I'd thought.

She still hadn't run and remained where she was.

"A few years ago, I discovered a few of my men were running a trafficking ring and disguising it as part of the Omens. Like it was my ring, and I was in charge. They'd been doing it for years, right under my nose. I'd always wondered where those rumors came from, but I'd never imagined they had substance."

She rolled toward me. "Wait, you don't traffic women and children."

"Fuck no," I said. "I despise scum that get into that shit. I have a line I don't cross."

Irises of chocolate penetrated mine. "But everyone thinks—"

"Because I let them. I founded the Bad Omen on blood and death. My reputation is the most ruthless of any of the bosses, and I like it that way. People react better to me if they fear me. The rumor was there, and I didn't stop it. But I tried to stop the instigators. It was a brutal fight, and I lost five men that night."

She stayed quiet, letting me spill the secret that only Pack and Breaker knew.

"They slipped away, and we lost them. I thought that was the end of it until they resurfaced about two years ago. Only, I can't locate them. Their leader, Henley, is using the training we gave him and hiding too well. They're taunting me, luring my newer men away, slowly dismantling my empire, pretending to be me while fucking up because they aren't me."

"All the stuff in Armina? With Riley?" she asked.

"None of it was me." I rubbed my face. "Clint Randall was one of the originals who broke from me. He was an idiot. Sloppy and one mistake away from a bullet in his head. He knew it and left when the others fled. I don't step into my brother's territory. And It's been years since I've bothered taking over another family. I don't give a shit about the families in Armina as long as they continue to fear me. But these imbeciles are out there stirring up trouble, trying to turn enough families against me that there's no way for me to fight my way out."

She chewed her lip, her eyes keen. "That's why you wanted to kidnap Riley? To force your brother to talk to you?"

"Yeah. We've hated each other for so long that when we do

talk, it's quick and heated. I need him to hear me because these assholes are ruining my reputation."

"And threatening your empire?"

"Yes," I turned toward her. "But it's not just what I've built. There are people who count on me. Jill, my men. The cities in my territory benefit from my businesses. People work in those establishments. I put back into my territory, donate, invest in it even if no one knows it's me."

"And what if your brother doesn't help you?"

I cringed at the word help, hating that it had come to this. That my hands were tied, and I had resorted to begging my brother for help.

"You really hate him, don't you?" she asked, seeing my reaction.

"Loathe is a better word."

"But you're brothers. What did he do that was so bad?"

"Stole something." Bringing back memories of that day always spoiled my mood, but with Ava there, it didn't.

She waited for me to say more and when I didn't, she asked, "What could be that important to lose a brother over?"

"A woman," I admitted. But she hadn't been a woman. All of us had been kids. Just twenty years old and what had we known about the world? We were three years into building our empire. Rolling in money, power, and women.

"What kind of woman has that power?"

None, but it hadn't been her. It had been Greyson. "One I loved, and my brother decided to use to prove she didn't love me." Saying it sounded idiotic. "He called me, telling me I needed to see something, and when I walked in, she was on her knees with his cock filling her mouth. She didn't even pause as he told me she was nothing but the whore he'd warned me she was."

"Huh." I squinted at her reaction. "Seems like an asshole move to me."

"Yeah. I left that day, packed up and moved to Seagate to start my own business."

"How long, Emerson? How long has this rift gone on?"

"Twenty-five years. It seems like a lifetime ago."

"It was a shitty move, but maybe he thought you needed to see it to believe it?"

I rolled my eyes, but I couldn't help the nagging memories of him warning me over and over. Of not listening to what he was saying, that he'd seen her screwing another of our friends. Seen her going down on one of our guys after that. And each time I'd dismissed him, the rift already forming because I accused him of trying to take her from me, assumed he wanted her and was trying to make me give her up. Until he finally showed me the proof.

"Yeah, it was a shitty move."

"Does it help that the Greyson Tides I know is not that man? He loves Riley—"

"And I loved…" But I trailed off because I knew it hadn't been real love. I'd gotten over her in days, but the grudge had lasted for decades. The hate I had for Greyson had devoured the speck of love I'd had for the girl. But I'd never loved again, never gotten close enough. Maybe Ava was right, and I'd been waiting to find someone worth loving.

"Let's go back inside. I could use a drink." I didn't want to talk about my brother anymore or the situation that was drowning me.

"So you're not going to kill me?" she asked, changing the subject, seemingly reading my mood.

"No, I could never hurt you, Ava." Honest, raw. I didn't like the vulnerability, and I started to rise, but she grabbed my shirt and pulled me toward her. My hands went to either side of her head as I landed on top of her.

"Breaker said you went to your club the other night. You were gone a long time." There was a question in her statement.

"Yeah." I adjusted my legs so that I hovered over her. "I had business, and I needed to get away."

"From me?" A bold question and one I hesitated to answer. "Did you do business with a brunette?" Her brow quirked like she was trying to be cute, but her eyes shone with the expectation of hurt.

"There may have been a sexy brunette in an even sexier dress who had an impressive pair of tits."

The devastation flashed before she could hide it, and my pulse thumped hard in my veins. This was a moment where I could have stopped the madness, taken us back to hostage and captor, rid myself of the muddled thoughts and emotions. But that would have been the equivalent of ignoring my brother's warnings all those years ago. It would leave me wounded, and I suspected it would leave Ava just as hurt.

She swallowed, her eyes drifting from mine.

"But I told her to go away." Ava's eyes flew back, wide and hopeful.

"Why?" she asked, her voice barely a whisper.

Another moment, another decision. Be the man I'd always been, hard, cruel, unkind, or be the man I was when I was with her, vulnerable but happy. "Because there was an even sexier woman at home with a better pair of tits who promised a night of contentedly warming my bed as she read her dirty romance books."

The smile that formed reached the corners of her eyes, leaving them almost golden. "You think my tits are nice?"

"Fucking perfect like the rest of you."

She took a handful of my shirt and pulled me down, her head rising so that our mouths crashed. All thought of ending this fled along with any rationale that kissing the woman I'd kidnapped had complications. There was only Ava and the sensation of her lips against mine.

This woman who had come into my life like an unexpected

storm and captivated me, woken me, was now the one thing I desired above all else. A hunger had started and now I was ravenous for her. My hand tangled in her hair, gripping strands as our kiss grew heated. Her moan swept through me like an unrelenting blaze, and there was no longer any debate about what I wanted to do to her. I wanted all of Ava—to touch her, taste her, own her—and that recognition branded my very being.

Her hands tore at the buttons on my shirt while my hand slid over her curves, lingering on her breast and teasing her nipple until it was so taut, I tugged at the ring I'd been craving to feel. Another moan and she arched into my hand. The sound was like a lead jerking me and I ground into her, my hand skimming her waist and then pushing her shirt up. Her skin was soft, and I dug my fingers into it, causing her lips to part from mine.

Dropping my mouth to her neck, I ran my tongue over it. "Tell me what you want, wildcat," I said, moving my hand to her hip and pushing her underwear down.

"You," she murmured, her head dipping back when I sucked her nipple through her shirt, my teeth scraping over the ring. Everything about her turned me on and, after wanting her for so many days, I was ready to tear her clothes off and take her right there.

"What do you want me to do to you?" I asked, pushing her legs apart with my knee and slipping my fingers into her warmth. "Fuck," I grumbled at how wet she was. "You're drenched."

"You've had me soaked for days," she purred, and I lifted my eyes to meet hers. They were alive with lust, a dark golden brown like warm honey. "I want you to take me, Emerson."

I plunged my finger into her, loving how her back bowed into me. "What else do you want me to do to you?" Sliding out of her, I moved to her clit, finding the piercing I'd suspected she had. Two sexy balls of metal right above her clit. I'd never slept with a woman with more than a belly button piercing, but I was looking forward to doling out the pleasure I suspected each of Ava's would bring to her. Rubbing my thumb over her clit, I sucked her nipple back into my mouth.

She gasped, her hands pulling my hair.

"Tell me what you want, sweetheart." I tugged at her ring and shoved my finger back into her.

"I hate commands," she complained, her voice breathy.

"Time to get used to them. Now tell me what the fuck you want so I can watch you break."

Her legs trembled as I shoved another finger into her. "Make me come."

I bit her nipple gently and pulled my fingers free. "That sounds like a demand."

"God, you're an asshole," she mumbled.

Slamming my mouth into hers, I kissed her. Tongues battling, hearts pounding, her hands grabbed at me.

"Tell me what you want," I said, dragging her bottom lip between my teeth.

"I just did," she rasped.

"Nicer."

I brought my fingers up to my mouth and tasted them, regretting it the moment I did because I wanted more.

"You want me to beg?" she asked, her eyes following the movement of my fingers.

"Only for me, wildcat. And only when I tell you to."

Her mouth twisted. I smoothed my hand up her stomach, cupping her breast and rubbing my thumb over her nipple.

She groaned, and I gave her a wicked smile. "This better be worth it," she said. "Dammit, make me come, please Emerson."

"That's a good girl." Her eyes lit as her legs moved to clench. I stopped them with my knee. "Uh uh, that's my orgasm to free."

A beautiful sigh slipped from her lips, and I captured it, kissing her again. After giving her breast another squeeze, I moved back between her legs, rubbing her clit and piercing until I plunged two fingers back into her. Her cry was one I committed to memory.

"That's it, wildcat. Come for me." I picked up my pace, watching her until her head went back and she clamped down on my fingers. Seeing her fall apart had to be the most glorious thing I'd ever witnessed. She was ravishing, her cheeks flushed, eyes glossy, lips parted. Her chest heaved as I caught her cry with my mouth, kissing her until she calmed completely.

Moving from her, I rose, cleaning my fingers again and knowing exactly what my next move would be. Her eyes questioned me, but I only bent down and picked her up, tossing her over my shoulder. She squealed and I couldn't help but tease her. "Squealing doesn't sound like you, Ava. First, you let me command you and now you're squealing like a kid?"

"Screw you," she returned.

"I'm about to."

She shivered and wrapped her arms around my back.

"No fight this time?" I asked, rubbing her ass before I pulled her shirt down to cover it.

"Do you want me to fight? Do you get off on that, Emerson?"

"I get off on whatever makes you come that hard, wildcat. If fighting me does it, then fight away, as long as you're coming on my tongue next time."

"Shit," she breathed, and I caught the twitch in her legs.

I strolled across the lawn, my hard-on making it an uncomfortable walk, visions of what I had in store for the vixen on my shoulder speeding my steps. I glared at my men, who stepped back as I walked through the front door.

"Make sure her window is sealed and locked," I told Pack as the door shut behind me. He had followed me in, and I detected the understanding in his eyes.

"Punishment, boss?" he asked as I walked toward the stairs to my room.

"Depends on how well she makes up for her mistake."

"I'm right here, assholes."

"Keep calling me an asshole and you won't like my punishment."

Pack broke off and headed to her room as I continued toward mine. A nod from my man at the end of the hall reminded me he was the one who had freaked Ava out.

"Take rounds outside. Pack can handle the inside security," I told him.

"Yes, boss."

I continued up the stairs, slamming my door behind us. Three long strides and I tossed Ava onto the bed. Her breasts bounced seductively, her shirt pulling up to reveal her stomach and the purple rhinestone above her belly button.

"Be a good girl and take your shirt off," I told her. "I want to see that sexy body."

She narrowed her eyes at me before she pulled it over her head. My eyes swept over her, taking in the pert, full breasts, the hooped piercings in her dark nipples, the flower tattoo on her left breast, the tapered waist that flared out to luscious hips and thighs, the vine tattoo on her hip traveling up to her right breast, the long legs that surrounded the lace panties she wore. Ones I was about to rip from her.

"Fuck, you are the hottest thing I've ever seen," I said, crawling over her. Her cheeks flushed a darker hue. "How wet are you, sweetheart?"

"Extremely, and calling me a good girl is not helping."

I nudged her cheek with mine before kissing my way down her neck, devouring her inch by inch and deciding I'd call her a good girl often if it kept her this soaked. I took my time, exploring every freckle and tattoo, flicking my tongue over her nipple and pulling the metal into my mouth as my other hand tugged at her other nipple. Her head fell back, and I moved my hand up her neck, spreading my fingers around it and hearing the resulting moan that had my pants tenting.

Ava may not have enjoyed being commanded, but she liked it rough just like I did, and that was enough to make me even harder. My hands slipping over her hips, I kissed my way down her stomach, swirling my tongue over her belly button piercing before tearing her underwear from her and saying, "Be a good girl and spread those legs for me. It's time for you to come on my face, sweetheart."

Another tremble went through her, and I smiled against her skin. Her legs spread, and I ran my tongue down her thigh, relishing the sweet taste of her skin and the pounding in her pulse points. I sat back and took her in again, every fantastic inch of her. Tracing the tattoo on her hip with my hand, I squeezed when I got to her waist, seeing the expectation as I scraped my fingers down and lowered my head, jerking her body forward and running my tongue over her center. This time she groaned, feral and loud. And when I pushed my finger back into her, the sound only deepened. I sucked on her clit, then rolled my tongue over the piercing. Two tiny balls that had her digging her fingers into my hair when I tugged one with my teeth.

"Fuck," she muttered, fisting strands of my hair.

Smiling against her sweetness, I shoved another finger into her and continued to devour her until she was shaking, her breathing heavy. Removing my fingers, I grasped her thighs and pulled her closer, plunging my tongue into her depths.

Her entire body rose, and she pushed me further into her.

"It's time to come for me again…like a good girl."

Her cry snaked around my limbs, paralyzing me as she came. Her body convulsed, her hands remained buried in my hair, and she let out the most beautiful whimper.

Giving her one last lick, I kissed my way up her stomach until I was hovering over her.

"Kiss me, wildcat, and taste how fucking delicious you are."

Her shiver cascaded through her body and as I lowered my face to hers, she reached her hands up and pulled my mouth down. It took all of another minute of kissing before I could no longer take it. I needed her with a desperation that was gripping my chest. Lifting myself, I stood, my eyes lazily gliding over her body as she propped herself on her elbows. Her eyes held a glazed look that only made her more ravishing.

With deliberate slowness, I unbuttoned my shirt and removed it. Her sight drifted over my chest, her tongue gliding over her top lip.

"Put that away before I put it to use," I told her, unhooking my belt.

She shifted to her knees, crawling over to me. The jump in my pants was painful and when she slid her hands up my legs then over my chest, her warm eyes laced with seduction, it only worsened. I took a chunk of her hair and tilted her head back.

"Careful, sweetheart, I'm not one to tease."

"And I'm not one to threaten." A flicker of danger lit her eyes, and that unhinged craving for her grew. Tracing the tattoos on my chest, she followed her hands with her mouth, dragging it lower. I released her hair and unbuttoned my pants. Her eyes flitted to me when I unzipped them and let them drop to the floor. I freed my dick from my boxers, loving how those chocolate irises drifted down to watch me stroke myself. Swiping my finger over my tip, I brought it to her lips and watched as her tongue circled it.

Damn, she was sexy, and she was destroying me. She lowered her mouth to me, her eyes glancing up just as I tipped my pelvis and filled her waiting mouth. I hadn't intended to use her mouth yet, but the invitation was there, and I wasn't turning it down. Fisting her hair again, I let her guide the pace, closing my eyes at the sensation of her tongue gliding over my shaft. She took more of me, and I couldn't help the thrusts of my hips that sent me so deep she was gagging. I held her head steady until I yanked her from me, loving the string of saliva that fell from her mouth and landed on her chest. She sucked in a deep breath, and I shoved her back to the bed.

"I'll let you know when I'm ready to fill that mouth. Right now. I want to be buried deep inside of you until you're coming so hard around me that you milk the cum from me."

Her lips, now red and swollen, parted with a quiet gasp. I opened the drawer to my bedside table and pulled out a condom, noticing her raised brow as I ripped it open with my teeth.

"Keeping condoms in your drawer for all the women you bring home? How many women have slept in this bed, Emerson?"

Every time she used my name, it burrowed deeper into me like some claim she had on me.

Rolling the condom out, I crawled over her, nudging her legs apart. I rested my tip at her opening, groaning at the sensation.

"How many?" she asked.

I nibbled at her neck, then dragged my cheek over hers. "Not many, wildcat. I rarely make it out of the club before I'm fucking them."

She hissed. A glorious sound that meant more than I thought she wanted to admit. I moved an inch further into her, burying my face in her hair as I tried to pace myself. "And how many men have slept in your bed, sweetheart?"

As soon as the question was out of my mouth, I regretted it. Intense envy sat on its haunches, ready to pounce.

"A few," she said. "But seeing as you have fifteen years on me, Emerson, I think your body count is bigger."

I lifted my head, pinning her wrists with my hands and pulling out of her. Eyes wide, mouth parting, she waited for my reaction. Envy had its talons in me. "I'm going to wipe their memories from you." I thrust into her, gritting my teeth at how good it felt. Her body bowed, her head flew back, but I grabbed it and forced her to look at me. Pulling back out of her against my body's protests, I said, "Every stroke." I thrust back into her, growling, "Every thrust." Sliding out again then plowing into her, I knew there was no way I was leaving her warmth again until both of us were satisfied. "Every time I fill you, wildcat, I will erase another memory."

I released her wrists, and she clawed at my back, her legs circling me and forcing me deeper. "And all those gorgeous brunettes?" Her mouth captured mine in a breathless kiss that had me thrusting with abandon.

"Never existed," I grunted, moving my hand to her neck and hearing her breath hitch. The jealousy, the possessive claims, the need to own her and accept the claim she'd somehow just made on me should have stopped me, but I was too far gone. Had been for days.

My hand followed the curve of her body, wrapping under her knee and pushing it into her chest. She cried out when I sank into her full depths, driving into her with heated thrusts. The only thing that could have been better than being inside of Ava was if I'd been riding her bare. The thought of spilling freely into her had my rhythm increasing, my release barreling down on me. Her heel was digging into me, pushing me deeper and I grabbed it, raising it up like I had the other and pinning her with her legs. A moan so animalistic it called to my pending climax, coaxing it closer, fell from her mouth.

"Are you going to come for me again?"

She gave me a devious grin. "Are you going to make me?"

I was too close for games, but I wanted her to come for me... no, I wanted her to come with me. It was something I'd never cared about, but the thought of Ava clamping down on me as I chased her release had my balls swelling.

"Good girls don't make demands," I said, freeing her legs and sitting back, ignoring the uncomfortable throbbing of my lower body and the need that had me in its grasp.

She grabbed the back of my neck and pulled my mouth to hers. "Please make me come again, Emerson. I want to come with you."

She could have said anything, and I would have obliged, but

those words, along with my name, had my mouth on her breast and my thumb on her clit. I slowed my rhythm, taking deep, steady strokes inside of her, hindering my release until her legs were quaking and her nails were digging into the sheets. When she was so close that I noted her muscles tightening around me, I drove into her harder. She came, her scream loud until I smothered it with my lips. Grabbing one hand with mine and her leg with my other, I tore into her, my climax thundering through me and joining hers in a symphony of groans.

Rapture. Ecstasy. They were words I'd used lightly, but now I knew their true meaning. Never had I come so intensely, never had I wanted to stay buried in a woman, to never have to separate from her, to never need to let her go. Until now. Until Ava.

I dropped my head to hers, our breaths rapid and unsteady. We had crossed a line, one that had faded with each passing day but one that now changed who we were. No longer hostage and captor, but something more. I couldn't deny it, even if defining it terrified me.

Erase all others. That's what Emerson Tides had vowed to do, and he had done it. He had wiped every other man from memory and replaced them with him. Sex with Emerson was more than sex and, given his knitted brows and serious expression, I suspected it was more than that for him as well.

A blissful calm sat in my body and mind, a sense that this was what I'd blindly searched for in every man I'd ever hooked up with. But that admission came with complications, which likely explained the pained look that now tainted his mood. He tried to move from me, but I tightened my legs around him. A small groan led to a look of annoyance, but I took his face in my hands and picked my head up so that my mouth met his. Kissing Emerson was like finding my center. He relaxed, the tension fading from his jaw. His arm reached under me and pulled me against his body.

Emotions crossed paths in that kiss, but they were too new, too dangerous, to be voiced or even contemplated. Our mouths separated, and he untangled himself from my limbs, rolling over and removing the condom with a quick flick of it to the floor. I was content to lie there and leave the distance between us, one I thought we both might need, but his arm came under my neck, and he pulled me into his chest. I wanted to fight it, but being in his arms felt too good. I lazily traced the pattern of his Omens tattoo, the skull and dagger my uncle had shown me, a sign of Emerson's power.

"Would now be a bad time to tell you I'm not a natural blonde?" I asked, peeking up at him.

Blue eyes of a sunny day looked down at me. His frown lifted, the smile lighting his features and emphasizing his strong jawline. "Are you shitting me?"

I shook my head. "I bleached it a few years ago and liked it. The pink's not natural either," I said, giving him a wink.

"Damn, I shoulda guessed that, given how I just memorized every detail between your legs."

I smacked his chest, but he grabbed my hand. "You didn't like that?" he asked.

Shit, had I ever. This man knew how to use his tongue and all the right spots to hit to make me scream. "I didn't say that."

I followed the skull's outline with my index finger. "Why don't you frighten me?" I asked him, meeting his dusty irises. I pushed myself up, placing my hand on his chest.

"I should," he said, his fingers twirling one of my curls. "You should have run from me that first day. Fuck, you should have run when I gave you the chance, but you sat in front of the door. Why didn't you run, Ava?"

Emotion specked his blue orbs with hints of navy.

"I don't know," I admitted. "I thought about it but then..." I dropped my head, but he tipped my chin up, forcing my sight to meet his.

"Then what?"

The inhale dragged through my throat, burning as it scraped its way to my lungs. "I didn't think I could sleep alone that night." My words came out so softly that I hoped he didn't hear them.

"Just that night?"

Avoiding the question, I brought myself up, straddling him and leaning on the solid wall of muscle. "I didn't run for the same reason you came to my room when you knew my meds would keep my dreams away. The same reason you don't scare me. The same reason you spent the day playing in the sand with me."

His hand skimmed down my chest, lingering on the curve of my breast. His lips pursed, darkness eclipsing his eyes. "But you ran tonight."

"And you said you were going to kill me. Stupid miscommunication. Damn, I hate that trope."

His eyes creased before a smile formed. "Another book reference?"

"Maybe," I answered, noting the flush of my cheeks.

His fingers weaved into my hair, and he brought my face closer to his. "Does this mean you won't run?"

"If it means you won't kill me."

"I could never hurt you, Ava. I had every intention that first night, but you opened your mouth and damn if I couldn't stop myself from hearing more."

"And now?" I held my breath, knowing the future was a convoluted mess of cobwebs I didn't think either of us could find our way through. I had a life outside of his world, a reality that didn't mesh with his, distance separating those lives.

"Now..." Torn like a ragged edge of paper, his expression dug into me with claws I couldn't remove, gutting me. This wasn't the ruthless bastard who terrorized the other families. This was Emerson. My Emerson—sweet, thoughtful, protective, amazing in bed, and the rock I never knew I needed. The placebo for my medication, the calm to the trauma I couldn't escape.

Whatever he wanted to say, he couldn't, just like I couldn't. We were something that couldn't be, something irrational, something we couldn't define. His fingers dug further into my hair, and he dragged my mouth to his, ravaging it with a force that sent my breath fleeing and my heart thundering against its confines. Touches followed that left my mind blank and the conversation like sand swept away with the tide. Raw, desperate, insatiable. He took me again, coaxing climaxes from my exhausted body until it was numb with pleasure. And once more, as if separating our bodies would cause physical harm. The commands and the dominating aggression returned, melting me completely and making me putty in his hands. If anyone else had called me a good girl, I would have punched them, but from Emerson, it left me craving more.

Worn and exhausted, I listened to his pounding heart and the steady rhythm of his breaths until I closed my eyes and dreamed of him.

MY EYES WERE HEAVY, my body like a limp noodle, and I groaned as I rolled onto my back. Blinking against the morning light, I looked over to find the other side of the bed empty. As much as I would have loved Emerson to have woken me with his mouth or his body, I was so worn out I didn't think I'd make a very active partner.

Swinging my legs over the side of the bed, I rubbed my sore thighs, enjoying the soreness like I would have a good workout. It was proof that last night had been real and amazing. Good God, had it been amazing. That man was made to please women, and the thought stirred the green coils of jealousy. I rubbed the sleepers from my eyes and made my way to the bathroom, chastising myself for being jealous when I was just as bad.

After assuring Emerson had indeed left me, I tiptoed down the stairs, pulling my shirt down further to cover the lace undies I'd retrieved from where he'd thrown them. A glance toward the garage had me flinching. The same guard who had creeped me out was standing there, his hands folded in front of him, his brown eyes so dark I mistook them for black. I had no clue what it was about him, but my instincts told me to be far away from him. Which seemed strange since I was in a house owned by a notorious mob boss and surrounded by his men, who were just as brutal and quick to kill. No one else gave me the creeps like this guy did.

I backed away and turned around, making sure my steps were quick. No one was in the main room as I passed through, and I didn't see Emerson on the deck. The door to his office was wide open, the office empty, so I hurried to my room to shower and change. Wherever he was, I was sure he was off doing whatever illegal things he did.

"How does that not freak you out?" I asked myself as I pulled my hair up in the clips Jill had gotten me—cute little butterflies with colorful rhinestones decorating the silver. After hopping in the shower, I checked out the bruises on my hips and thighs, not ugly or hurtful but a sign that he'd brought the aggression I loved and left his mark on me. My stomach flipped at the sight, and I rolled my eyes at it.

In revolt, it growled, so I gave it a scalding look before I left the room, my bare feet chilly on the tile floor. I spent the morning watching television and munching on the sweet potato chips I found in the kitchen. For someone with so much money, Emerson's pantry was sorely lacking good snack options.

Never once in the hours I wandered the house and the deck, watched movies and raided his kitchen, did it ever cross my mind to run again. I was content to forget there was an expiration date to this arrangement. That in days, my uncle and his boss would be here to trade for me or kill for me. It was almost like I didn't want to face the reality, to comprehend the fact that this wasn't the plot of some romance book where I knew the ending would be happy. Because the truth was too difficult to admit—there was no happy ending in this. I was falling for Greyson Tides' enemy, a man who had kidnapped me with the intention of kidnapping Greyson's wife. It didn't matter that he had taken me in her place. Her husband would want retribution.

I flopped my head back on the couch and stared at the vaulted ceiling, thinking it was such a waste of space and how a nice loft would make better use of the upper windows. A small studio where I could paint with the view as my backdrop. My fingers twitched in the movement of my paintbrush, missing it. Knowing how competitive the art space was, I had opted to focus my master's on museum work, still a competitive space, but it had seemed the more realistic option. Now I rarely had time to draw or paint.

Turning the television off, I snuck into Emerson's office. I tugged on the drawers, discovering he kept them all locked but the middle one. Finding a ballpoint pen, I snagged a notebook from deep in the drawer. It was old, with pages torn from it and otherwise empty. Passing through the main room, I pushed the sliding glass doors open and stepped onto the deck. A guard stood at the end of the deck; another made his rounds below on the far right side of the house.

"Ah, this is where he has you guys hiding. I knew he wouldn't leave me alone." Even if he had widened the cage bars, it was still a cage.

He only nodded, then canvassed the area, his eyes hidden by his sunglasses.

The sun was fantastic on my skin, but I knew to stay on the shaded edge of the deck. Scooting the table over some, I sat and tucked my legs under me, pulling the cute skirt I was wearing down to cover my thighs. I stared at the blank page. It had been too long since I'd sketched. My years between graduating and starting grad school had given me a taste of how brutal the art scene was. I'd scraped by until I'd given up and started taking odd jobs through the years. My uncle had hated it, trying over and over to give me money, but I had left the account he established for me untouched. I needed to figure myself out on my own. He had done so much for me, and now it was my turn. But his offer two years ago to pay for an apartment and grad school, an offer he'd given multiple times, and I had turned down just as many, was too tempting this last time.

By then, the lead in my pencils had gone dull and my desire to draw had lost its luster.

The first lines of the horizon marred the paper, the pen scratching uncomfortably in my hand. But then they continued, taking form until I had duplicated the view before me on the page. I sat back, flexing my fingers, and stared at the sketch. When was the last time I'd sat quietly? Given my head the space to allow creativity to spark? Too long. For so many years, drawing, like reading, had been my escape and then it had been a reminder, and I'd left it behind.

Lifting my eyes to the ocean, the waves crashing against the shore, I realized this was the first time my mind had been quiet. Calm and at peace. I could have blamed it on the meds, but I had taken them for years and still the noise, the constant thoughts, continued to come. Flipping the page, I let my pen lead the way, forms taking shape until I had filled a quarter of the book with sketches.

The shade had receded, the sun too harsh, so I rose and stretched, leaving the notebook and pen with every intention of returning later, once the sun shifted again. My stomach rumbled, and I realized I hadn't eaten lunch, only snacks. I trudged into the kitchen, finding one of Emerson's men there, grabbing water.

"So, you guys are human," I joked.

He squinted in confusion, and I motioned to the water.

"I never see you guys do anything but stand around and look scary."

He shrugged. "It wouldn't be good for us to look anything but threatening."

"Wow, and you talk. I thought Breaker and Pack were the only ones who still had their tongues."

"Only the rookies lose their tongues."

"Did you just make a joke?" I asked, pushing past him to grab some lunchmeat from the fridge, which could have fit three of my fridges in it.

"Don't let the boss know that." He gave me a wink, and I wasn't sure how to take it. This guy was not typical of the men who worked for Emerson, but at least he wasn't the creepy guy.

"Secret's safe with me," I said, pulling some turkey out. After rummaging through the condiments, I found something resembling mayonnaise but fancied up with some healthy shit that I usually avoided at all costs. "Who puts avocado in mayo?" I grumbled.

"Guys like Cade Slaughter."

My head jerked toward him. Slaughter? That was the last name Emerson used? But it was the candor this guy had that caused the reaction. There was something off about him, but I couldn't put my finger on it other than he seemed to be flirting with me, and I knew that was off-limits because even his boss had difficulty allowing himself to do it. This guy was asking for a beating if he continued. As strange as his behavior seemed, it was still nice to talk to someone. I'd been alone all day and with no idea when Emerson would return, this was a pleasant reprieve.

"Where is your boss, anyway?" I asked, curious if his men knew.

"Last I heard, he was at the club."

My gut twisted, my hand squeezing the bottle too hard so that a giant mound of mayonnaise-like substance flooded my bread. "Shit," I mumbled, placing the bottle on the counter and wiping the extra goo from my bread. It shouldn't have bothered me that he was at the club, but I suspected what went on there behind private doors. What he'd done for years with women he met there.

Maybe last night had been nothing. Maybe I was just another notch in his belt, another conquest.

"Having trouble?" the guy asked.

"Seems like it." *Yeah, I let my guard down and started falling for your boss. Like a fool, I slept with him and fell for the nicknames. But otherwise, I'm good.*

I wanted to scream at myself for letting Emerson in and thinking this might be something different. For him, it hadn't been. I rubbed my cheek, hating how used I now felt.

Maybe his being at the club was nothing more than work. Maybe I was looking for an excuse to make what we'd done into something trivial. To keep a distance there when he was doing nothing wrong.

But he had left so early, with no good morning, no morning kiss. It was more likely that he'd played me. Used and discarded me like every woman he took. Like every man I slept with. Damned karma.

"So do you have a name, or should I call you water guy?" I took a bite of my sandwich and turned to him.

"Chad."

"No fancy mob name?"

He smiled, another unusual occurrence, and shook his head. "Nothing fancy."

"Well, Chad. No one has talked to me all day and your boss left me stranded." And fucked over. "Since you seem to be the only outlier in this dysfunctional group, sit and talk to me."

He didn't hesitate, which again seemed odd. Maybe he had a death wish or maybe he enjoyed the pain Emerson would dole out on him if he discovered him slacking on the job. I might have had some regret for asking him, knowing what Emerson might do to him, but I was so peeved at Emerson and the idea that he was currently screwing some random woman at his club that I didn't care.

Chad ended up being a chatterbox. I thought I was talkative.

He could have run circles around me. We sat in the kitchen, talking about everything from sports to art to sneakers. The man had an opinion on everything. I was mid-laugh at his story about running into the net and stumbling over it headfirst while playing tennis when I heard a gruff, "Having fun?"

I swiveled to find Emerson, his arms crossed, his eyes so dark I could barely tell they were blue. His eyes swept to me, then to Chad, before they narrowed. Chad was standing now, his face blank, but I could see the fear there.

"We were just talking," I said, picking at the label on my water bottle. "It was harmless. He was keeping me company while you were at the club." I made sure to emphasize the word club.

"How sweet." That voice was low and gravely. The sound I imagined came from a demon. Or a man possessed. He strolled through the kitchen and grabbed a knife from the counter. Chad now had his back to me, his hand resting on the island where we'd been sitting. With moves so fast they were hard to follow, Emerson punched him and plunged the knife into his hand. I scrambled from my chair as Emerson grabbed him by the throat.

"You're new to my team, so let me make this clear. You now have one strike against you. It's more than most get. One more fuck up and I will cut your hand off and choke you with it. You ever leave your post again, you ever open your mouth while on duty, you ever so much as look at her, and I will make sure your death is slow and miserable. Understood?"

"Yes, boss."

Emerson yanked the knife from his hand, and I tried not to scream at the blood. "Get the fuck out of my sight."

Chad scrambled away, but as he got close to the door, Emerson threw the knife. Its track came so close to Chad that it sliced the tip of his ear. "Go find Pack and tell him you're on outside rotations from now on. The next time you even look at her, I'll rip your eyes from their sockets."

I swallowed back my fear, telling myself this was the monster he had warned me about, telling me I should be afraid of him. My eyes flashed to meet his. Cold and steeled.

"We were just talking," I said. "It's more than I can say about you." Why had I added that? God, he already looked feral. I didn't want to provoke him.

He stalked over to me. "What the fuck does that mean?"

His towering presence made my knees shake, but I wasn't about to let him see that. "Did you enjoy your time at the club?" What was I doing? Antagonizing the devil. I had to have lost my mind.

Eyes narrowing, his hand grasped my neck, and he shoved me across the room into the wall. The hold on my neck was more gentle than I would have expected, forceful, but not enough to leave marks. It was the thud of my spine against the wall that rattled my teeth and sent the air from my lungs.

"What are you suggesting, Ava?" His blue orbs were piercing, his question a snarl.

"That you've been gone all day. That you got what you wanted and now you've moved on..." I couldn't say more because it hurt for reasons I didn't understand.

"Do you think I was fucking someone?"

I lowered my sight, nodding and hating how it looked and sounded. His hold on my neck tightened and my eyes flew to his.

"You thought I was fucking some woman at my club, so you flirted with one of my men?"

"I wasn't flirting."

He stepped into my space, pressing his hard body against mine.

"What does it matter, Emerson? It shouldn't. You don't own me, and I don't own you. It shouldn't matter that it meant nothing to you."

A wounded look passed over his features. He released my neck, his hands sliding down my arms until they locked on my wrists. With a quick move, he pinned them above my head, the fingers of one hand holding them tight as his other dragged down my body, causing trailing goosebumps. An exhale slipped from my lips, and he gave me a devious smirk.

"I'm disappointed, wildcat." I sucked the breath back in as he lifted my shirt, moving over my hip and cupping my breast, rubbing my nipple through the fabric of my bra. "That you would accuse me of something I didn't do." A pinch to my nipple caused me to lurch into him.

"But you—"

He lowered his face to mine, dragging his stubble over my cheek and his hand back down my body. "Have several clubs to run and oversee." He pushed my skirt up, his hand tracing my thigh until it shoved my underwear aside. "I stopped in to have a drink and do business."

I started to respond, but his finger slid through me.

"Shit, you're wet, sweetheart."

I groaned, hating how easily he destroyed me with his words and touches. "Did that business include a woman?" I snapped in response.

A finger drove into me, and I cried out. "No, because I thought I had a woman here who could satisfy me. But then I come home to find her flirting with one of my men and completely soaked."

Another finger and the motion had me chasing the pleasure they promised me.

"Are you drenched because of another man?"

"You're an asshole," I said, my teeth gritted.

"I never said I wasn't." His fingers rushed from me, and I whined like a freaking idiot. "Now be a good girl and tell me who has you so wet."

"Damn it," I grumbled. "You do."

"Good girl," he murmured in my ear before his fingers drove back into me. "Tell me who owns you, Ava."

"Nobody owns me," I said, trying to think straight when all I wanted to do was come.

His fingers freed from me and circled my clit, putting pressure on just the right spot so my body became his to command.

"Do you want me to claim you, wildcat?" Fingers filled me again and my legs trembled. "To own you?"

It went against everything I was, but every part of me screamed yes. That I wanted to be his and only his. That this was so much more than some confusion about how our relationship had started.

"Tell me what you want, Ava." He drew his fingers from me and grabbed my chin with them. "Tell me you want that, and I will protect you from every demon out there and claim you as mine."

"And if I don't?" I searched his eyes, seeing the emotion behind them, the words he wasn't saying.

"Then I'll walk away now. Lock you back in your room and never touch you or speak to you again. Send you home when I have what I need."

He dropped his hand and lowered his head, licking my chin where moisture still sat. His hand wrapped around my waist and pulled me into his firmness. "Tell me." There was a desperation to his demand, a pained sound.

His hand caressed my ass, then pushed my skirt over my hips until his fingers settled between my legs again.

What did I want? To run like I always did, to pretend this was nothing, that he hadn't already left a brand on me? To deny that his touches were all I would ever crave if I said no.

His fingers drove back into me as his mouth draped over my cheek. I was tired of running, tired of searching, and to pretend my search hadn't led me to him would leave me empty.

"Tell me, wildcat. Who owns you?" he demanded as he kissed my neck.

My body trembled from the building climax and the revelation that I was about to voice.

"You do," I breathed just as I crumbled. My orgasm hit me like a rogue wave that pulled me under and drowned me. A cry tore from me, but he silenced it with a kiss that destroyed me to my core. I was still convulsing, coming down from my bliss, when he removed his fingers. He lifted me and filled me, sending the residual bursts of my climax riveting through me.

His mouth devoured mine as I clutched to his back and squeezed my legs around him. Scratching at him, I said, "But only if you're mine Emerson Tides," between kisses. "Mine to own and mine to claim."

He pulled back, his blue eyes sparkling amid the lust that darkened them. "Are you claiming me, wildcat?"

I bunched his shirt in my fist and yanked his mouth back to mine. Nipping his lip, I said, "Yes."

"Fuck." He kissed me so hard it stole the breath from me. "Done."

Lost in the heat, the intensity of the inferno that engulfed us, I didn't think about the condoms that had been so prominent the night before. I was sure he had one in his wallet like just about every man I'd ever slept with, but if he did, it was forgotten. Only the consuming desire that constricted my thinking existed alongside the pleasure that was assailing me in electric currents. He fumbled with my bra, then ripped it as if it were nothing more than a flimsy piece of paper. And I did the same to his shirt, spraying buttons across the floor, their tiny pops as they hit the floor lost beneath my moans and his growls. Flesh to flesh, I pulled him as close as our bodies would allow, forcing him deeper in me with my heels.

A second climax sat in my periphery, rising with each twist of my nipple between his fingers, every bite to my neck, and every thrust he gave me. It grew and grew until I could deny its presence no more and it leaped, attacking me with such fervor that my scream reverberated through the room. Emerson came with a roar that eclipsed my scream, his body going tense as he exploded in me. I turned my head, our mouths meeting and locking in a kiss that sent the last vestibules of my resistance to tatters. I could no longer deny what this man did to me, what we were together, how perfectly our disfigured pieces fit.

He pushed into me two more times, his hand so tangled in my hair that he gave up on removing it and lowered his forehead to mine. Heaving breaths made it challenging to talk, so I simply clung to him with my legs, my bottom supported by his one hand, my body by the wall.

When I could finally get air to enter my lungs in more than ragged gulps, I draped my hands up his back and weaved them into his hair.

"That's a first," I said, letting my head fall back.

"Never been fucked against a wall?" he said, and I looked back at him to see his sly grin.

"No, I've had plenty of that."

His smile shifted quickly to a frown, his hold on my hair more a tug now. "When I say you're mine, Ava, that means no mention of another man touching you."

"Mmm, well, that goes both ways, Mr. Tides." He grimaced at the name. "I guess you didn't fuck the memory of them from me completely, so we might need to do that a few more times."

This time, the smile spread to light his features. He kissed me and lowered my body, slipping from me and only then glancing down. "Shit, that's what you meant. Yeah, that's a first in a very long time." His eyes shot back to me. "Please tell me you're on some kind of birth control."

I shook my head.

"Damn." His mood switched like the flick of a light switch, and he had his pants zipped and his phone out before I could stop him. "I'll get something for you to take. A pre—"

"Emerson, stop." I pushed his phone down, receiving a nasty glare in response.

"I don't need birth control. I can't have children."

He stared at me, something like suspicion in his eyes.

"I'm serious." I'd never shared the truth, continued to insist any man use protection to protect myself from whatever they might unknowingly share with me. But no one but my uncle knew the extent of my injuries.

I pulled my skirt down and fixed the underwear he hadn't bothered to remove, giving him a curious look as I adjusted it.

"I was caught up in the moment." He ran his hands through his hair, looking suddenly unsure of himself. "I've never let that happen before."

"Let me clean up and I'll explain." His cum was slowly leaking out of me, and the thought had those obnoxious butterflies cascading through my belly again.

He picked me up and sat me on the counter just as I walked away. "Talk before I make a phone call and get you medicine."

"So worried about getting me pregnant?" I asked.

His expression tightened, and he moved to stand between my legs. He tucked a strand of my hair behind my ears and said, "Not as worried as I should be, but I don't want children Ava and you and I...we don't know what this is between us."

"You don't want children?"

"No. It's one reason I've never even entertained getting serious with someone. I don't live that kind of life, and kids annoy the shit out of me."

Inclining my head to the side, I smiled. "Is it odd that we're having the kid conversation already?"

He snorted, the tension fading from his jawline. "Probably. Now tell me why I shouldn't worry that my cum is dripping out of you right now." He shook his head and rubbed his temple. "I don't make mistakes, Ava. But every time I turn around now, it's another mistake."

I placed my hand over his and lowered it. "I wasn't ready for this conversation either, Emerson. It's not something I readily share, like anything in my past."

His eyes darted to mine, suddenly serious. Taking a deep breath, I said, "When my stepfather beat me, he would hit my stomach and pelvis. It was a place that guaranteed no one would see the bruises. It was a regular occurrence. The worst beating was the night he locked me in the basement for those endless days. I knew something was wrong. I was bleeding even though my period wasn't due for two more weeks. The pain was likely a blessing because I blacked out for some of the time." He brushed his fingers over my cheek, making a path down my arm. It wasn't sexual, but more reassuring. Telling me it was okay to continue, to give him my burden to carry. That was the thing about Emerson Tides. He looked like the biggest bad boy, and he was, but there was a side to him that was sweet and caring. Maybe it was a part of him he didn't let others see. One that was special for me or because of me. "There was so much scar tissue in my uterus they had to remove it. I can't have children."

"If I could dig his body up and kill him again, I would," he said, his eyes darkening.

"Well, you can't, and it was a long time ago. Therapy and meds, remember." Although part of me was certain Emerson Tides had become another form of therapy.

"So," he started, his brow quirking as he tilted his head, "all those condoms last night and I didn't need them?"

Chuckling, I wrapped my arms around his neck. "I always insist on protection, so yes, you needed them." I had until today when my hormones had raged in rebellion and blinded me to the fact that there was no condom separating us. Goosebumps pebbled on my skin, and he rubbed his finger over them.

Those blue eyes, so calculating and perceptive, flitted to mine. Letting my fingers trace his jawline, I said, "What is this, Emerson?"

The muscle in his jaw twitched. "I don't know but I do know I will kill anyone who even looks at you, that I couldn't get you off my mind all day, and that I plan to fuck you bare repeatedly tonight so I can feel you coming on my cock again."

I gave him a questioning look. "Was that a pickup line? Because if it was, you're no longer allowed to use that on anyone but me because it's entirely too hot."

He threw his head back and laughed before he pulled me in for a kiss. "Have you eaten dinner?"

A glance out the window told me it had gotten dark without me even knowing it.

"Nope. Although I raided your boring pantry earlier and had half a sandwich while talking to that poor guy you just scarred for life."

His eyes scrunched. "My men are used to scars and he should have known better. Too many damn new guys."

"To replace the ones who are being recruited?"

"Yeah." He kissed my nose. "No more business talk. I'm making you dinner and you're going to sit here and talk to me."

A flush of warmth filled my chest, and I pulled him in for another kiss. "What do you want to talk about?"

"Anything, as long as I get to hear your voice."

His words struck at the defenses I'd been fighting to maintain, sending them tumbling into the caverns of my being. It didn't matter how we had started, who he was, what his past or my past held. I was free-falling with no possibility of stopping and, with every small thing Emerson Tides did, no desire to stop myself.

Chapter Nineteen

EMERSON

I didn't know what I was doing, but I was tired of battling with myself. Last night had been enough for me to reconsider the fight, but today had solidified the fact that I had no choice but to surrender to it. Ava had wheedled her way into my being with every smart comeback, every cute look, every free-spirited laugh and action. And I couldn't remove her if I wanted to.

My mind had done nothing but wander to her, thinking of what we'd done and how amazing it had been. So that when I'd walked into the kitchen and seen her with another man, a possessive need had overtaken me. I knew then that I was lost. There was no going back. I would kill any man who so much as looked wrong at her without hesitation and if he dared to touch her, I would gut the son of a bitch and fuck her while he died a slow and painful death watching me take what belonged to me and not him. The thoughts were irrational, and I'd never had them with any woman, not even the one that had come between Greyson and me.

Now as she sat across from me, talking about how she'd lost a serving job because she'd poured coffee on some ass who had pinched her, taking bites of pasta between breaths, her feet tucked under her, hands animating her story, I realized the tension of the day and even the last year had eased. Like she was a salve that removed the strain in my life and filled it with something I hadn't experienced in far too long: joy. There was a part of me who even thought he could give it all up to keep her smiles and her laughter, to hear her voice, and see the gold highlights in her eyes.

She stretched, her shirt lifting to reveal the piercing in her belly button, and I nearly salivated at the thought of licking my way up that lush skin. Dressed in a short plaid skirt and a shirt that had some logo I didn't recognize on it, she tempted me to lift her back on the counter and take her again. I'd shredded her bra, which left her perfect tits too visible below her shirt. And that skirt...that skirt was dangerous. She hopped from the stool and my eyes followed her swishing hips, then trailed the path of her thick thighs. Wiping my hand down my face, I pushed away the thought of bending her over the sink and taking her again. That body was killing me.

"You look like you're still hungry," she said. My eyes flew from her legs to see her giving me a knowing smile.

Flashing her a coy grin, I replied, "I might need dessert soon." She took my hand and dragged me from the kitchen. "I guess you do, too?" I asked, curious why we weren't heading to my bedroom like I'd expected.

"I do, but I want to go outside for a little." She turned to me, walking backward. "Can we make the night last just a little longer?"

"That's what I was planning to do," I answered. I grabbed for her, but she slipped out of my hold and ran toward the glass doors, her giggle trailing behind her.

Stopping in my tracks, I watched her open them, then look back at me. Moonlight shimmered in her hair, making the strands white, the pink ones almost crimson. My breath caught as I took her in, realization dawning that every small thing Ava did made her unique. She lived life with wide eyes and no expectations but that she would enjoy it. She didn't carry her past like baggage, didn't let it bend her spine or tear her down. To her, life was a challenge, and she ran into the danger and possibilities without recoiling. Everything about her was so different from me, yet there were subtle similarities.

"What?" she asked, her chestnut eyes holding so much life.

In two strides, I threaded my hand through her hair and brought her lips to mine. Whatever was happening between us, I wouldn't run from it. I would spread my arms wide and let it barrel through me. Change me, own me, devour me. Because if it meant this woman was mine, if it meant her smiles were for me, her laugh echoing in the chambers of my black heart, her touches washing the stains from my body, then I would give up everything else in my life to keep her.

I recognized the sensation in my chest, the bellowing emotion that demanded I acknowledge it, but I kept it silent, kissing Ava like she was the last breath of air that would fill my lungs. That kiss washed over every other, drowning them in a sea of oblivion to never return to my memory again. Leaving only Ava in their place.

Lips separating so slowly they seemed to cling, I rested my head against hers, moving my fingers further into her curls. It was too soon for this to be something definitive, yet it was. I wouldn't voice it, and I doubted she would, but the knowledge was there in the power of that kiss, in how her hands clung to my open shirt, its buttons still on the floor of my kitchen.

Giving her forehead a kiss, I looked down at her, seeing it there. The same understanding I carried and with it, the danger of voicing that truth.

"What happens in five days, Emerson?"

A jolt of uncomfortable currents hit my chest. Five days until I traded her for my brother. Sent her home to the other side of the country to resume her life. I didn't want to think about it and so I didn't answer her.

"Let's go out on the deck like you wanted."

Her eyes flitted between mine and she gave me a quick nod before taking my hand and leading me out. The moon was high and full, its beams lighting the beach below, its body leaving a warped mirror image on the water. Ava leaned over the rail, her sight on the moon, but a shape on the table caught my attention. Dropping her hand, I headed to it and picked up the notebook.

"Oh, that's nothing," she said as I flipped through it.

Even in the moonlight, I could see the talent on the pages.

"Should I punish you for going through my desk, or failing to tell me how talented you are?"

"I guess it depends on the punishment," she teased.

I glanced from the sketch of a man who looked too much like me to think it was anyone else.

"I would have gotten you art supplies if you'd asked," I told her. It bothered me that she'd gone through my drawers, but I kept the valuable information locked away and I knew her intentions had been innocent.

She gave me a shrug. "I haven't drawn in years."

Scrunching my brow, I asked, "Why? And why go back to school for art history when you're this good?"

The scratching at her arm gave me insight into her vulnerable side, a side she kept hidden below confidence and a bubbly demeanor.

"The art world is competitive. I tried after school but having to sell myself, to market pieces of myself as if I was selling stolen watches on a street corner, got to me. I started working more at all those odd jobs and when Uncle Den offered me the chance to go to grad school for the fiftieth time, I took it with the goal of enjoying other people's art. I left that part of me behind."

"You ran away from it." I closed the distance between us, keeping the journal in my hand. "Ava Shelton, who never runs from anything but an unhinged mob boss she thinks is going to kill her, ran."

"I didn't run. I just woke up. They were dreams of a little girl who wanted an escape from her cruel life. That's all they were."

I took her chin between my fingers. "You ran and from the looks of it," I shook the notebook, "you decided to stop running."

She looked away from me, and I tossed the book on the table. "You don't run, wildcat. From anything." Her sight shot back to me. "Remember that because it's one of the things I..." I caught myself before the wrong word shed the locks I had on it. "...adore about you."

Neck tipping, she studied me, and I knew she could see what I didn't want her to.

"I want to go to the beach," she said, surprising me with the change of subject.

"Running from the truth?" I asked.

"As much as you are," she retorted, and I snapped my mouth shut, hating how she was calling me out, although, if I was reading her right, she was calling herself out as well.

"It's too dark to go down to the beach."

"Ha, are you kidding me? The ruthless boss is afraid of going to the beach at night?"

"I'm not afraid of anything," I said, stepping back from her. A small voice in the back of my head told me I was afraid of one thing now—losing her. "I'm older—"

"Pfft, that's an excuse. You're how old, Emerson?"

"Forty-five, Ava."

"Okay, so that is a bit older than me. Shit, fifteen years? I thought Riley was the only one into older men. With..." Her eyes went wide, and I saw her figuring it out, surprised she hadn't earlier. "Wait. She told me Greyson was forty-five. How can you be the same age...unless...oh my God, you're twins?" I'd never seen her eyes so large, and she reminded me of one of those caricatures artists drew at the fairs our parents used to take us to.

She took my face in her hands and moved my head back and forth, inspecting me.

"You won't find any similarities except our eyes."

"I thought you were his older brother."

"I am. I claim those damn five minutes."

She laughed, still looking for some sign that what she'd discovered was true. "That's crazy. You look nothing alike."

It was true. Only our eyes matched. I stood an inch taller, my build broader and more muscular—although I hadn't seen my brother in twenty-five years—my hair was black like our father's and his brown like our mother's.

Her hand fell, her expression shifting, her eyes growing concerned and losing the wide-eyed excitement. "How do you not speak to your brother for decades when you're twins? Isn't there some kind of twin bond they talk about?"

There was and always had been, but I would never admit it and I had blocked it out the day I'd left. Refusing to admit that it seemed like I had ripped a part of myself apart that day, a part that had never healed, and so I had filled it with hate and anger.

"No," I answered a bit too gruffly. "Come on. If you're going to make me go down these stairs in the pitch black, then let's get it over with."

"Why don't you have lights?" She kept staring at me as we walked and I rolled my shoulders, noticing the tension returning.

"Because lights show my enemy there's another way into my house."

"Like they couldn't just come through the front door?"

I shot her a look and opened the gate.

I led the way, listening to her ramble on about twins and me and my brother. Each word reminded me of the regret that had been building since she had come into my life. The same that had reared its annoying head from time to time throughout my life but was now a steady aggravation. When we made it to the bottom, she ran to the water and dipped her toes in.

"Now what?" I asked, not having been down here at night in years. At times, the rush of the waves and the vastness of the ocean called me, and I would stand in that same spot, wondering how my life had come to this. Lonely, corrupt, a tangled web I couldn't escape even though I wanted to.

She lifted her shirt over her head. "Now I rinse the dried mess you left from my thighs, and you fuck me in the water."

It was my turn to gape at her. The skirt came off along with the underwear and I looked up to make sure none of my men were watching her. It was too dark from where they stood, but still the moonlight left little to the imagination. She removed the clips from her hair and sent it tumbling before she plunged into the water.

"I thought you couldn't swim," I said, watching her move further from me and hating the fear that lanced my insides.

"I can't, so you'd better come in and save me."

She brought her finger up and beckoned for me to follow. If it was one thing I was learning about Ava, it was that she would challenge my routines and test me at every turn. My fearless wildcat.

Ignoring the voice that told me this was ridiculous, I stripped and made my way to her. Scooping her into my arms, I proceeded to do exactly what she'd suggested, taking her right there with the waves intensifying my every thrust and the moonlight illuminating her face as she climaxed for me.

FOUR DAYS. That's all I had left before my world went to hell. I raked my fingers through my hair. Who was I kidding? It had already gone to hell and Ava was the only light left in it. The voices on the other end of my phone continued to argue. I usually stayed out of disagreements between families that sat on the border of my province. Leaving it to them and hoping one would wipe the other out so I wouldn't have to hear their bitching about stupid shit I couldn't care less about. This was how territory wars started. Someone looked at someone else the wrong way and feathers got ruffled. I would have just killed them both, but with my situation as fragile as it was, I didn't have the men to deal with a takeover. In fact, it had been years since I'd even threatened such a thing. The threat still stood, but I hadn't bothered stepping out of my province for another family's territory. It wasn't worth the trouble at this point.

The door to my office cracked open and Ava's grin popped in. I'd left her in the main room, curled up on the couch when my phone rang. Her hair was rumpled, her shirt wrinkled, but it was the devious sparkle to her eyes that had me forgiving her for interrupting me during a call. She closed the door behind her, and I mouthed, "What are you doing, sweetheart?"

The grin lifted further, and she strutted over to me, her hips sashaying hypnotically. The shouting grew on the phone, and I shook my head at Ava. Gesture ignored, she pulled her shirt over her head, bumped my legs apart and dropped to her knees.

"Fuck," I muttered, watching her undo my pants.

"You agree it was an undercut, Cade?" I heard on the other end. Damn if I did, but I really didn't care because Ava's mouth was now warming my cock, her tongue drifting under my shaft. I sank my hand into her hair.

"I think it was an attempt at an undercut that was more insulting than anything," I answered, trying not to groan when she took me all the way and drew back with a gag. There was no way I would make it through this call if she kept it up, but I wasn't about to stop her. "Stop pussyfooting around and just tell him you want a share of the market, Hansen."

The line went silent except for the huff. I looked down to see Ava's head bobbing up and down, her brown eyes on me. I pulled her hair, forcing her from me, and stood. She looked so sexy I just about came looking at her.

"You two figure it out and call me when you have a solution.

Otherwise, I'll be the solution, and you won't like it when I come out there and put your bodies in the river." I hung up on them and tossed my phone onto the desk.

"That was a risky thing to do, wildcat."

She licked her lips and stroked me with her hand. "I like risks."

"There are consequences to interrupting my business calls."

"I'm sure I'll enjoy every one of them."

My hard-on jumped in her hand, and I took it from her, fisting it a few times before I said, "Open up like a good girl."

A shiver made its way through her, and she opened her mouth wide for me. I pushed her head forward, my eyes on her as she took every inch of me, struggling not to gag and losing the battle once I shoved her further. The sound had my balls tingling. I let her work me until I couldn't stop myself from stilling her head and moving with swift, long thrusts in and out of her mouth. Her gags and tears sent my release thrumming through me, and it hit me with an intensity that had me bumping the back of her throat and ripping gags from her. But as much as I hated that she was uncomfortable, it felt too good to stop.

"That's it, wildcat. Swallow every drop of me," I growled, completely out of control as my release ricocheted through me.

When my climax freed its hold on me, I backed away, a pop sound coming when her mouth released me.

I brushed the tears from her cheek, saying, "Open that sexy mouth for me and show me what a good girl you are."

She opened, sticking her tongue out at me and smiling despite the tears and swollen lips. The sight was riveting, and I knew I wanted more. I tucked myself away, completely drained but still able to lift her onto my desk.

"Lay back, sweetheart. I think you deserve a reward for that."

I swiped my hand behind her and cleared my desk, sending whatever was there falling to the floor. Her back hit the desk, my mouth hit her skin, kissing my way up her chest and then her neck. Yanking her bra down, I cupped her breasts, teasing her nipples until they were rigid in my fingers.

Tugging one, I nibbled her ear before saying, "The next time you interrupt my meeting, Ava, I will edge you on until you beg me to bring you to climax."

"I don't beg," she whimpered as I sucked her nipple ring into my mouth and flicked my tongue at it.

"You will for me because you're a wildcat who needs to be reminded of who's in charge."

My hands tore at her pants, shoving them down while I bit her hip, leaving teeth marks. Her groan reverberated in the air. I spread her legs further, bending them and ordering her to hold them before I went to my knees. I jerked her to my face and feasted on her as her cries filled the room and her body shook. Minutes before, I hadn't thought it possible to get hard again, but my erection was throbbing against my pants by the time her back bowed off the desk and she came in a frenzy of convulsions.

Seeing her like that was too much, and I unzipped my pants, freeing myself again. Her body was limp when I flipped her and yanked her to me, thrusting into her. Throwing my head back, I gripped her hips, reveling in how her muscles were still pulsing around me.

Smoothing my hand down until I reached her ass, I grunted out, "You still have consequences to deal with for walking in on me, sweetheart."

"What?" She tried to lift her head, but I moved my hand from her hip and pushed her back down with my palm.

"You don't make the rules around here. I do and you follow them."

The crack of my hand hitting her ass echoed through the room.

"Ow," she whined, and I smoothed the spot.

"You don't like that?" I said, hands going to her hips again as I pounded into her so hard her body slid back and forth on the desk.

"I might have liked it." This time, her words came out in a purr.

That was all I needed. Hips released, I leaned forward and wrapped my hand around her neck. "Good, because I'm going to leave my print on this ass like a brand." I smacked it again, enough to sting, but not enough to bruise. Her body jumped. A few more hits and I was so close to coming that I moved my hands to her waist and drove into her.

"Are you going to come with me?" I asked, my breathing ragged.

"Only if you say it the right way." Her words were hoarse and broken.

"Come for me like a good girl." And she did, baring down on me so that I lost it. My climax wrecked me this time. Clutching to her hips, I rode the waves of it until they pounded me so badly, I fell on top of her, thrusting into her with the last of my release. I laid my cheek on her back and stretched my hands to cover hers.

"If that's my punishment," she heaved, "then I'm interrupting every meeting from now on."

Her skin muffled my laugh. "If I get to come in your mouth each time, you have my permission to storm into every meeting and drop to your knees."

"Even when you have other people in that meeting?"

I raised myself up and hovered there, tracing the dragon tattoo on her shoulder blade with my tongue. "You can, but I'll have to blind them all before you do. Maybe gouge their eardrums, too, so they don't hear those beautiful gags."

"That's gross," she said, trying to see me over her shoulder.

"That's me staking my claim. No one sees or hears any part of you, or I'll have to kill them. Plain and simple."

Finally finding my strength, I slid from her and fixed my pants. "Why don't you keep my cum in you the rest of the day?

I'm just going to fill you up again, so there's no reason to clean up."

"You're going to take me again right now?" she asked, her eyes going from the chair and to the desk she was resting against. She was wriggling into her jeans, her tits bouncing in the lace bra she wore. It was white and sheer enough for me to see right through it.

"This guy needs a breather. You just drained him dry. Let's get a drink and turn on one of your boring small town love stories while I recover." Of all the tastes in movies I could have guessed for her, it would not have been those. They made me want to gouge my own eyes out, but since she had no reservations about making herself comfortable any time I sat with her, I was willing to put up with it.

I threw her shirt at her. "Cover those up before I make you come again."

Pouting her lips, she retorted, "I might leave it off then."

With a shake of my head, I stepped across the room and opened the door for her. My phone interrupted my steps. Seeing my brother's name on the screen, I told her, "I'll be out in a minute. This one I take alone."

"Decided to come crawling to me early?" I asked Greyson when I answered, hoping that wasn't the case. I wasn't ready to part with Ava yet, nor did I have a plan to keep her.

"What's wrong, Mer?"

Our parents had never let us shorten our names, insisting we remain formal, even with our friends. The only rebellion we had was between ourselves. Up to the day I changed my name, he was the only one I allowed to use that nickname, and I was the only one who called him Grey. Anyone who thought otherwise had found themselves black and blue.

"Nothing other than you not following my timeline. I should kill her just for this." Saying the words caused knots in my stomach.

"I'm serious. Cut the shit for five minutes. Brother to brother, tell me what's going on before this escalates."

I squeezed the bridge of my nose. "It already escalated. And we haven't been brothers since the day you back stabbed me."

"It's been twenty-five years, Mer. Let it go. She ran off with a bookie who knocked her up six months after I tossed her out. She was a slut who was using you."

I let the silence hang between us, tempted for just a moment to leave it in the past and tell him everything. It was what I'd wanted, to have him listen to me, to help me wipe the scum from my territory and make some kind of peace agreement between us. But I wasn't ready. Too proud to admit my failure to handle the mutiny in my ranks, the failures as everything I'd built slipped through my fingers and turned to ash. Too fearful of losing Ava.

"And you were the bastard who stole her from me." The words were empty, the rage hanging on by a tattered thread. I was tired of the fight, of clinging to the past. Ready for something more. Scraping my hand through my hair, I said, "You have four days. Call me again before that and I'll ensure she's dead before you even hang up."

I disconnected and stared at the phone, contemplating dialing him back. But I wanted to hang on to the next four days, to pretend things were good. To hold on to Ava just a little longer and to my pride before I had to tuck my tail between my legs and admit that I'd fucked up. That everything I had was now just a façade.

There had been times through the years where I'd thought of leaving it all behind. Taking enough money to live off and slip away, travel the world, live like a normal person. Leave the killing, the constant stress, the high adrenaline and live. But there had been no one worth living for until now.

Phone back in my pocket, I left my office and found Ava throwing popcorn into the air and catching it in her mouth.

Hearing me, she turned, missing one. I watched as it bounced off her nose and onto the floor.

"Come on." She patted the seat next to her, then bent and picked up the rogue piece, popping it in her mouth and mumbling, "Five second rule."

"And you call me gross," I teased, sitting beside her. She curled up to me and shoved a piece of popcorn in my mouth.

"You are. Now shush. She just left her high paying finance job and moved home to help her father run the inn."

"Let me guess. There's a buff handy-man who wouldn't last two minutes in a street fight?"

She bumped me with her elbow, then snuggled into my lap as if it was a natural thing we'd been doing for years. That's what it was with Ava—everything about her was new, but almost like she'd been doing it with me for a lifetime. My fingers played in her hair as the movie continued, but my mind wasn't on the predictable plot. It was on the woman who sucked in a breath when the characters had their first kiss, who squeezed my leg when some accident happened, and wiped her eyes when the damn thing finally ended. She added life to my bleak world. A lonely world with no attachments, women who came and went because none had been her, blood and violence. But in the days she'd been in my life, she had grounded it, tethering herself to me and I couldn't begin to unravel her from me, nor did I want to.

Chapter Twenty

AVA

Emerson had left me in bed after ravaging me to the point that I needed another hour of sleep just to replenish my energy. The man had stamina. My fingers draped over his pillow as I thought about him. Another day had passed, and I was in even deeper than I ever imagined. I wanted to stay here with him, to continue in my ignorant bliss and pretend we were a normal couple on the cusp of our romance, that I didn't have a life beyond the doors of his home, and he didn't have some bastards trying to destroy him.

I rolled onto my back and stared at the ceiling. If he didn't have someone dismantling his empire piece by piece, I would never have met him. It seemed ironic and I still couldn't convince myself to forget that our situation may have changed, but our dynamic hadn't. I was still the hostage, he the warden. Closing my eyes, I tried to forget that fact and what it entailed. The possibility that Greyson Tides would kill him, with my uncle at his side. Revenge for taking me. Or that he wouldn't and Emerson would send me home, too many miles to count separating me from him. Either way, I lost, and I didn't want to lose.

Footsteps brought a smile to my face, and I stretched, my eyes still closed. "Did you grow hungry and leave your meeting early?" I asked. My body may have been sore, but I was more than willing to deal with a little more soreness if it promised the ecstasy Emerson brought me.

A hand came over my mouth and my eyes flew open.

The guy with the face tattoo and beady eyes stood over me. "No, but you keep that pretty body ready. I have buyers who will pay extra to own Cade Slaughter's woman."

I scratched at his hand, but a pinch to my neck had my muscles going slack and my world going dark.

Chapter Twenty-One

EMERSON

The pictures were grainy, but they were more than I'd had. I sat back and scratched my chin.

"So you think they're holed up in Ludburough?" I asked Rudy, a man I kept in my pocket for surveillance and special ops projects. He was ex-military, tough as nails, and an expert at finding people who didn't want to be found. Only now admitting I'd been unsuccessful in my hunt, I had asked for his help. Pride was a dangerous thing.

Pack stood behind me, focused on the picture of Henley, the man who had been a thorn in my side for too long.

I'd been hunting the bastards who had escaped my grasp. When the rumors about the trafficking didn't disappear, I knew they had set up shop somewhere else in the territory. But they went underground, too deep for me to find. The more they smeared my name and had my enemies thinking I had gotten sloppy, the harder I looked. After the debacle with the Donelli's, I called Rudy in. He'd been digging for two months and I'd almost had him call off the hunt.

"Yeah. They're using the warehouse as a front. I'm sure of it."

I sat back, flipping the photo on the desk. "We checked that warehouse. Everything checked out as legitimate and we found no trace of them."

"Because they know how to hide," said Pack. "We trained them, Cade. They're shadows, like we trained them to be."

Like we trained every one of our men. Ghosts to go unseen and do my bidding. It differentiated me from other families and left them terrified of me. My men could infiltrate any family and unravel them from the inside. They were efficient, skilled, and deadly. And these assholes had taken that gift I'd given them and turned on me.

My fist bunched, my knuckles straining against my skin.

"What's the second location?" I asked, gnashing my teeth.

Rudy held his phone out. Another picture, this time detailed. A house in the hills, hidden enough to go unnoticed in the dense forest.

"Kingsport, about thirty minutes out from the warehouse."

I knew Kingsport well. It was where I first planted roots in Seagate before I built enough power to run down the other families and settle south where I now lived.

"What do you want to do, boss?" Pack asked.

I wanted to run them down, destroy them, leave nothing behind to even know they had existed.

"Thank you, Rudy. Keep up the surveillance. We'll strike soon. I want to know every move they make until then."

"Got it, Cade." He put his phone away, adjusting his leather jacket. Creases forming in his forehead, he said, "They're running the trafficking from below ground. There's no sign of them moving victims in or out. No meetings, no sign of buyers. It's like they have tunnels below and we haven't found where they empty. If we hadn't spotted Henley emerging when we never saw him go in, we would have never found them."

My jaw ticked. No wonder we hadn't found them. If they were running their business underground, it would be impossible to track them. That it had taken Rudy this long to pin them down told me how entrenched they were. Henley had been one of my best men, so it made sense. But he'd slipped up and now I had him.

"All the more reason to act swiftly," said Pack.

I nodded in agreement. "I'll be in touch with the next step. And I'll wire your bonus today. I'll add another for keeping them under your sight until we flush them out."

With a curt acknowledgment, Rudy left, closing the door behind him.

Rubbing my temples, I said, "I know what you want to do, but we don't have the men."

"If you hadn't killed two the night they brought Ava, we'd have more," he said.

Drawing my eyes from the door to him, I stood. "Don't push me, Pack. You know why they needed to die. I don't accept mistakes."

"Yet you're making them, Cade."

I slammed him against the wall, my gun to his head, but he didn't flinch. If he had, I would have killed him. No attachments. It was the way I'd lived my life until Ava had stepped into it.

"You won't do it," he taunted. "She's gotten to you." Punching him, I put my gun away. He rubbed his cheek. "It's not a bad thing, Cade. Rage has blinded you for years."

"If you were anyone else, your blood would be staining my floor right now," I told him.

"I know," he said, rolling his neck. "Don't expect me to hold hands with you and spout out some best friend's shit as we admit our feelings for each other."

"Fuck off," I snarled.

Had I gone soft? Pack was the closest thing to a friend, the only one who knew me, yet I'd never admitted we were anything more than boss and second. Best friend seemed like some wimpy thing my brother would admit. Something Ava would say. My lips fought my smile. Just thinking about her brought them too easily.

"What do you want to do, Cade?"

"Don't get all fucking mushy on me, Pack. Yeah, you're probably my best friend, if I had one. But don't let it go to your head."

I dropped into my seat as he laughed. "That's not what I meant, boss, but yeah, I've been stuck with your ass for too long not to notice, even if you don't say it." He gave me a goofy grin.

"Leave," I said, rubbing my temples. "Just leave and let me think."

"About how that woman is changing you?"

"She's not changing me." But it was a flat out lie because my perspective was shifting with every minute she was in my life.

"Keep telling yourself that. What do you want to do about what Rudy brought us?"

I rested my head on the chair. "I don't have the men to just go barging in there." And if Henley had shown himself, he wanted to be seen. He was too smart for it to be a mistake, like I'd originally thought.

"But you will."

Lifting my head, I looked at him with his crossed arms and menacing stance. "You put this plan in motion for this moment. In three days, Greyson Tides will be here."

"With Brinks and Raines in tow." I was sure of it.

"And an army behind them. He's your chance to finally take these assholes down."

I scraped my hand through my hair. "How did I get to this point? Relying on my enemy to save my ass."

He shrugged. "Mistakes you and I can't take back. Maybe it's for the best." Squinting my eyes, I tried to determine what he meant. "You've been at this a long time, Cade. Carrying this grudge against your brother. Ruling this territory alone, segregating yourself. Maybe it's time you have a queen at your side to help you rule. And time you bury the grudge with your brother and make him an ally instead of an enemy."

"I don't pay you for your opinions," I snarled.

"But I give them anyway," he replied with a wink before walking to the door.

"Pack," I called to him just as he threw the door open.

"Yeah, boss." He craned his neck to look back at me.

"I appreciate you hiring new men, but you always run them by me first. I know Ava has had me preoccupied, but go by me before you bring anyone else in. And that guy with the snake tat on his cheek gives Ava the creeps. Keep him on outside duty from now on."

I'd meant to mention it earlier, but like everything now, my mind wasn't as hyper-focused as it normally was. Every time the thought occurred, one of Ava had pushed it to the periphery.

The way his brows continued to pinch with every word left me concerned.

"I haven't hired any new guys. I have candidates, but I'm still running checks on them."

Standing quickly, I stared at him. "You didn't hire a guy with a shaved head and a snake tattoo on his cheek? Been here at least a week?"

"No," he said, the word drawn out as realization struck us both.

"What about the suave looking one? Looks like he could model. Green eyes, blonde hair, has a hole in his hand where I put a knife through it the other day."

"No."

"Fuck." I ran through the office, past him, pulling my gun out. "Check the house and the grounds. I need to check on Ava." My heart hammered so hard it was like a throbbing pain. Instinct screamed that she wouldn't be there as I took the stairs two at a time.

The bed was empty, the room silent. I crashed through the bathroom, finding it just as empty. Running down the stairs, I looked in all the rooms, scanning the beach for her. Every empty space caused the pain in my chest to swell. Pack came in the front door as I ran into the foyer, dragging another of my men with him.

"Tell him," he demanded, shoving him toward me.

"I thought it was you, boss."

My gun was at his head before he could blink. "Choose your next words wisely."

His throat bobbed, but he kept his fear in check. It was a requirement of my men. Fear was your death sentence. "Your car left. One of our men was driving. It looked like you were in the back on your phone. The windows are dark, so I just assumed."

My fist hit his jaw, splitting his lip. "You don't assume," I growled. "When did they leave?"

Hesitation told me I wouldn't like his answer. "A few minutes after your guest."

"That's a good twenty minutes," Pack said.

I roared, slamming the butt of my gun into the man's head where he collapsed, blood pooling where the force had split his skin.

"Don't kill him, Cade. We need every body we have if we're going to find her."

"I want the roads checked, the airport. Check everywhere."

"We won't find them, and you know it."

I bunched the collar of his shirt in my fists. "I will, and if they hurt her, they'll find out why I'm considered the most unhinged boss in all the provinces."

"That's the man I know. Call your brother, Cade. Get it over with. We need him and his men if we're going to win this war and get her back."

Letting him go, I stepped back, my heel hitting the unconscious man.

"I'm going after her."

"Think about it, Cade. That's exactly what they want. This is a trap. Henley wanted us to spot him. He's making the plays and if you run after him, you're playing right into his hands." His thought mirrored my own, that Henley had purposely exposed himself. "They taunted you all this time. Now they're playing with you, making sure you know they were close enough to kill you. This is their end game and taking Ava ensures you'll lose your shit and run to your death and if you don't, your brother kills you for losing Ava. A war between the two strongest families."

"A war." I remembered Ava lingering on that word like she was thinking the word meant more. "Greyson has Brinks and Raines on his side. By default, they have Donelli and Strint. All of whom think I've been targeting them. They kill Ava and guarantee everyone turns on me." I calmed my urge to run after her, forcing myself to be strategic. Henley thought by taking my most important belonging, that I would do exactly what I had intended —go after her without thinking it through. He knew I ran into danger. That I wasn't a patient man. "A war with me as the target. Every family they've been taunting and…shit, deliberately fucking up, so it looks like I'm growing weak. All of them coming to my door to kill me."

I was fucked, as was Ava.

"It's more likely they'll sell her," he said, his tone heavy. "And make it seem like you sold her off."

The thought gutted me. "Even more reason for everyone to come after me."

"But there's one thing they don't know."

I met his eyes. "That Greyson Tides is my little brother." Only my closest, most loyal men knew that truth.

"Call him, tell him the truth. There's no more game to get him here and talk to him. No more stringing Ava in front of him to control him and force him to cooperate. It's time to tell him everything."

"Get out of here and take this guy with you. I want every man we can spare searching the roads for them." But I knew where they'd taken her. To the warehouse Rudy had shown me. Sending my men out gave the appearance of desperation and would make Henley believe I was falling into his trap. Rushing to my death.

"And you?"

"Need to make a phone call."

He dragged the man out, and I paced the floor, feeling helpless again. They had kidnapped her right under my nose. Infiltrated my ranks. Arrogant enough to be seen by me. Playing a game that only I had ever mastered. A game that was coming to a head. Every part of me wanted to recklessly go after her, to burst into that warehouse and kill everyone in it. But that's what they expected me to do, and I'd be dead, leaving Ava to suffer for my impulsiveness.

Then there was the fact that they were using an actual business as a front, which meant the people in that factory could be innocent. It was something they had learned from me. Blend in, hide in the obvious places, be a ghost in a crowd.

I needed to get to her, but for the first time in my life, I needed help in getting what I wanted. I pulled up my brother's number, willing to be the one crawling and begging this time if it meant Ava was safe. Hitting his number, I waited, my throat constricting until he answered, and I said the three words I'd been dreading.

"I'm in trouble."

Chapter Twenty-Two

GREYSON

I rose to my feet, walking to the large window of my office. People were walking the street below, enjoying the warm day, unaware a predator watched them from above.

"I'm listening," I told my brother. He sounded sincere for the first time in the years we'd been apart, and that worried me more than it should have, considering the bad blood between us.

"They took her." A distinctive crack in his voice had my brow furrowing.

"Who?" I asked, although my gut told me the answer.

"Ava. Stole her from me and I didn't see it coming." I could hear the thud of him punching something. "Grey, I need to get her back, and these assholes have me cornered."

The nickname only he had ever called me until Riley had claimed it. An endearment when we were kids, a reminder of our rift when we got older.

"Slow down. Who has her, and how did they take her from you?" The suspicions that Mason and his girl had raised pawed at my thoughts, and as Emerson spilled the truth, he confirmed them.

I listened to the unraveling of a man who had once been my

brother and my partner, my best friend, and had become my adversary in a sequence of events that had spiraled from my one poorly choiced lesson.

"So, these guys have been masquerading as Omens, pissing everyone off, and now they have Ava. And you let them in right under your nose?" He was off his game, and I could only imagine it had started with the Randall incident, then spiraled from there. "What the fuck were you thinking?"

"I was distracted. She..." He paused, and I didn't have to see him to know he was searching for words.

"You fell for her. Damn it, Riley was right." I heard a smug 'hmm' and looked up to see her leaning on the doorframe with just as smug a look. That door had been closed when I'd taken the call, and I shot her a scowl to remind her of what I thought about her sneaking up on me.

"*Close the door,*" I mouthed to her. Even if my secretary was part of the business, this was a conversation I didn't want anyone hearing.

Emerson said nothing, but he didn't need to. My brother had never asked for help. It was beneath him. Especially from me.

"So you took Ava, intending to take my wife..." A growl accentuated those two words. "To force my hand, giving me no choice but to listen to how your empire is in the tank and you want me to bail you out? Am I understanding that correctly, Emerson?"

"Yes," he snarled, the man I knew returning with my curt summary of his actions.

"Idiot. You never did understand the art of subtlety or manipulation."

"I don't need manipulation or subtlety. People fear me because I act swiftly and with force."

Two halves of the same coin our parents had called us. I used my brains. Emerson preferred his muscles. It was what made us the perfect team, one very similar to Brinks and Raines. Only when Emerson flexed his muscles, he had already calculated every outcome and decided on the most lethal course. He was too smart for his own good, with a need to strike quick.

"You fucked up," I told him. "And you almost fucked it up with me. You had no guarantees that I would help you, especially if you had taken Riley. A bullet would have been in your head before a word left your mouth."

"And mine would have been in yours. And I didn't fuck up. I cleaned house, and it went wrong."

I turned from the window to see Riley perched on my desk, watching me with those sharp green eyes.

"Then how did you end up with Ava?" I snapped, frustrated that he was such a mess when he'd never been this way.

"My men grabbed her, thinking she was Riley."

I laughed, and Riley's head inclined to the side while she studied me. Two strides and I was in front of her, rubbing my hand up her thigh. I'd forgotten she was meeting me for lunch. Now that she worked for the smaller firm in town, she was no longer in the same building as me and the few blocks of distance grated on me. Her insistence on maintaining her independence and continuing her career had been a point of contention until I had agreed with the condition that she stay heavily guarded and I run a check on every client she met with. Arguments about client privacy fell on deaf ears and she conceded to my requirements.

"Another fuck up? Are those the two who took Ava today?" I pushed her skirt up, sinking my fingers into her skin.

"No. I shot them as soon as I discovered they brought me a blonde and pink haired vixen with a mouth and a fast right hook."

My snort had Riley's brows crinkling. I brought my finger to her mouth and shook my head.

"That sounds more like the man I know. Shoot and ask questions later."

"Exactly."

More silence. He was waiting for my decision, and it wasn't an easy one. His reputation went against everything I prided myself on. Especially now that these imposters had botched so many attacks in his name. Even without the suspected trafficking ring he'd never denounced, even if he wasn't involved, it still looked bad. I dropped my hand back to Riley's leg, thinking about what Emerson had said about the reasons behind the sloppy attacks. A war to turn us all against him and wipe him out.

"It's more than that," I mumbled, the pieces falling into place.

"What?" he asked, confusion in his voice.

"They know you'll call me. Your bargaining chip is gone. They may not know we're brothers or why you had Ava, but they know she belongs to my family. That I'll hunt down anyone who hurts her."

"And bring your force on me when they know I'm weak."

I shook my head, my hand frozen on Riley's skin. "No, you taught these guys better than that and they've taken what you taught them and are using it on all of us. This isn't a play to take you out. It's a move to take all the top families out."

"It's a trap?"

"You're too far into it, too focused on what they've been doing to your dynasty to look outward and see their true aim. By taking Ava, they know I'll come for you. Your bargaining chip is gone. By proxy, Brinks comes with Raines because Riley is involved, and they'll want payback for hurting her friend. Brinks might be an asshole, but he's as protective of Riley as I am." She pouted her lips and crossed her arms. "Donelli has been waiting to get a piece of you. With Tony in charge, he'll bite at the chance to get revenge for the attack on his family and for the shit with Tirenti they think you masterminded. And by proxy, Strint will join in as well as Rinagi who they placed in Tirenti's seat."

"All of Armina and the power of the east coast gunning me down and not noticing the real threat is surrounding them," he muttered. "Shit, this is a disaster."

"Yeah."

"Stay there, Grey. I'll get her back. I can't drag you into this if it's a trap."

I could hear the stress rising at the speed of his speech and knew he was pacing the room.

"Suddenly getting a conscience, Mer?"

Riley's hand played with the buttons on my shirt, and I suddenly had the urge to shorten this call.

"Maybe. Forget I called."

"Mer," I said to stop him from hanging up. "I'm in and I'll bring Brinks and Raines. But this needs to stop. We put the past behind us, and you let your grudge go. Maybe I'll forgive you for shooting me when I tried to stop you from leaving."

Riley's brow rose. I'd never told her the story behind the scar that reminded me every day of what had broken between me and my brother. What we'd both lost that day.

Silence was my answer. A silence that almost had me hanging up.

"Fine. You're still an asshole."

"And you're a shithead whose aim sucks." Thankfully. "Clean house, Mer. I'll call Brinks. But we'll need someplace safe to fly in. They'll be expecting us to use the closest airport, and they'll have eyes on Armina."

"I'll text you the coordinates to my safe house. There's a landing strip behind it. Only my top men know it exists."

"Good."

"Grey." He caught me right before I disconnected. "Thank you."

"I'm doing this for Ava. If you prove yourself and don't turn on me like I suspect you will, then I'll accept your apology and your thanks."

I put my phone in my pocket and met Riley's eyes.

"So, I finally get to meet the infamous brother?"

Tipping her chin, I said, "No. You're staying here."

"Nope. We're a team, Grey. Where you go, I go."

She was stubborn, but there was no way I would take her to Seagate. "I know we are, but this is too dangerous. My brother can't be trusted. I could walk off that plane and he could gun me down in seconds. I don't want you there for that, and I won't risk losing you if this shit about the trafficking is all a ruse."

"What shit?"

I rested my head on hers and sighed. "Lunch is off, baby girl. Let's call your brother and I'll fill you both in."

Her arms wrapped around my neck. "And then we leave for Seagate?"

My jaw tightened, but I saw the resolve in her eyes. Once she had it in her head to do something, there was no talking her out of it. She was the only one who had ever gotten her way with me. It was the reason she now worked out of my sight and too far from me for comfort.

"There will be consequences if you insist on defying my order to stay here," I said. My fingers draped down her arm, causing goosebumps to rise.

"I like your consequences," she said with a grin, those green irises sparkling with mischief.

There was no winning this argument. The situation was dangerous. Emerson could turn on me, kill me and everyone I brought with me, but my gut told me otherwise. That my brother needed me and this was a chance I couldn't turn away from. To mend the gulf between us. If we survived.

"Ready to save Ava?"

Her smile faltered, worry coating her eyes. "What happened to Ava?"

Chapter Twenty-Three

EMERSON

Relief and hope mingled with the fear that held me in its grip. Every minute Ava was in their hands was a minute closer to losing her for good. But if it was one thing I admired about my brother, it was his precision and patience. He had gained his power by taking his time. His enemies looked over their shoulders for months and sometimes years before he struck. And when he struck, he was methodical and deadly.

I clutched my desk, hating that I'd dragged Ava into this mess. Hating that she was in trouble and possibly hurt, that she wasn't here with me, that I had told her I would protect her and instead I'd let her slip through my fingers.

A knock at the door halted the bombarding thoughts.

"Enter," I said, pulling my gun and stepping to the side of the door. I didn't trust anyone now. No one but Pack and the few men who had remained loyal to me since the beginning. The ones those fools hadn't dared approach to betray me because they would have been dead within seconds of voicing any thought of mutiny.

"It's me," Pack said, coming into the office. I lowered the gun as he closed the door. His muscles were tight with tension, his face lined with anger. "We flushed out another traitor." He threw a patch of bloody skin onto my desk.

I walked over and studied the snake tattoo on it. The same that had been on the cheek of the man who took Ava. Flashes of white rage tore across my vision.

"Looks like they have their own brand," he said. "I've had every man on the property stripped and searched for the tattoo. The one I found it on was kind enough to tell me they all have it, before I cut his tongue out when he failed to give me anything else of use."

"Copying everything from us," I mumbled. "Our moves, our strategies, our brand."

"Looks like it."

Rolling out the strain in my neck, I looked over at Pack. "I think it's time we change our ways, Pack. Think you're up for it?"

"I've been by your side since the beginning, Cade. I'll be there till the end."

"Emerson," I said. "Emerson Tides."

He gave me a goofy grin. "You never looked much like a Cade."

I would have laughed, but there was too much at stake to let my guard down.

"What's the plan, Emerson?"

"Something new and something unexpected. It's time to take my power back and show these assholes they can't break me."

For the first time in months, I felt like myself. The same, yet different. Still powerful and terrifying but changed by a spirited woman who saw below the identity I had created and into the man I'd forgotten I was. Letting my hatred and need to show I was stronger than my brother drive me. Now I had a new drive: Ava. And a new future that offered a remedy to the loneliness I'd covered with brutality, greed, and one-night stands. The possibility of a woman at my side and of a reconciliation I'd never imagined I needed.

"Pull six men. Only the ones who have been with us from the early days. No one else. Breaker, included." There was no doubt of where his loyalty was. His cousin had been Jill's husband. He would fight to the death by my side. "They're watching us, expecting me to attack, but instead, we'll go to the safe house. We tell every man to load into the cars. Each car takes a different direction to the safe house in Umberg. That way, we all head in different directions. Ours is the only one that heads to Newpen instead."

Newpen was the only safe house my men didn't know about. Only me and Pack. It was there only for emergency. An empty estate with twenty-four-seven security by an elite team of ex militia I had hired years ago. They kept the house secure and stocked, ran it like it was theirs and even lived in the west wing of the house. I hadn't stepped into it more than twice in the last ten years that I'd owned it. And none of my men even knew it or the team existed. I could have called them in to help me raid the warehouse and get Ava, but I suspected those four men wouldn't be enough in addition to the few I had left.

The house and the team were my last resort backup. If things ever went to hell and there were no options but to run, that was the place. A final stop before I slipped away and disappeared. An emergency plan that I had never used...until now.

"Got it." He was out of the office before I could say more. He'd get everything in order, giving me time to send coordinates to Greyson.

I left the office, heading to my bedroom to grab a few things. I didn't know if I'd ever come back to this house. If things didn't work out, I never would. Reminders of Ava were all over the room. Her scent, her book, the lotions and beauty products she'd moved from the guest room. The clothes she'd worn the night before strewn on the floor where I'd ripped them from her. My eyes leaped to the bed, eyeing the wrinkled sheets shoved back. I moved closer, seeing the syringe tossed to the side.

They had drugged her and taken her. Naked. The ire snapped through me like the end of a whip. They'd touched her naked body and taken her out of my home that way. When I was through killing the others, I would torture the ones who touched her until they were pleading for death. Starting with their hands and then their eyes.

With a renewed sense of purpose, I threw a few things in a bag. I stared at the bed, remembering how I'd curled her body into mine and held her all night. Wishing I had stayed in bed with her. I could almost feel her skin under my fingers, hear her steady breaths, smell the fragrance of her shampoo. The moment left me riven until I picked my head up and remembered my purpose. I would bring her home and bring my wrath down upon the shit-heads who had dared take what was mine. They wanted a war. Well, I was about to bring that war to their front door and trample them with the force of it.

Chapter Twenty-Four

AVA

My head throbbed, and a heavy sense of grogginess sat over me. Groaning, I opened my eyes, squinting at how blurry they were. I tried to move my hands, but someone had tied them behind me. The rope dug painfully into my skin. My ankles were also bound. The room came into focus, but it was too dark to make much out. A single dull yellow light hung from the ceiling. I was on a cot in an empty room the size of a cell. And I was still naked.

Fear trampled any fight that might have been in me. My bindings were too tight to even offer wiggle room, and my captives had no qualms about leaving me naked and alone in a grungy cell. Had they touched me? Raped me? All kinds of thoughts raced through my head and panic eked its way in. The numbness started, and I knew a panic attack was coming, but this wasn't the place for it. My heart raced, so I forced myself to take slow and steady breaths, counting to five with each before releasing them. Remembering all the meditation sessions I'd had with my therapist. The wave of panic subsided, the tingling fading as my heartbeat slowed.

Swallowing down the fear, I took a mental check of my body.

Nothing hurt but the few bruises I knew were from Emerson, distinctly around my hips and on the insides of my thighs. But there was no pain or sense that someone had touched me, not that I had any idea if I would know since they'd knocked me out. I pushed the thought aside and tried sitting up. It took a few tries, but I managed just in time for a figure to enter the room.

"Look who's awake." The creepy man with the snake tattoo came closer. His grin caused the hair on my arms to rise, and I backed away as his hand reached for my breast.

"Get away from me," I said, hitting the wall behind me.

His hand met the skin of my cheek in a flash that sent me falling onto the thin, dingy mattress and my jaw aching. He climbed over me and held my chin, squeezing it so hard tears sprung in my eyes.

"You better be glad the buyers don't want us sampling the goods or I'd fuck you so hard you'd be pleading for me to stop." His tongue ran over my cheek and licked away the tears. "Fucking Cade Slaughter's woman would be something to brag about."

He rose and adjusted himself, cupping the small bulge in his pants like he was proud of it.

"Too bad you have to hold your dick to make it look big," I said, because I never knew when to keep my mouth shut.

With a handful of hair, he tugged me up and hit me again. This time my ears rang, and I tasted the tang of blood in my mouth.

"Get your hands off her," another voice came from the doorway. "You bruise her too much and we'll lose money."

"She's got a smart mouth on her. I might need to use it to show her some respect."

"And I might have to bite to teach you respect," I retorted.

A hand caught his before he brought it down on me again. "Get out. If I catch you in here with her again, I'll take your fingers and send them as an apology to the buyer for touching his property."

"We have a buyer?" The excitement in his voice had me cringing just as much as the fact that someone had paid money for me.

"They liked the pictures we sent, and the bids are high." Oh shit, pictures? They had taken pictures of my naked body and sent it to their list of buyers? Pervs who bought women and girls to use for their pleasure. I was going to be sick. "There's a bidding war going on. Everyone wants the honor of owning Cade Slaughter's woman. A piece of the mighty and a fuck you to his power."

"We struck gold."

"Damn right we did. Now get out of here. There's another hour of bidding, then we'll get her ready for transport. She'll ship out tonight."

The snake guy left, his steps too bouncy, his hands rubbing together like some maniacal cartoon character. The new guy stooped down and pushed the hair back from my face.

"So, you're the one in charge?" I asked, trying to keep my voice steady and my mind clear. Get them talking. That's what they always told us. If we couldn't fight back, then get them to talk.

But he didn't fall for it. He picked up my hair and pulled it for me to see. Gone was the blonde and pink replaced by a dark brown so close to my natural color it was shocking. "We had to pretty you up a bit. Our high rollers are particular and if you look like you might bite, then the lower bids come in. Those are the men who want to break you and not play with you. Any other time, I would have left you as is and sent you out for breaking. But since you belong to Cade, I want him to know how much I sold you for. To know that some other man will be fucking his girl and enjoying every second of being balls deep in her wet cunt."

I spat at him, and he pulled my hair harder. Wiping his face, he said, "Your new owner may not like a woman with spirit, but I can guarantee if he needs to break it from you, he will. Even if it means he sends you back to us so we can pass you around until you're begging for just his cock."

Standing, he wiped his hands on his pants, ignoring my glare.

"Don't tempt me, sweetheart." My stomach turned at the word. "I had fun pulling that piercing from your pussy." This time my stomach lurched, and bile filled my throat. "I was tempted to shove my cock in there, but I have my rules." He yanked me up by my hair and slammed me against the wall, pulling my hair so hard my neck craned. "I might have to break that rule and give you a good fucking if you continue to be a nuisance."

"Nuisance is my middle name. You might want to warn your buyer that I don't play nice."

His lips curled into a snarl. "I have one buyer who pulls the teeth from his girls so they can't bite him when he shoves his cock down their throat. I blocked him from this bid, but I think I'll add him back. He's a high bidder and likes the feisty ones."

Terror held me prisoner, the vileness of what he'd told me leaving me stunned. This was why men like Greyson Tides detested men like this. Why Emerson had tried taking these men down. If I made it out of this, I would ensure he struck down the rumors that he was responsible for the trafficking. Struck it down and cleared his name, because any association with this was horrid. I'd lived in a bubble, never really understanding what these men were doing to women, but here I was in the middle of it, and it was even more grotesque than I'd thought.

"Now be a good girl and shut up, or I'll knock you out again."

Hearing good girl from him made the vomit want to spill from where it perched in my throat. He stomped out of the room, closing the door behind him. I heard a lock and thought about how different this prison was from the one Emerson had put me in. Did he know I was gone? He had to have realized it by now, but did he know who had taken me? Or where I was?

The panic rose when I realized he'd been hunting these men

and hadn't found them. He might never find me. I might never see him again, experience his touches again, touches that horrid unwanted ones would soon replace. I squeezed my eyes closed, trying to fight the panic and desperation, calling on the strength I'd prided myself on for years. Strength these asses had stripped from me so easily it terrified me.

Keeping my eyes closed, I prayed Emerson would find me, keeping that thought in my mind and curling into a ball to shove away the knowledge that countless men had seen me naked and at least one had touched me as he'd removed my piercings. I let the thought of what Emerson would do to them when he rescued me, of what I would do to them when I was finally free, take over the all-consuming hopelessness that threatened to drown me.

Chapter Twenty-Five

GREYSON

Mason was resting on the wheel of my plane, Tyson standing rigid next to him when we pulled into my hangar. His plane was on the tarmac, his men on guard. Three men stood in the hangar on guard with mine.

"Is it party time?" Tyson said, rubbing his hands.

"There is no party." I stepped from the car, Riley emerging after me.

"What the hell is my sister doing here?" Mason asked, pushing from his spot and closing in on us.

"She's pig-headed and won't listen. That's why she's here."

"I'm not pig-headed," she quipped. "And stop talking about me like I can't hear you both."

"Get back in the car, Ri. There's no way you're going into something this dangerous."

"This plane is better stocked than ours." I tipped my head to see Angie emerging with a bottle of wine and a bag of chips. Casey's curls peeked out after her.

"Angie's right. Riley gets cheese curls. I want cheese curls."

"And you have the nerve to lecture me for bringing Riley?" I asked Mason.

He sighed, plowing his fingers into his hair. His green eyes that were the match to Riley's met mine. "They're all stubborn."

"Ang threatened to cut me off for a week if I didn't take her," Tyson grumbled.

"Yeah, and we had to hear the blow job she gave you on the way here," Casey said with a disgusted look. "You're lucky I didn't throw up."

Tyson smirked as Angie wrapped her arms around his neck, the bottle thudding against his chest. "It was worth it," he teased, bringing her hand to his mouth.

"It's like dealing with a bunch of juveniles," I muttered. "Did you get the coordinates I sent you?" I needed to bring the focus back, and if I didn't know better, I would have questioned why Mason kept Tyson around. But I knew better and as much as the man played, he was a beast.

"Got 'em. But you and Riley are hitching a ride on my plane."

My hands clenched. "No. We go separately."

Mason stepped forward, rolling his neck. "I know you like to think you're in charge—"

"I am in charge," I sneered, my hackles rising. As much as Riley had forced a truce between us, the feud still existed between me and Mason. It always would. Two alphas trying to lead the pack were bound to butt heads. Raines was the only one content with assuming the beta position.

Riley wrapped her arm in mine, running her hand down my bicep.

"So you keep assuming." He crossed his arms. "But I'm dissenting on this. We fly as a team, keep your top men with us and I've got Ty. My men and the rest of yours take your plane. They fly in first, in case it's a setup. We land after, giving us time to know if your brother ambushed the first plane. The Omens won't know you aren't on it."

It was a valid point and a smart move. One my brother would likely not expect. That sixth sense I had about Emerson told me this wasn't a setup, that he was being truthful, but taking precautions was something I never failed to do.

"Fine, but if Raines pulls his dick out, expect my bullet to rupture his balls."

"Damn, that's low even for you, Tides," Tyson said. "But not a bad idea the next time I need to teach someone a lesson."

"So no cheese curls for the ride to Seagate? Then I'm snagging some from this plane." Casey said, her cheerful personality grating on my patience already. Ava exuded that same constant excitement, like she'd combust if she wasn't bouncing around and chattering. I usually hid in my office the days she came to visit or sent Riley to her apartment so they could do their girl's day out thing.

Thinking of Ava reminded me of the time crunch, and I glanced back at Den, who looked about ready to explode he was so eager to go.

"Den," I called to him. "You oversee Mason's men. When you land, you are not to leave the plane. No one gets trigger-happy. If they do, you put them down. I'm sure Brinks understands the importance of his men having constraint."

"I do. But it's Tyson you need to worry about, not my other men."

Den gave me a nod of understanding and gathered up the men. It would keep his mind off Ava if he was in charge. Otherwise, I would have had him with me. He needed the distraction.

I turned back to see Tyson flexing his muscles. He was ready to hit something and if he was this wound up after a blow job, I didn't want to think of him without the release.

With everyone rounded up, we boarded Mason's plane. Riley guided me to a seat she assured me Tyson wouldn't have been in and waited for my plane to take off. I leaned forward, my nerves high. We were walking into enemy territory on the guarantee of safety from a man who had been my adversary for twenty-five years. The chance was high that this could blow up in my face. That I would end up dead, taking everyone else with me.

"This isn't like you, Tides," Mason said, leaning back in his seat and crossing his ankle over his leg. Casey sat next to him, her feet tucked under her, a bag of cheese curls in her hand. "You don't rush into things."

I didn't. The only time I ever had was when I chased Clint Randall down to save Riley. "This is more your thing, but that doesn't mean I haven't done it. Remember, I was taking down my enemies when you were still running around the schoolyard."

Angie's shrill laugh came from the other side of Tyson. Her head peeked around him. "You mean when Riley was running around the playground." My jaw ticked at the dig. I narrowed my eyes at her and she shrank back. "Damn, I thought Mason was scary."

"Does she ever shut up?" I asked Mason.

"No," Casey said randomly, her eyes focused on her snack, her fingers poised to grab her next victim.

"Ouch, Casey."

"It's true."

"And why don't you defend me?" Angie asked, elbowing Tyson.

"Cause it's true, little viper. Your mouth only stops when my cock is filling it."

My head thumped back in the seat, and I glanced over at Riley, who gave me an understanding smile. She took my face in her hands and gave me a kiss.

"Dealing with your family is going to be the death of me," I mumbled.

Mason snickered, but I kept my focus on Riley. Taking her hand, I rubbed her thumb with mine. "How are you doing?"

She was worried about Ava but wasn't showing it. My strong girl, who wanted to run with the big boys and play our game. It killed me that I was putting her in danger, but it had been no use arguing with her.

"We're going to save her, right?"

The mood turned like a storm on a sunny day. "Yes."

She swallowed, giving me a nod before she rested her head on my shoulder. I pulled her into my chest, glancing over to see Mason, his brows knitted. He knew just as I did that with every hour that passed, our chance of getting Ava back slimmed. My brother knew it too and waiting wasn't his strength. I just hoped he didn't do something stupid before we arrived.

THE FIRST PLANE landed fifteen minutes before ours. Safely. After ten minutes, my phone buzzed.

What the fuck are you doing out there? Emerson's text came through.

Making sure you don't do something stupid, I replied.

Get the fuck out of the plane. I have a plan.

Be there in five.

We landed shortly after, coming to a stop a little too close to my plane for comfort.

"Your pilot sucks," I told Mason, looking out the window.

Emerson stood at the back of the sprawling house, a pair of large French doors behind him. He had his arms crossed, his muscles bulging below his button down, the sleeves rolled up to show his tattoos. He looked as menacing as he always had.

"Shit, that's your brother?" Angie asked. "He's hot."

"Shut up Anj," Tyson griped. "He's old like Tides."

"If I make it through this day without shooting you, it will be a miracle," I muttered, standing.

"I'd like to see you try," he said, taunting me.

I removed my gun and set it on my seat, reading the question in Riley's eyes.

"Grey?" She rose, but I shook my head.

"What are you doing, Tides?" Mason asked.

"Going to meet my brother."

Riley's emerald eyes grew large.

"Look, as much as I'd like to see you dead, Tides, it would crush Riley, so pick your gun up and let's go."

I turned my attention to Tyson. "That's the closest thing to sentiment I'm going to get from you, so I'll accept your concern, Raines."

Riley hadn't sat down, and she shifted my focus to her. "What are you doing?" But I could see in her eyes she knew exactly what I planned.

I pulled my phone out and dialed Den. "Stand down and do not open that plane. You're going to want to, but no guns, no one but me walks toward that house. Understood?"

"Boss, what are you doing?" he repeated Riley's question.

"They're Omens, Den. You can't see them, but they're out there." Everyone's sight shifted out the plane window. "Stay put until you get a call from me."

I disconnected and pocketed my phone.

"You're not going out there alone," Mason said, standing.

"I appreciate the support, but I am. It may look like only my brother is out there, but Omens are ghosts. My brother taught his men everything he knew. They infiltrate and take down others because they're good. If we all go out there, guns drawn, every one of you will be dead before you can get the first shot off."

"Not gonna happen," Tyson said, moving next to Mason.

"Stay put and do not leave this plane under any circumstance until I tell you to."

I pulled Riley into my arms and kissed her, knowing it might be my last, knowing I was risking everything on a dim connection that told me Emerson was really in trouble, that he needed me. She clung to my shirt while Mason argued with Tyson.

"Stay put, baby girl. If you leave that seat before I give you permission, you'll suffer the consequences." She shivered delectably, and Mason grumbled.

Releasing her, I motioned for Mason to come with me to the door. "Open it," I told the pilot. He started the process as I pulled Mason aside.

"This door gets sealed the minute I'm out. If anything goes wrong, I want her out of here. I don't care that it goes against your code to not fight your way out. Your sister is my only priority, and you will turn this plane around and get her as far from here as you can."

He glanced toward the door where the stairs were being lowered. "I don't run, Tides."

"For your sister, you will. And if she's in danger, Casey's in danger. This is why I didn't want to bring her, and you didn't want to bring Casey or Angie." I looked behind him, seeing Riley with her arms crossed, her eyes creased with worry. "Promise me you'll protect her."

"She's my sister. That's all I've ever done."

"Then we have an understanding," I said, heading toward the stairs.

"Tides."

I turned back to him.

"Good luck."

Giving him a nod, I descended the stairs, every step I took, heightening my alarms. I was an open target. One easily taken down. I could almost sense Den's discomfort. His number one job since we'd met had been to keep me safe. He was likely watching my every step, his hand on his gun. I was sure every one of our men was doing the same. I didn't take risks. Mason was right. That was Emerson's move, not mine. Slow, deliberate, calculated. That was me. Not this. Not walking into the depths of hell, vulnerable with every step that led me to the devil.

The wait was excruciating. Every second that ticked by was another inch Ava slipped from my grasp. And Greyson was sitting on his plane like this was some game. The hours I'd spent waiting for him to arrive, I had put to use. A renewed energy filled me and with Pack's help, I'd come up with a plan. But standing there watching a plane sitting on my runway was enough to drive me mad. It wasn't until the second plane landed that I understood.

A decoy. How like my brother to not trust me. But then, why would he? He had no proof that anything I'd told him was the truth. But I'd stood there with no weapon, my hands in the pockets of my pants, an open target, hoping that was enough to give him some kind of proof this was not a trap. The door opened on the second plane, stairs unfolding, and within minutes, Greyson descended them. Alone with no weapon, His sign of trust on display to meet mine.

The stairs pulled back in, the door shut, and I wondered who was on that plane that he needed to lock it back up. His steps were confident and steady. I remained where I was, at the top of the deck, the doors behind me. Pack was inside, the others all hidden in the shadows of the property and the house.

With every step closer he came, the tightness in my chest grew. The hatred had disguised the fact that I had missed my brother all these years. And only now, seeing him, no longer the young boy of twenty but a man, his features so like our father's, creases in the corners of his eyes, gray along his temples. How much of our life had we missed because of his decision and my anger?

"Emerson," he greeted me once he stepped on the deck. He kept his distance, and I stayed in place, but a tugging in my chest had me rethinking all the years of loathing that had sunk into my bones and my being. Until Ava had lifted it from me, replacing it with a lightness I hadn't had since my youth.

"Grey."

"You have me here." The wariness was clear in his voice. The trust was still on a delicate branch, so easy to send tumbling. "Call your men in so mine can relax."

"Ah, but you know I can't because the minute anyone moves but you and me, your men will blast those windows out of the plane and an all out war will start."

"True. So then what do you suggest we do, big brother?"

The term had me reeling back, and I caught myself, understanding the opening he was offering. This was it, the only one he would present and if I did the wrong thing, he would recant it and turn around and leave. Find Ava on his own, competing with me to get to her first. Our competition would hurt her in the long run and all of us would lose.

"You look good, little brother. Almost like dad."

He chuckled. "That's because I got the good genes. One of us had to be the good-looking one."

"Fuck off. I was always better looking. With more muscle."

His forehead creased, his eyes growing serious. "I'm sorry for being such an ass. If I'd known what it would do, I would never have done it."

I shrugged. "I was thick-headed, and she did give good head, so..."

This time, he laughed, and I joined him.

"Sorry for shooting you," I added.

"Now that was a dick move."

"I purposely missed your vital organs, and I doubt you would have become such an expert shot if I hadn't motivated you."

His head shook, and he said, "So, Cade Slaughter is calling a truce with Greyson Tides?"

I put my hand out, offering it to him. "I think it's time for Cade Slaughter to retire. Emerson Tides is making a truce with his brother."

He stared at me for a second before he extended his hand. When our hands met, I had a sense that I was returning home after being adrift for decades. The bond between us repaired, the frayed edges of it sealed, and emotion washed through me.

"Let's get your girl back," he said, a knowing twinkle in his eyes as he released my hand.

"Tell your men to come off the plane and tell Brinks to stop being such a baby and grow some balls."

Another laugh as he pulled his phone out, and I took mine out. My muscles twitched for just a second before I saw the phone and his grip on the phone clenched until he saw mine. I called my men off, telling them to stand down, and he did the same.

"Brinks, you and Raines come out first. No guns. His men are standing down, but if they see a gun, I can't guarantee they won't shoot. And I may not stop them if it means I won't have Raines aggravating me anymore."

I heard the bitching on the other end, then listened to him make another call. This one to Den, Ava's uncle. The doors opened, the stairs folding out.

"How safe are we out here, Mer?" he asked me. His eyes trailed on the plane he'd emerged from and when I saw the familiar black hair of Riley Brinks, I knew why he was still on edge.

"Very. No one, not even my regular men, knows about this place. They're all at my other safe house. Only my most loyal are here."

"If any of your men shoot, I won't hesitate to kill you," he said, glancing over at me.

"Understood. Why did you bring your woman with you? And two other women? Is that Angela Donelli?"

"Yes. It's a long story, but all three of them are stubborn."

"Must be something in the water because Ava's the same way." Saying her name hurt, and I rubbed my chest.

"You fell in love with her," he stated, as if it was nothing, his eyes still fixed on Riley.

"I don't know what I did." It was an honest answer. We'd never said the word, although I'd sensed it pushing for recognition. It had seemed too early, although now I wished I had told her it had been taking root and burrowing into my heart.

"So this is the infamous Cade Slaughter." Mason Brinks was a tall man, solid build, muscles that weren't as prominent as his partner's, but still imposing. His green eyes mirrored the ones on his sister.

"And this is the not so infamous Mason Brinks and his lapdog, Tyson Raines."

Raines snarled, but Brinks put his hand out to stop him. "We're here because you let a rat into your ranks and now you've lost Ava. Don't go pulling some kind of rank of me, Slaughter."

"Considering you let a rat in your ranks who took your sister, I wouldn't trade barbs with me, Brinks."

"Enough," Greyson said, his voice with an authority he had still been developing when I'd seen him last.

A pile of ebony hair ducked around Greyson's arm, her green eyes so bright they almost shimmered. She was a beauty, but I'd known that from pictures even if they didn't do her justice.

"Did you two make up?" she asked. Serious and confident. This woman matched my brother perfectly. Not the spirited bundle of energy that Ava was, but still just as bold.

"Yes," I answered. "Let's go inside."

I led them into the house.

"So that makes you my brother-in-law," she said, her eyes perceptively taking in the room.

"Where are your other men?" Brinks asked, stepping in front of Riley.

"She seems like she can defend herself, Brinks. And I'm sure if I made a move, Grey would break my hand and then I'd break his neck, of course."

He sneered, and I evaluated him, seeing the striking similarities to his sister. They looked more alike than Greyson and I did.

"My men are around."

Donelli's daughter screamed as Pack stepped from a corner.

"Like I said, they're around. Stand down Raines, if you shoot my second, I'll have to kill you to even the odds."

"Angie, get over here," he scolded, and I could see the relief as he tucked his gun back in his pants.

"It's like gathering children for story-time," Greyson muttered. I could see the reflexive twitch in Riley's arm like she wanted to elbow him, but she stayed in control. This was still a serious situation, one that could erupt at any second.

"There's so much testosterone in this room it's smothering." I surveyed a mop of curls that bounced as a curvy petite woman walked around the room, her eyes fixed on the computer and map set up in the center.

"And you are?" I asked. She was the only one I didn't know, although I vaguely remembered seeing her in intel pictures on the Donelli's. Something about her being Donelli's accountant nudged the back of my mind, but I couldn't place her name.

"My sister," Raines said.

"Casey," she said, hopping over to Mason, who threw his arm around her shoulder.

That piece of information I didn't know, other than hearing her name from Ava, but then, my intel had been off since this debacle began. I looked between the two men. "Bet that went over well," I muttered.

"Oh, he's so like you, Grey," Riley said, and my sight flew to her. I had never heard anyone call him Grey except me.

"We're nothing alike," he grumbled.

"Keep telling yourself that," she said, giving me a smile.

I suddenly sensed the loss of Ava's presence even heavier than I had and my mood dropped further.

"We're losing time," I said, my words terse. "The imposters are using a warehouse as a front for their business. I have men scouting it and the residence of their leader, Henley." I walked over to the map we had spread out on the table. "He's the one who was running the trafficking business under my nose. We flushed him out, but he went underground, and we only just found him again. We haven't figured out how they're getting the girls in or out but suspect it's some kind of tunnel system below the warehouse."

"How many men does he have?" Brinks asked, coming closer to the map, his eyes sharp as they flicked over it.

"The estimate is fifty, spread between the two locations, based on what our operative has reported," Pack said, coming over to the table.

"This is Pack. He's my second."

Nods around, then focuses returned to the map.

"Fifty is a lot more than we have," Raines said.

"And more than I have left. With the team here, I have eleven. The rest of my men are at my second safe house and they only make up another ten."

"You don't have them here because you don't trust them." Greyson met my sight.

"Correct. Their crew all have a tattoo of a snake on them in different spots on their bodies. Damn copycats trying to replicate what I've built." Crimson slashed my vision, and I fisted my hand. "We checked all our guys and only found one, which we eliminated, but the rest of my team is new, replacements brought in to cover the losses and I won't risk one of them betraying me while I'm trying to get to Ava."

"So that makes twenty with our men, not counting the three of us," Brinks said.

"Numbers that could work." It was Casey who spoke this time. "If you play it right and time it right. They'll have their guard up, especially if this is a trap to lure you in." She sat on the corner of a chair, pulling her curls into a knot on her head as she talked. "Ava is a valuable commodity and if they're smart enough to pull off all the shit they pulled in Armina and at home, they'll have double the security."

"But they messed up in Armina," Angie said.

"Who runs your family, Brinks? You or your women?"

He glared at me, but it was Riley who said, "I wouldn't let Ava hear that. She'd surely lecture you about how insulting that was."

I couldn't help but chuckle. "All while standing with her hands on her hips."

"Exactly," she said, giving me another smile. I suddenly knew why my brother loved her. The warmth of that smile bled through layers of ice that only Ava had ever melted.

"Does the warehouse shut down for the day?" Raines asked, his finger moving between the warehouse and the home that was marked on the map.

"No. Twenty-four-seven, so we have to contend with civilians. Although they run on a skeleton crew at night."

"Smart," Greyson observed. "What do they make?"

I rubbed my head. "Furniture. Mostly tables and chairs. Some overly ornate bed frames specialty made. All their furniture is oversized and almost gaudy. They call the beds princess frames so you can tell the clientele they cater to."

"Oh! I have one of those!" Angie Donelli had a pitch to her voice that reminded me of nails on a chalkboard when she hit the right tone. She was a true mafia princess. Spoiled by her father. Beautiful by any standard, with freckles that splashed over her cheeks and a distinct birthmark that gave her character. But as beautiful as any of these women were, they weren't Ava and didn't hold a candle to her in my eyes.

The thought had that ache in my chest growing. I wanted her back so badly it was almost debilitating.

"You do?" Raines asked her.

"Yeah, Daddy bought it for me years ago. I told him I didn't want that style because it was too frumpy, but he insisted, saying I needed it because of what it did. I had to get a pink bed skirt to cover it so no one would know it was so ugly on the bottom."

"Focus, Angela," he said to her. "What do you mean, what it did?"

"The bottom is a hiding place." She looked at us like we should have known that, but we all just stared at her. "He said if anyone ever stormed the house, I was to run to my room and hide in it. There's a tiny hole at the end of the frame to slip your finger in and slide it open. He had me try it over and over until I could do it in under two minutes. But it's tiny and so cramped."

My heart pounded, my skin getting clammy. "That's how they've been shipping the girls out." Ava was terrified of enclosed, dark spaces. The thought of her in one had me gripping the table so I didn't stumble.

"The perfect hiding spot," Mason mused as Greyson held my gaze, keen to my emotions. "Ensure the truck is temperature regulated, there's enough air for breathing, and you're doing nothing more than delivering furniture. No questions from the authorities. No suspicion turned to the buyer if there are any witnesses."

Riley moved closer to Greyson, whose sight was still on me.

"If we don't get to her in time, they'll put her in one of those," I told him. "It will kill her." The need to get to her spiraled, climbing through my limbs and causing the blood to thrum through my veins.

"I know. We'll get her in time, Mer."

I couldn't answer.

Mason flipped through the pictures Rudy had given me. Pulling out one of the tables being loaded into a delivery truck, he said, "The compartments are in the tables, too."

He tilted the picture, studying it before he put it down and pointed to the space where the tabletop extended down in thick pieces of wood. To the untrained eye, they looked like expensive maple tables with an inside lip with decorative engravings on it. But in reality, that space contained one, maybe two women, cramped into the box until they could get them to the buyer.

I rubbed my hand over my chin. Light was fading, and the warehouse was an hour from our location.

"What's the plan?" Mason asked, looking up at me.

"One they won't expect," I answered, shaking off the fear and remembering who I was, who we were dealing with, and what was at stake.

Chapter Twenty-Seven

AVA

I didn't know how long I laid there, but the longer I did, the more the room closed around me. The light flickered often, leaving me in the pitch black for seconds that lasted an eternity. Suddenly I was young again and thrust into that basement, my nails breaking against the door, then just as quickly, the sensation was gone. Over and over, this continued until I squeezed my eyes tight. All my years of training fled, leaving me as helpless as a female character in a bad horror movie. Not that I could do much. My hands kept falling asleep because the binds were so tight and there was no hope of freeing my ankles from the rope that bound them.

I dozed, the exhaustion of the last few hours getting to me, but the sound of a lock jolted me from my sleep. Raising my eyes toward the door, I watched as the flirty guy from Emerson's house strolled into the room.

"Hello cutie." He waved a bandaged hand. "Remember me?"

"You're vile," I spouted as he stooped down in front of me.

"If I'd known your tits were that nice, I would have fucked you in his kitchen."

Anger, like boiling lava, bubbled in my veins. "When he finds me, I'll make sure he takes your entire hand this time."

"Oh, he won't find you, Ava." He stood and pulled a syringe from his pocket.

I bucked and struggled to get away from him, but he put his palm over my face, holding it into the mattress. Another sting of the needle and I couldn't keep my eyes open anymore.

"It's time to get you ready for your new owner." His last words bounced through my consciousness until they faded with everything else.

PITCH ENVELOPED ME. Something pinned my body. My hands were to my side, my legs straight out. I could wiggle and pick my head up about an inch, but nothing more before I hit something solid. I turned my head back and forth but could see nothing. My chest seized, my breaths so shallow, my heart pounding so rapidly I thought I was dying.

I was trapped. In the dark. Terror crawled from my belly, its sharp claws leaving a trail until it scraped through my throat and out of my mouth with a screech I didn't recognize. I turned my arms over and pressed my palms to the solidness, detecting wood grains.

A box. I was in some kind of wooden box. A compact, dark box. My mind raced in competition with my heart and all stability I had left whooshed from my body as horror replaced it. My screams were loud. My tears as wet as the blood from my nails that were splitting. With panic and terror encompassing me, I continued to scream until my throat was raw and my voice was hoarse. When the screams stopped, my hold on my body broke and panic swept through it, triggering my body's preservation mode, and I blacked out.

Chapter Twenty-Eight

EMERSON

The drive to the warehouse seemed never ending. My thoughts raced, my nerves were on edge, and my muscles were so tight I could feel the strain of them in my neck and shoulders. I stored only a few cars at my safe house, but there were enough to fit us all. After a heated debate, Casey stayed back with Riley and Angie. Her brother and Mason went a few rounds with her before she gave in. One look from Greyson had Riley stopping her own attempt and Angie had already sprawled on my couch filing her nails and watching television with no desire to leave her spot.

Greyson tapped his fingers on his knees next to me. "Ava told you about her stepfather. That's why you called that day."

I kept my eyes trained on the passing scenery. "Yes. I'd like to drain the lake he's in and kill him a few more times."

"Trust me, Den made him pay. There wasn't much left of his face when Den brought the head to Bridgeville. I didn't ask where he put the eyes and tongue." He flicked a speck of dirt from his pants.

"Good." It offered me some relief to know the man had suffered.

"When did you fall for her?" he asked.

It was a valid question. One I wasn't certain I could quantify. "I don't really know. The minute she opened her mouth?"

"Figures. Of all the women to tame you, Ava, with her constant chattering would be the one."

"I like the chattering."

"You would." He tipped his head back. "You always liked mouthy women."

"And Riley's not?"

His laugh was deep. "No. Don't get me wrong, she's tougher than she looks, but she's more like me."

"It's you silent types who are always the ones to watch," I joked.

A truck rumbled by, its lights blinding. Pack looked at me through the rearview mirror. Den sat next to him, his neck thick with strain. He hadn't sat still since Greyson introduced him, but the menacing glares he'd given me let me know his opinion of me. Not that I hadn't returned them with my own.

"We're five minutes out, boss."

The light mood disappeared, the anticipation and adrenaline returning. My phone buzzed, and I looked down to see Rudy's message that he and his men had cleared out. I had warned him we were on our way, not wanting them in the crossfire. This was my fight, not his.

A second text covered his before I could finish reading it. This one was from the team who had guarded my safe house. They were in place, ready to clear the workers out. The road crested and the town of Ludburough appeared. It was a small, industrial town that sat in the open hills of Kingsport. A few factories, one stop-light, and a handful of residents.

"If they're hiding the girls in the tables, then the workers aren't as oblivious as we assumed," Greyson said.

"Unless they only ship them at certain times."

"After the key staff has left." He pulled his phone up and I watched over his shoulder as he searched the company Henley was using as his front. "Working hours are seven to six." He scrolled further, tapping to a new screen. "I think it's safe to assume anyone on that factory floor is armed and dangerous."

I texted the team leader in place just as we pulled into sight. *How many guards on the perimeter? How many people inside?*

Five outside. Four inside, two are definitely on patrol.

Assume the others are armed and proceed with caution once we're in place.

I sent the same message to my men in the third SUV just as another message came in. Confirmation that the men from my second safe house were in place to raid Henley's home. I hadn't given them any details on Greyson's arrival or our plans, hoping if there was a traitor in that team, they would alert Henley and distract his attention from the warehouse. Either way, it worked in my favor. Henley would be nervous for the first time since this began, or he would be unaware of the battle I was bringing to him, still expecting me to come storming in by myself.

Pack pulled up just short of the warehouse and we all peeled out of the cars. Checking my guns, I walked over to Brinks and Raines.

"My men go in first." I gestured for Pack to take the team we had discussed. Pulling down his mask, he disappeared with them into the night.

"Ski masks?"

"There's a reason my men are called ghosts, Brinks."

"Then why not do this on your own?"

The flood lights went out. "Because the men in that warehouse know everything my men know. Training for my men is extensive and military style. Only recently did I have to take shortcuts and turn to on-the-job training. Those men down there are the best of my team, but many of the men in that building match their skill. They may have fooled you into believing they were sloppy, but they played you."

The emergency system kicked in and dull yellow lit the building. I sent a quick text to my man leading the team at Henley's house with the okay to attack, then pointed to the ten men who filed out of the warehouse, guns drawn.

"That's why I needed more men."

"Den, take the next team in." Greyson's order was terse and emotionless. This was business, and my brother was as cool and collected as ever.

"I'm ready to cause some damage," Raines said. He had a reputation for violence. The muscle of Mason's family. No one crossed him and lived, so no one dared cross him just like they didn't dare cross me or my brother. Until these assholes got arrogant and thought they could take all of us on. Their mistake.

"Let's get my wildcat back," I said, pulling out my gun and rising from my spot.

"Wildcat?" asked Raines.

"Better than viper," I taunted, hearing the rumbled growl from him.

"Time to do some damage like old times, brother?" Greyson asked, slapping his hand on my shoulder.

"Just don't get yourself killed before we can sit down with a glass of scotch and hash our differences out."

"Yeah, I don't want to see my sister all ragged and depressed again, Tides. No dying."

Greyson tucked two guns under his suit jacket and took the safety off the one in his hand. "Considering you and Raines are the ones with recent gunshot wounds, I think it's you two who need to be careful."

"Fuck you, Tides." I could tell Mason meant the response to be harsh, but there was an undercurrent of humor in his words.

As we stalked into the fight, I considered the irony that Henley and the other traitors had intended to turn us against each other, but had instead succeeded in bringing us together.

Our men cleared out the exterior guards, but inside was a

chaos of gunshots and yelling. I'd taken time to run the other teams through what to look for from Henley's men. Tricks and moves that made the Omens so lethal. I'd hated to lose the valuable time but if I lost Grey and Mason's men within the first few minutes of the fight, I would never make it to Ava.

We ran into the fray, avoiding bodies and bullets. Mason and Raines took the right flank, while Greyson and I took the left. A bullet clipped my shoulder, and I cursed at the sting of pain. As I moved further into the chaos, I lost sight of Greyson and the others. The fight was brutal, but the thought of Ava hurt, or worse, fed my fury. It seemed a never ending battle, and the bruises were compounding with every punch I took and gave and every bullet that narrowly missed me.

The flow of Henley's men slowed, but I spotted the door they were emerging from. A stairway that led to the tunnels we'd suspected housed the true operation. I found Pack and motioned for him to follow me, but I spotted the gun raised across from me too late. A bullet tore through the shooter's head before his finger could release the trigger at his target: me. The bullet freed as his body fell, just missing my head. Greyson's intense eyes held mine for an instant before he turned his gun on another victim. My brother had always been an excellent shot, but I suspected the scar he carried from my bullet had encouraged him to become the best.

I rushed to the stairs with Pack at my rear. There had been no sign of Henley or the two who had taken Ava. Pointing my gun down the hole, I started down the stairs. It was too quiet. The fight was slowing above, but down below, there was silence. Stepping over the first body, I suspected I was late to the party. A trail of bodies, some with smashed faces, others with bullet wounds, all dead.

As I reached an open space, I found Raines lounging against the doorframe, his legs crossed, a smirk that was in stark contrast to the blood that covered him including some of his own where a bullet had grazed his temple.

"You Omen with your fancy ghost moves took too long. Rage and muscles do just as much damage."

Mason stood in the room with his arms crossed, blood dripping from a wound in his arm. "These your guys?"

The face tattoo guy and the flirty one were on their knees, their hands tied in front of them, their faces bruised and bloody. Henley was next to them. Emotionless and hard, he stared ahead. I was glad he hadn't been in the crossfire at the house because I had plans for him. Brutal and lengthy plans.

"Remind me to never get on your bad side, Raines," I muttered. "Did you find her?"

"No. There are plenty of other women and girls locked down here, but no Ava."

"You won't find her," Henley sneered.

I walked over to him. He had been one of my best. Too smart and cocky for his own good. Too proud and confident, thinking he could run a business without me noticing, then run me out of town. He had hidden the business under my nose for years and been close to taking me down, but he had underestimated me like my enemies always did.

"Where is she?" I placed my gun to his temple, but I knew he wouldn't tell me. He was too tough, no amount of torture would break him.

"She'll be entertaining her new owner soon. I was going to sell her to a decent buyer, but that mouth of hers let me know she needs a man who can put her in her place, on her knees where she belongs. He'll make sure that mouth is only good for one thing."

My fist met snapping cartilage when I punched him right before the blunt end of my gun hit the side of his temple and sent him crumbling on the floor. I walked past the face tattoo, going to the one who had blatantly flirted with Ava. The pretty boy.

"Pack, you got that knife with you? The one with the good blade?"

Pretty boy blanched.

"Don't tell him anything, Chad," the other guy said.

"Chad?" I snickered. "You really are out of your element, aren't you? One of Henley's hires, because if you'd worked for me, your terror wouldn't be so obvious."

Pack's knife was smooth in my hand, and I rubbed my finger along the blade, drawing blood at the tip and licking it.

"Hold him for me and someone shut that other one up."

"Kill him?" Brinks asked.

I glanced over at him, seeing the lethal gleam in his eyes. As much as I'd teased him when we met, Mason Brinks had earned his place among the families with as much skill and brutality as my brother and I had.

"Nah, that would be too easy."

He knocked the guy out within seconds. Pack had a firm hold on Chad, who was doing a terrible job fighting him.

"Raines, kick that crate over here, will you? I like a little leverage."

He sent the crate toward me, and I stopped it with my foot.

Chad thrashed more, but Pack was a wall of solid muscle. There was no getting free of him. I grabbed Chad's hand that still had the bandage on it from where I'd impaled it with my knife, spread his middle finger out and took it off with one swipe of the knife.

His scream was piercing as I evaluated the knife. "It always cuts so smooth," I said to Pack, hearing Raines snicker.

Chad continued to scream, and I took his face in my hand, holding the bloody knife to his neck. "You're going to tell me where my girl is, and I'll have your finger bagged on ice so you can get it reattached. If you don't, then I'll continue to hack you up piece by piece, starting with your dick until you're ready to talk."

"They shipped her out already," he cried, too easily because he hadn't been one of my guys, trained by Pack. This was one Henley had hired on his own.

I tightened my hold on his face. "When and where?"

"Right before you got here. I don't know where."

"The truck," Greyson said from behind us. I looked over my shoulder at him. He looked like he'd just come from a board meeting, not a gunfight. "It passed us when we were on the road."

I remembered the truck rumbling by us. "Damn it. We need to find out where it's going and stop it."

I stormed away from Chad.

"Wait, my finger. You said—"

"I know what I said, but there's no sense in reattaching it if I'm just going to take it back off again. You three touched my girl. I plan to take a part of you for every look and every touch." I stalked closer and stooped before him. "And if any of you dared put your cock near her, I will cut it off inch by inch and feed it to you."

An embarrassing whimper came from him, along with a puddle of piss. "You picked the wrong business, Chad," I said as I walked away. "You should have stuck with modeling."

Greyson was at the computer console on the other end of the room, Den over his shoulder.

"Fuck," he muttered, "there's an entire database on here of all their buyers."

"Who doesn't lock their computer and their files?" Raines asked, joining us. "Nice job with the finger. I would have taken the entire hand, but the finger move had finesse."

I shook my head before responding to Greyson, "Novices who think they can run a business better than me." I leaned over Greyson as screens and names swept by. He stopped on a browser window, expanding it to reveal the name and dollar amount along with a delivery address. To anyone else, it looked like a simple furniture purchase. Only the ten million dollars wired as payment would have aroused suspicion.

"Ten million to get a piece of Cade Slaughter," Raines muttered. "That's impressive."

"They'll have stayed on back roads to avoid province police. If I take the highways, the destination is only two hours from here. I can catch them." I tucked my gun in my waistband and turned to go when Greyson's hand encompassed my shoulder.

"I'm going with you," he said.

Den stepped behind him. "As am I." His shirt was off, and he was wrapping a bandage around his stomach where blood ran from his side. "And I want a piece of the assholes who took her."

I blinked. "You're wounded."

"So are you," he returned. I rolled my shoulder in response, glad the bullet hadn't hit anything important.

"We'll stay here and clean up," Brinks said, ending the debate.

I didn't care to waste more time. I gave Mason a curt nod and stalked away with one thing on my mind: hunting down that truck and saving Ava.

Chapter Twenty-Nine

My mind flittered in and out of consciousness. My body was stiff and shaking uncontrollably. It was cold, but my anxiety had me sweating and my teeth chattered at the chill that wouldn't leave. I kept telling myself I was no longer a teenager locked in the basement, no longer a child easily frightened with an overactive imagination. That there were no monsters. But that was a lie. There were monsters. These men were prime examples. And they were shipping me off like I was a piece of property and not a person. To be owned when I didn't want to be owned. Another lie. I wanted Emerson to own me because I knew I was safe with him, that he would treat me like I was valuable, not a thing to be traded.

I wanted to go back to the prior night when he was bringing me to ecstasy, worshiping me like I was his goddess. Tears came again, and I fought them for only a few seconds. If I was going to cry, now was the time. I wouldn't let these men see me cry. They didn't deserve to see my tears or my fear. I wouldn't let them break me.

There was constant movement, rumbling under me like I was in a vehicle, and more tears spilled as I realized Emerson wouldn't find me now. Not with me locked away like this, on my way to a life that would be worse than anything I had experienced as a child. This couldn't be happening. It had to be a nightmare, and I would wake up soon to find Emerson's arms around me. I hadn't taken my medicine. That was all it was. A nightmare.

I continued to tell myself that, to convince myself that none of this was real, but the longer I did, the less confident my words became.

A jarring motion sent my body crashing hard into the side of the box and pain shooting up my arm. The vehicle had stopped, and my heart hammered. Fear shredded any remnants of positivity. The man who had bought me was out there and panic collapsed over me, stealing the air from my lungs and sending me into terror mode. I screamed and scraped, a final adrenaline surge flooding through me. I pounded my knuckles against the wood until they were bloody. What remained of my voice was a high-pitched squeak, but I kept screaming. Promising myself that I would fight this, that I would not let this man have me without a battle and if he killed me, then it was better than what he could do to me.

A loud rattling sound broke through the constant hum of the vehicle, and I heard shouting. Every instinct kicked in and I pounded more, screaming and crying. Terror seized me at the thought of what was coming, but the shouting escalated, raised and familiar. My fear changed to desperation, and I continued to fight against the restraint of the box, my screams raw screeches.

"Cut the unit!" I knew that voice and with it, an ache swelled in my chest. "I hear something!"

The hum stopped, and I screamed so loud my voice cracked. I hit the wood with my knees, ignoring how the skin split further, determined they would find me.

"Back here!"

Emerson. I recognized the low baritone of his voice, the emotion in it. He'd found me. Tears rushed from me as I yelled for him. Sounds of screeches and tumbling until my box shook. I pounded and bellowed until light streamed in at my head and hands pulled me out, enveloping me into arms I knew too well. I clutched at his shirt and inhaled his scent, letting his arms curl me into his body.

"Shh, I've got you, wildcat," he said, never letting go. Someone put a heavy blanket over me, but I didn't lift my head. My tears were flowing too freely, my body shaking too severely to do anything but cling to Emerson.

He stood and carried me. He tried to hand me to someone else at some point, but I clutched at him, curling further into his hold, and he relented. I felt him sit then drop down, the landing shaking me, but still he didn't let go. Hushed voices spoke, and I thought I recognized my uncle's voice. The soothing motion of a car and his embrace lulled me to sleep, exhaustion sweeping through me as the last of my adrenaline slipped away.

SPLASHES of consciousness mingled with a sleep so heavy I couldn't ignore it. Each time I came to, an oppressive fog weighed on me, but just beyond it, I sensed Emerson's presence. A calm in the storm that pulled me back under each time. There were times when I opened my eyes and his worried face came into focus. When I sensed his touch on my face before whatever drugs they had given me stole me away. Those lucid moments were short but enough for me to realize that the trauma had been so bad they had needed to give me sedatives.

Reality came and went, but Emerson was the steady beacon that kept me reaching back through the fog. I needed to stay conscious long enough to let him know I would be all right. That just knowing he was there, that I was safe now because of him, was enough to assuage the damage. When the darkness began to abate again, I fought to stay aware. A ragged breath filled my throat, and I sat up, only to have Emerson wrap me into his arms and lower me back to the bed. I opened my eyes fully to see him there.

"You found me," I said, my voice so raw I could barely hear it.

"I promised I would protect you." His eyes held such sadness. "I failed you, but I won't fail you again."

I reached my hand up to his cheek, seeing bandages over my knuckles and some of my fingers. The effort to hold it up was trying, and I was relieved when he took it and brought it to his mouth.

"You didn't fail me," I said, even though speaking hurt.

"You're hurt," he said, softly. "They hurt you, touched you, and I let that happen."

Guilt twisted his features, making them harder.

"No, Emerson. You saved me." I ran my finger over a cut on his cheek, eyeing the bruises on his face. "You fought for me, and you saved me."

"But you're still hurt, Ava," he said, dropping his head. "Shh, go back to sleep." He moved me against his chest, and I fought the heaviness of my eyes, losing my battle.

I BLINKED my eyes open again, this time without the heavy exhaustion that had weighed me down. Emerson was next to me, and as I moved toward him, he opened his eyes. A pained expression lined his features, and I wanted to remove it, knowing I was the cause.

"My life is dangerous, Ava."

I wasn't sure why he was telling me that, why it mattered.

"I like danger," I said, putting my hand on his cheek and kissing him. The kiss was so gentle, no sign of the aggressive man who left bruises from his intensity. This man thought I was fragile now, and I hated that he did.

"How long have I been sleeping, Emerson?"

"Three days." The regret in his voice was palpable.

His fingers pulled my hair forward.

"I told you I was a brunette," I said, trying to make his grimace disappear.

"I miss the blonde and pink." His thumb brushed over the side of my nose. "And the rhinestone."

"All of them," I said, frowning as I thought of what those assholes had done.

Eyes creasing further, he said, "All of them." He knew. Knew they'd touched me to take my piercings out. Based on my clean skin, he must have bathed me when we returned. Another soft, sweet side to a man who had killed for me.

Stretching, I sat up, swinging my legs over the side of the bed and waiting for my head to stop spinning. I felt like I'd been sleeping for days. But then again, I had.

"Careful," he said and his hand came to my back. "Let me help you."

"No, I'm fine. I just need to use the bathroom and..." I brought my hand to my mouth and breathed. "...find a toothbrush."

He chuckled, telling me there was one in the bathroom for me as I stood, ignoring the wobbling in my legs. My knees ached as the scabs on my cuts stretched, and my walk across the room was slow. By the time I peed and brushed my teeth, I felt human again. Taming my unruly hair proved futile, so I gave up and returned to the bed where Emerson was lying in the same spot, his hand behind his head, waiting for me.

Fully awake after so many days of rest, I climbed onto him, sitting on his chest and ignoring the slight discomfort in my knees. His shirt was off, and a bandage was on his shoulder. My fingers traced the bandage edge, hating that he'd been hurt.

Between the bruises on his face and this, I knew it had been a fight to the death to save me. He brought his hands to my waist, tentatively, like he was afraid to touch me.

"Did you kill them all?" I asked.

"Yes."

I captured his bottom lip, dragging my teeth over it. "Torture the ones who took me?"

A twitch of his lips and he said, "Still torturing. I expect they might bleed to death before I remove any more parts, but maybe another day or so of suffering before I send them to hell."

I lifted the T-shirt he must have put on me, watching his eyes light, then dim when I threw it aside.

"My therapist once told me to find ways to distract myself from my terrible memories," I said, bringing his hands to my breasts. "I think it's time for distraction, Emerson."

"Ava, I don't think—"

"I don't want you to think, Emerson. We take risks. You and me. It's what we do. We don't play it safe, and we don't let the past do anything but feed our need to conquer more of life." His hands moved, caressing my breasts. "I want you to distract me. To remove their unwelcome touches from me and replace them with yours."

His eyes darkened, his hands stilling. "Did they..."

This was the man who killed without remorse and now killed for me. The unhinged mafia boss who took no prisoners and left a trail of bodies in his wake.

"No, they just stole my piercings. Assholes. That's gonna be a pain in the ass to replace them all."

"I'll buy you diamonds for the next ones."

His hands moved to my waist, squeezing it and causing a gasp to flee my mouth. He picked me up and pulled me forward so that my hands hit the wall to stop my movement.

"Sit on my face, wildcat. Let me lick that clit while it's bare, so I can see if you taste any different."

A storm of flurries ricocheted through my stomach. I lifted and settled over him as his fingers dug into my thighs. I let thoughts of all that had happened go and closed my eyes as his tongue reminded me of his claim on my body. He licked and sucked and kissed until my climax roared through me with a ferocity that burned away the memory of any other hands on me.

His hand moved past my leg as I rode out the remaining waves of my release and I heard his zipper. Picking me up, he positioned me over him. I guided him into me, throwing my head back as he filled me completely. He pulled me down, his mouth capturing mine, and I lost myself further to him. Touches that were powerful and firm drove my body closer to another climax.

"That's it, sweetheart. Come for me again." His blue irises were as dark as a stormy day, his hoarse voice so sexy it sent my desire climbing. My body was no longer mine to control. It was his. He owned it and it would bow to his every wish. I leaned back on his thighs while his hands twisted my nipples and squeezed my breasts.

"Fuck, you're gorgeous," he muttered. Hands on my waist, his eyes stayed on me, watching me climax for him.

Every rise and fall of my body brought me closer to falling apart and as my release hit, I watched him crumble with me, our bodies destroyed as one. He yanked me down, kissing me so fiercely it was like a brand on my soul. He held my hips down, exploding inside of me, filling me while my body convulsed around him.

I collapsed completely on him and his hands slid up my back. They played in my hair as my head rested on his chest. His hold on me was so powerful, it almost seemed like he was soaking me in, like he would never hold me again. I snuggled into that hold, worry invading and shoving the rapture aside.

"You're letting me go," I said into his chest. I didn't know how I knew, but I did. His comment about danger earlier, the intense way he was holding me, revealed more than he wanted.

He didn't answer me. "Get some sleep, Ava."

I tried to pick my head up, but he kept me against him.

"Emerson…" But I didn't know what to say. We'd known this was going to happen. Two weeks. Separate lives, separate coasts. "Did I hear my uncle's voice?"

"He's here with Greyson. They'll take you home tomorrow."

"I don't have a choice in that?"

His hold loosened, and I looked up at him.

"You have a life, Ava. Family, friends, school. All I have is danger. There's nothing for you here, and I won't endanger your safety by keeping you here."

"We take chances, Emerson. That's who we are."

The space between his eyes knitted. "With business, but not with you. I won't take a chance of you getting hurt again."

We were risk takers and both of us had taken a risk with this. And now he was pulling away because that risk had been too great. On all fronts. This was why we never got close. Why he never let women in, and I never let men in. There hadn't been one worth letting in before.

"So, you save my life and then it's goodbye?" I moved from him, but he rolled over, caging me. His beautiful eyes looked between mine and he brushed his thumb over my cheek.

"I don't want to give you up, Ava, but you were never mine to own."

Yes, I was. The words sought to leave my mouth, but I couldn't let them. I had no fight left in me and I didn't think I had the words to change a fate that had sat over us since the moment I fell for Emerson Tides.

I pulled him to me, hating this, hating that he was right. That we had our separate lives, and they didn't coincide. I kissed him, resigned to not fight it like I hadn't fought falling for him, but knowing that walking away from this would hurt me more than anything those men could have done to me.

I WOKE THE NEXT MORNING, my body blissfully satisfied. Emerson's touches and kisses like a lingering ghost on my skin. Looking over at the empty space in the bed, my chest caved. He had made love to me, the emotion fierce, the touches deliberate and slow, soaking in the memory of my skin. And now he was gone.

A note sat on his pillow, and I sat up, pulling the sheets to my chest.

For all that I didn't say, I'm sorry. You have changed me forever, wildcat.

Conquer the world, and when you're done, if my mark remains, find me.

I understood then why he had pulled away. Left me. It wasn't just to keep me out of danger. It was a chance for space. To test if it had been real or something that only existed because I'd developed some attachment to him as my captor. That damned syndrome I couldn't remember the name of.

My head hit the pillow hard, sending the down puffing around it. He was right. We needed time apart. Our lives were so different. Even if we had met each other under different circumstances, becoming involved with a man like Emerson Tides was like stepping into a hornet's nest and hoping you didn't get stung. It meant danger and more. He didn't want me in that danger, but if I chose to face it, he would be there. Only if it was my choice and not some byproduct of a kidnapping.

I held the note to my chest. This had happened so fast that it couldn't be real. But every part of me screamed it was. That no matter the space and time apart, I would still need him. I looked over, seeing my meds on the side table and knowing he had ensured I took them even when I slept. Always taking care of me, putting me before his needs. My morally gray man who had taken down his enemy with no hesitation to save me.

The energy to get up was hard to muster, but I managed to, finding a clean set of clothes in the bathroom along with a small box. I left it there, showering first, not ready to open it, to say my last goodbye to him. I knew he was gone. Understood that last night had been his goodbye, but this was one last gesture from him like the note on the pillow.

After dressing, I sat on the side of the bed and opened the box. In a nest of black velvet sat a collection of diamonds to replace my piercings. I tugged the tiny note below them. *No other man gets to see these. You wear them only when you're ready for me to see them.*

I closed the lid, shaking my head. "Confusing bastard." Letting me go, but still laying a claim. An offer to come back to him just like the note. The promise for me to clear my head, let the events of the last two weeks settle, then see if I still loved him.

The note scrunched in my hand, a swelling pressure building in my chest. Love? Was that what this was? He loved me enough to let me go, and I loved him enough to let him go. To test that love and see if it lasted when distance and life stood between us.

Sadness had seeped its way into my bones while I'd been in the shower, but now it crept away because I knew this wasn't good-bye. Knew no matter how many beautiful brunettes crossed his path, Emerson Tides would only have his mind on me. That the hottest man could tempt me at the bar and I'd know there was no temptation because the only man who could truly worship my body was on the other side of the country, thinking about me.

Taking the box, I made my way downstairs. Hugs from Den and Riley. A curt nod with a half-smile from Greyson, which was more than I usually got. The plane ride was long and the further I traveled from Emerson, the greater the tug at my core that reminded me I would always be tethered to that place on the coast and the man who filled it.

Riley chatted about how Greyson had arranged for me to make up the missed time at school. I had already finished my thesis, but I had missed my presentation. They would overlook my time away and reschedule, allowing me to walk and collect my degree in a special ceremony. My job was still there, my boss not caring that I had missed so many days. Life would return, but I wasn't sure it would ever be normal again. Emerson had said I changed him, but he had changed me, too.

As the conversation died down, I pulled the new drawing book out that Emerson had left for me and began to draw.

Chapter Thirty

EMERSON

Leaving Ava had been the toughest thing I'd ever faced. I hadn't intended to, had wanted to keep her with me, to never let her go. But seeing her so fragile and hurt that night had opened my eyes to the dangers she faced with me. I couldn't keep her in this world. She had stayed sheltered for so many years and she was safer under my brother's watch. Her uncle would ensure she stayed that way, just like he always had.

But that excuse had only been part of the reason I'd left her. I needed to know if it had been real. If the emotions would remain with distance and time or fade because it had only been the situation causing them. And if they remained, then to offer her the power to return on her own. Not me forcing her into my life like I had, but her choosing that life. A life with me, a life of danger. As much as I hated the thought of being without her, I wanted her safe. The thought of anything else happening to her killed me, but if she decided I was worth taking the chance, then I would accept her decision and find every way in my power to ensure no one hurt her again.

Needing my mind off her, which was difficult to do, I threw myself into rebuilding my businesses, cleaning up the messes

Henley and his idiots had made. I denounced all association with trafficking after seeing for myself how horrendous it was. My reputation didn't need that stain. The girls we found we had freed, returning them to their homes and giving funds to those who had no home so they could start a new life. A convenient fire at the warehouse had left it in ashes and in its place, I was building a women's shelter, with Jill leading the helm. The men in Henley's database had suffered for their crimes and I had buried the remains of Henley and the other two who had touched Ava in the caved in tunnels. Every one of their last breaths had given me exquisite satisfaction.

Being in the house without Ava was miserable. All the little places she had left her mark reminded me of her. I kept the gray scarf I had taken from her the fateful night she'd come into my life next to my bed, picking it up every so often and inhaling her scent just to keep me sane.

My phone rang, and I picked up Greyson's call. "Have you given it any thought?" Always right to the point.

"Hello to you, too, Grey."

"I don't have time for formalities, jackass. You know who it is."

Chuckling, I said, "Yes. It's a good offer."

"Good? I don't take partners, Mer. This offer is the only one you'll ever get from me and the best."

"Maybe, but I don't like partners either, Grey. Too messy and you can't trust them."

His growl had me laughing harder. "Fine. I accept. Partners again, but this time dominating both coasts. It's an empire that will be hard to take down, Grey."

"Exactly. Just play nice. With Brinks in my life, Donelli and Strint are allies. Don't piss them off and don't get in their territories."

"I don't play nice."

"Neither do I, but apparently we both do now."

"How was she?" I asked, watching a car come down the street.

"Why don't you ask her yourself? She should be there about now to change before the party."

The car pulled up to the curb.

"You're so whipped now. Parties? Since when do you do parties?"

He hung up on me, and I laughed, knowing I'd pissed him off. One of Greyson's men left the car and looked around, his eyes landing on me. He had known to expect me and gave me a gesture of acknowledgement. He opened the door, and my heart leaped so hard against my chest that I almost lurched forward. Ava gave him a big smile, talking about something as she reached back into the car and grabbed her things. He said something to her and her eyes flitted to me, growing large. Her smile spread to light every part of her face.

The car left. Greyson's man knew I had her covered. I had my men hidden in enough places to take out anyone who got within ten feet of her.

She strolled toward me, and I took her in. She looked beautiful in a black dress that flattered her curves. The hem came to her mid-thigh, the sleeves short and leaving enough skin to turn me on. Her brown hair darkened her eyes to a rich chocolate and the diamond in her nose sparkled in the sun.

A single text had flashed on my phone that morning. *I'm ready to conquer the world, but only if you're with me.* And I had dropped everything to get there. It was the message I'd been waiting for, but one I hadn't expected for months. Not one month later. Not the morning of her graduation.

"I thought I told you no wearing my diamonds for anyone but me?" I said when she was close enough. She held her gown, cap, and diploma in her hand.

"I didn't break that rule," she said. "You're here, aren't you?"

"So, I am."

"Are your ready for me, Emerson Tides?"

I reached out and weaved my hand around her neck, then pulled her to me. "I've been ready for you my entire life, Avani Shelton."

She scrunched her nose. "That's gross, considering I wasn't even born when you were a teenager."

I shut her up with a kiss, digging my fingers into her curls and wrapping my other hand around her waist to bring her flush against me. Her things fell and her hands came up over my shoulders and into my hair, pulling my head down closer. If anything in my life had ever felt right, it was this moment. Being away from her had been like having half my soul stripped from me and stretched across endless miles, clinging by a fragile string. Now that string wove through me, repairing the damage and ensuring it would forever be whole as long as she remained with me.

"I love you, Emerson Tides," she said, our lips parting. Her words resounded through me like a storm, washing over the broken pieces of the man I'd been before her and securing them. "It has nothing to do with how we met and everything to do with you. No amount of time apart will change that, so please don't leave me again."

I brushed her hair back, tucking it behind her ear. "I miss the pink," I said, kissing her smile. "I didn't tell you the truth that night." Her eyes dimmed, smile dropping. "Because I couldn't even admit it to myself. It wasn't until you were gone that I realized how real it was. How every woman I saw only reminded me more of what I had set free."

"Did you..."

"No. Shit, Ava, that's where your mind went?" My eyes narrowed. "Did you?"

She shook her head. "There's only you now."

I took her face in my hands. "And there is only you. I loved you the moment you opened your mouth and looked up defiantly at me, wildcat. But I couldn't admit it because it was too soon, too convoluted and only when I drove away from you did I realize how wrong I was in not telling you. I love you Ava and if you really want to conquer the world with me at your side, I'm here and I will never leave."

She reached her hands around my neck and pulled me into another kiss. This time, I wrapped both arms around her waist and picked her up the last few inches, holding her against me like I never wanted to release her.

"So, do you have all my diamonds in?" I asked, nibbling her lip.

"Yes." Her response was breathless.

"Then I think it's time for me to see them, sweetheart." I scooped her into my arms.

"My things!" she squealed.

"Don't worry, one of my guys will get them." I opened the door and took her upstairs, letting her guide me until we were in her apartment and I couldn't control myself.

I pressed her against the wall, hiking her skirt up and finding every piercing with my mouth. Her cries I put to memory with the tug of my hair in her hands and the feel of her thighs quaking around my shoulders as I held her up. As she tumbled, I caught her, thrusting into her while she rode out the climax around me. I lost myself in her, knowing I would never be apart from her again, that nothing in this world would bring me the pleasure of her warmth, of her body, of her cries. She tugged my mouth to hers, clenching her heels into me and sending me so deep I grunted. My release perched on the precipice, waiting to chase hers and as I sensed hers climbing, I bit her lip and said, "Show me how much you missed me, sweetheart. Come for me again, like a good girl."

Her head fell back, her body swept up as she broke, taking me over the edge with her. I held her there, pinned against the wall, our bodies one as the rush of my orgasm thundered through me.

"You own me, Emerson," she breathed. "All of me."

"That's what I like to hear." I nuzzled her neck before letting her legs go. "Now be a good girl and clean up. We have a graduation party to attend and I'm going to have a tough time sharing you with anyone else for the day."

She pulled my head down and kissed me. "I promise I'm all yours when it's over."

"Damn right you are. And that dress stays on because I plan to strip it from you when we get back, although I might have you leave the heels. That's a sexy look."

I really wanted to keep her in her apartment for the rest of the day, but since I'd missed her graduation, I had to at least make it up to her by going to the party with her. She didn't have to know that was why I was subjecting myself to this, but it was the reason. Besides, it would give me time to talk more to my brother about this new venture we were about to enter. The Tides empire expanding across the provinces. Now that I'd taken my real name, people were even more frightened of me. It had me looking forward to the next chapter in my life, the one that would involve Ava at my side.

Later that night, after hours of discussion with Greyson and Brinks that unfortunately involved Raines, after hours of keeping my eye on Ava as she bounced around the party, talking and laughing, drinking and eating, smiling like she was the center of the world, I took her back to her apartment and ravaged her a few more times.

My fingers ran through her hair as hers drifted over my tattoos. She lifted, studying my Omen tattoo and peeking up at me. "You changed it?"

I had. Adding that annoying snake Henley had used to the center of the dagger. Its head came out of the skull socket, its tail out the side of the mouth, but the dagger plunged into its middle, blood dripping from it. A sign that I had crushed my enemy and a warning to anyone else who wanted to fuck with me. Henley had left me at rock bottom, ready to give up, but Ava had brought me back to life.

"I added another one, too." I twisted to show her the new one on my shoulder blade she hadn't noticed in our frenzied lust for one another.

"A wildcat," she said, tracing the jaguar I'd added the day I returned home without her. She followed its movement, its hind feet springing, jaws wide and ready to attack its prey. "You got that for me?"

She looked back at me, her eyes misty.

"I needed a reminder of you," I admitted.

"I love you," she said, laying across my chest.

"Always," I said. "And forever."

Her kiss was soft, leading to more, and I realized this was what life with Ava would be. Filled with the danger that had always been there, but now with smiles and kisses, laughter and love. Things I'd never known I needed, but ones I knew I could no longer live without.

Epilogue

EMERSON

"Stop fidgeting," Greyson told me.

"I hate these monkey suits. This is why I don't do those fancy events you go to."

"Would you two stop?" Mason scolded, and I shot him a look. "The music is starting. Get your shit together up there."

I tugged at my necktie. Tuxes were confining, and I hated them. It was one reason I rarely wore full suits.

The doors opened and Angie walked in, her dress a soft blue that complimented the decorations of the venue. She wore a white scarf around her shoulders as a cape, its ends twisting over her arms where she held a bouquet of white roses with blue frosted tips.

"Damn, I'm going to enjoy ripping that off her later," Tyson muttered.

"Really?" I asked. "This is a wedding, not a frat party."

"Shut up Tides... Shit, I can't say that anymore without pissing you both off. Just keep your mouth shut or I might just fuck her while we're here."

I bunched my hands.

"Why are we doing this again?" he asked.

But my eyes were on Ava as Greyson hissed, "Because I promised Riley a Christmas wedding and since she didn't get it, we're renewing our vows this Christmas. Now shut up before my fist shuts you up."

I would have joined in, but I couldn't tear my eyes from how gorgeous Ava looked. She had bleached her hair blonde again, and added the pink streaks to it that I adored. Her diamond sparkled in the side of her nose, her brown eyes shimmering brightly with gold eyeshadow highlighting them. She gave me a ravishing smile and took her spot next to Angie. The rest of the ceremony went by in a blur because I couldn't stop looking at her. Even as Riley came down the aisle in a gown fit for a winter fairy and she and Grey exchanged vows, Ava was the only thing on my mind.

It seemed like I had come full circle. Standing in as my brother's best man for a wedding I had once tried to destroy in my desperation. Being accepted into this strange, sometimes high tension, family he now had and having the joy of my life standing across from me with a smile she reserved just for me.

The ceremony was small, just family, held at a winter resort I owned in the mountains. My offering to make up for the damper I'd put on their first wedding. No big party, just a celebration of my brother and his wife. Some skiing, lots of drinking, some business, and plenty of time to relax.

As the priest declared them wed again, snow falling against the wall of windows behind them, they sealed their vows with a kiss. They made their way into the small group that included Tony Donelli and his father. Another addition to the extended family I had inherited when Greyson and I had reconciled.

Greyson threw a glance back at me, a look shared between us that affirmed the bond we'd repaired. Giving him a nod, I tucked my hands in my pocket and made my way to Ava. My new reason for living. She had moved to Seagate with me and while I'd offered to buy her a gallery to run, she'd turned me down. Instead, she spent her days working in the women's shelter I'd built, teaching art classes for the residents, and drawing in her spare time. There wasn't a night when I didn't have her tucked in my hold, nor a night that I didn't worry about the danger my life held for her. And while she argued that the danger was something we both embraced, I had decided there was one risk I would no longer take: losing her.

Which was why I was unwinding the illegal parts of my business and had found a protégé to eventually take over my territory. I'd wanted to step away for years, and Ava had provided the incentive. Within three years, I would retire, acting as a consultant to my brother and to Mason Brinks, but spending most of my time by Ava's side as she conquered the world. There was just one last thing I needed to do.

"You must be the sexiest man here," she said, wrapping her arms around my neck.

"And you are the most beautiful woman here," I answered, scooping her into my arms.

"I don't know, Angie's pretty sexy." She was taunting me, but I wasn't about to bite because nothing tempted me like Ava did.

"Not my type anymore, remember? Plus, I'm only into blondes when it's you."

She giggled. "I love you, Emerson."

"I know. That's why we're going to return here next summer and you're going to marry me."

Her mouth fell open. I walked her into a corner away from the others and took her face in my hands. "I'm serious, Ava. Marry me. Next May to mark our year anniversary. We can elope if you want or have an enormous party. I don't care, as long as you're happy. Marry me, Avani Liliya Shelton."

"Aren't you supposed to be on your knee, Mr. Tides?"

"Is that a yes?" My heart was racing erratically. I had intended to ask her the next morning, but with the snow falling behind her, the blush of excitement on her cheeks, and how ravishing she looked in her bridesmaid's dress, I couldn't wait.

"Maybe, but I want to see some dedication to this."

I couldn't help laughing as I dragged my hands down her body and got to my knee. Pulling the ring from my jacket pocket, I said, "Is this better?"

She fell to her knees and took the ring before tugging me to her. "Yes, and yes. I will marry you Emerson Tides."

Our lips met, and I pulled her into my arms, standing and picking her up as I continued to kiss her.

"So, was that a yes?" Greyson asked from across the room.

I gave him a thumbs up as Ava giggled.

"Why wait?" she asked.

This time, it was my turn to gape.

"We have a priest. Everyone is here. I don't want some big fancy wedding and it's not like we were doing anything now but having dinner." It was true, there was no party, nothing planned but dinner and drinks.

"We don't have rings, you don't have a dress…" A million thoughts were going through my mind.

"I don't need anything but you, Emerson. We're risk takers, right?"

My lips twitched as my grin grew. "Yes, we are. Hey Grey, you mind if we squeeze in on your special night?"

"Had a suspicion that would happen with as impulsive as you two are," he said, coming over to me and holding out two rings. "Riley and Casey are good at reading these things and when I told her what you planned, well, we all figured you'd pop the question today and the two of them took it a step further."

Ava shot a look around me, giving Riley a huge grin.

Greyson put his hand on my shoulder. "The priest is waiting when you're ready."

I watched him take his place where I had stood earlier. Pack took Den's place. Riley stood across from Greyson, followed by the other two women, and even Mason and Tyson took their places.

"Damn, that is one messed up family I'm marrying into, isn't it?" Ava said.

"You sure you want to do this?" I asked her.

"Are you?"

I searched her chestnut eyes, looking for any sign of doubt and seeing only what was in my heart. Love, endless and raw. There for me and only me. The piece of myself I had never known I was missing. I scooped her into my arms, loving the cute squeal she made.

"I've been sure since the day you walked into my life, wildcat."

I carried her to the priest, and we took our places where Greyson and Riley had stood. Exchanging our own vows and declaring our love to those we now called family and friends. Greyson handed me the rings and as Ava and I completed our vows, slipping on our rings and sealing our fates with a kiss, I knew there was nothing more I wanted in life. I had everything I needed now. I had my brother back, and I had Ava. There was nothing else that mattered in my life but those two things, and I would spend the rest of my life proving that.

Thank you for reading Unhinged Cravings. If you enjoyed Emerson and Ava's story, please consider leaving a review. Reviews are like priceless gems to authors.

Be sure to read on for a BONUS EPILOGUE from Greyson.

Piles of books were everywhere when I returned home from the office. I scanned the living room, scratching my head at the scene. Riley had taken the day off, telling me she wasn't feeling well and insisting I go into the office even after I argued I could take my calls from home. After working until noon, I had stopped to get her some chicken noodle soup at the deli she loved and headed home...to an unexpected scene of chaos. It almost looked like a bookstore had exploded all over the main floor of our house.

Sidestepping the piles, I put the soup in the kitchen and made my way upstairs, marveling at the number of books stashed on the stairs. Either she'd gone on a book buying spree, which wasn't that hard to believe, or she was reorganizing her library. It amazed me how many ways she could shelve books: by color, by author, by size, by decorated edges. In the five years we'd been married, she had to have changed it at least ten times.

"Riley?" I called as I hit the landing. Her bookshelves were blocking most of the hallway, and I squeezed my way to the room.

"Grey?" Surprise edged her voice and as I stepped into the room, I saw why.

The walls were no longer rich green with the forest wallpaper accenting one side. Instead, a light shade of sage covered them, softening the space. Riley stood on the left side with a tangle of limbs sticking to her from a tree decal she was sticking to the wall. She blew a strand of ebony hair that had slipped from her ponytail as her bright eyes met mine.

"You weren't supposed to be home yet," she complained, pouting her lips.

"What are you up to? If you'd wanted to re-do your library, I would have called the decorator." I narrowed my eyes. "Is this why you took the day off?"

Guilt creased her eyes. "You were supposed to be at the office all day."

"I brought you soup and thought I'd spend the afternoon with you," I explained, wondering why I was on the defensive and what she was up to.

She disentangled herself with a huff and wiped her hands on her jeans. "It was supposed to be a surprise."

The sadness in her voice had my irritation soothing and as she stepped toward me, my eyes landed on something that made my heart race frantically.

Swallowing, I looked back at her and asked, "Is that what I think it is?"

She nodded. "I wanted to have it all done when you came home."

I glanced back at the mahogany crib, feeling unsteady. "Are you sure?" I said, my voice coming out in a whisper, afraid to say it too loud for fear she would say no. We'd been trying for three years and the two times we'd succeeded, she'd miscarried in her first trimester. The loss had been devastating, but knowing how badly she suffered through each one made it unbearable. Knowing I couldn't protect her from it, that I couldn't take her anguish away, had left me feeling helpless.

"I wanted to wait until I made it past week twelve before I told you. I'm fourteen weeks, Grey."

Relief washed through me, followed by exhilaration, and I closed the distance between us and scooped her into my arms, twirling her around.

She laughed, urging me to put her down, but I stopped her fight with a kiss, pulling her tighter into my embrace until I worried I might hurt her. Releasing her, I gently lowered her to the ground.

"You've been keeping secrets from me, baby girl," I said, planting another kiss on her nose.

"And it's been so hard. I thought for sure you'd notice I gained a few pounds."

Shrugging, I said, "I kind of liked it and thought if I mentioned it, you'd get worried and try to lose it."

Her smile lit her eyes. "I'm only going to get bigger."

"And sexier." I brought her to me, rubbing my hand over her stomach and marveling at the thought that our child was growing inside of her.

She tipped my head up so that our eyes met. "There's something else."

Furrowing my brows, I wondered how there could be more when this was already so much. She tilted her head to the other side of the room, and I followed the direction, my eyes landing on the box I had disregarded when I'd come into the room.

"I only had time to set one up," she said in a coy voice. "We're having twins."

Sight flying back to hers, mouth gaping, I struggled for words. Twins. Not just one child, but two. Like me and Emerson or maybe identical. My knees threatened to buckle on me and, as if she noticed, Riley threw her arms around my neck and brought my forehead to hers.

"Twins?"

A nod and an even bigger grin. "Twins."

I thought about what that meant. Two children we were bringing into the dangerous world I ruled, into the dysfunctional family we had. The family I could handle, but the danger I couldn't. Every day with Riley was another fraught with worry and the incessant nagging that I was pushing my luck, that things were going to come crashing down around me and I would lose her.

I didn't know how Raines was doing it. He and Angie had been the first to add a child to the mix, their daughter born a year after Riley and I had renewed our vows. The spitting image of Angie, Raines spoiled her just like he did her mother, like a true mafia princess.

"Grey?" Riley's voice brought me back from my thoughts.

"I think I need to call my brother," I mumbled.

"To let him know about the babies?" Babies. My world spun again, and I grasped onto her. "Because I can't wait to call Mason and Casey. We can have our baby showers together." She bounced up and down on her toes, my arms following her motion.

Mason had just shared the news that Casey was pregnant and now I knew why it hadn't devastated Riley like I'd worried it would. How she had kept her secret this long was a testament to her fortitude.

"No," I said, peeling my arms from around her and pulling my phone from my pocket. "To get his help winding down the business just like he did." Her bouncing stopped, and she stared at me. "It's time to retire, baby girl. Maybe buy a big house in the country where the kids can run around."

"But country life isn't you," she said.

I tucked a stray hair behind her ear. "My life is with you and now our children. Whether it's in the country, the city, the beach, or the mountains. It doesn't matter because all that matters is you and now..." I placed my hand on her stomach. "...them."

Tears welled behind her eyes, and I tipped her face up and kissed her again. She was my everything just as our children would be. I'd once told her I would give it all up for her and it had been the truth. Nothing else in this world mattered. It never would.

"Besides, we need another room to put your library back together and the guest room isn't big enough." Stepping away from her, I removed my suit jacket and rolled up my sleeves. "Let me make this call, then we'll call your brother. The rest of the day, you're going to put your feet up while you teach me how to build a crib." I glanced back at the hallway. "Did you really move all those shelves by yourself when you're pregnant?"

She put her hands on her hips. "I'm not fragile, Greyson."

"You are now. No more moving furniture or lifting anything. I'm pampering you for the duration of this pregnancy. Scratch that. For the duration of your life, baby girl."

The tug of a smile preceded her admission. "Den may have helped me move the heavy stuff."

"You told Den before me?" I wanted to be angry, but knowing she hadn't lifted the shelves or the crib boxes eased my irritation. "There will be repercussions for that," I added, giving her a smirk that had her blushing.

"Just call your brother."

She went back to fighting with the tree decal and I watched her with wonder. This woman who had unexpectedly come into my life, who had captivated me and challenged me, who now carried two precious pieces of our love inside of her, and had once told me she would let me burn the world down for her, was my everything. The piece of life that had been missing. And now that she had completed it, I needed nothing more. Because Riley made life worth living like nothing else in my life ever had.

I dialed my brother, the other piece of my life that was now complete, and leaned on the doorframe, my eyes still on Riley.

"Grey," he answered.

"I need your help."

"Anything." Concern strained his voice, and I could tell he was on guard from my comment.

"I'm ready to retire."

"It's about damn time. There's a house a few miles from our place with a perfect view of the ocean and nice weather year-round."

I chuckled, thinking it would be nice to be closer to him, but Riley would miss her brother too much. "I'll consider it for a vacation home."

"Good. I can be there in two days to discuss your retirement plan. Ava's teaching a class tomorrow that she can't miss." A bark sounded in the background. I'd never thought of my brother as a pet man, but he and Ava had adopted a pit bull they named Omen from a shelter, and Emerson treated the dog like it was his kid. I'd never seen a dog with so many toys and dog beds. Of course, Riley insisted on sending him Christmas and birthday presents every year.

"Sounds good. There's one more thing, Mer."

"Always is with you." It was good to hear his smile through the phone after years of only hearing his scowl.

"Are you ready to be an uncle?"

About the Author

J. L. Jackola is a writer of love stories with fantasy, darkness, feisty women, and morally gray men. She's an admitted sugar addict with a penchant for anything with salted caramel. When she's not weaving tales, snacking on sweets, or downing her morning cup of tea, you can find her logging miles in her running shoes, watching movies with her family, or curled up with a book.

She resides in Delaware with her husband and three children.

To learn more, visit her website at
www.jljackola.com